COLOR TOUR

COLOR TOUR

AARON STANDER

WRITERS & EDITORS
INTERLOCHEN, MICHIGAN

Publisher's Cataloging in Publication Data

Stander, Aaron.
   Color tour / Aaron Stander. -- Interlochen, Mich. : Writers & Editors, 2006.
     p. ; cm.
     ISBN-13: 978-0-9785732-0-1
     ISBN-10: 0-9785732-0-X

     1. Murder--Michigan--Fiction. 2. Murder--Investigation--Fiction.
   I. Title.

PS3619.T363 C65 2006   2006927249
813.6--dc22   0607

Printed and bound in the United States of America

Cover and interior design by Lori Hall Steele

Author photograph by Alicia Diane Walker

FOR BEACHWALKER,
WHO HELPS THIS ALL HAPPEN.

1

Prince Hal, an impeccably groomed Welsh terrier, led the way to the beach, barking and running in circles, allowing Nora to catch up, and then racing ahead through the dune grass. When he got to the water he poked at the waves for a few moments and then scampered back and forth along the shore, waiting for her arrival. Nora ambled along with Falstaff, her graying chocolate Labrador, who was content to walk by her side, a slimy tennis ball in his mouth.

Nora stopped, stood in the shallow water, and looked out across Lake Michigan, where the colors of the setting sun mirrored on the gently rolling surface. She knew that a storm had been predicted for later in the evening, but as her eyes ran along the gentle curve of the horizon, she couldn't see a hint of the approaching clouds—just the golds, reds, and darkening blues as the sun started to slip into the water.

She thought about how much she loved this beach, especially in the fall after the summer people left, when it was hers again. She turned and looked back at the ridgeline glowing in twilight—the radiant maples, golden poplars, gently browning oaks, and verdant conifers.

Nora was pulled back to the moment by Falstaff's sharp bark. He looked up at her hopefully, nudging her leg with his soft coat, his tennis ball laying at her feet. She threw the ball as far as she could—a girl-style throw, that's what Hugh, her late husband, used to call it. Without hesitation Falstaff splashed into cool water and was soon back, dropping the soggy ball at her feet and waiting for another throw.

Hal's participation in the game was limited to running back and forth and barking. Occasionally he would approach the water's edge, tentatively probe the gentle swell, poke at it with his right paw, and then jump back quickly. This getting wet in the pursuit of sport, he would have none of it.

Nora peered along the beach in both directions, shed her terry robe, and entered the cold lake. She moved quickly to the deeper water beyond the band of stones near the beach and then slid below the silver plane—thighs, sex, breasts—stopping with her arms floating on the surface. She shivered violently several times and then kicked off the bottom and started swimming toward the setting sun. When she reached the first sandbar she stood and panted until she caught her breath. She heard the rhythm of Falstaff's paddle and caught him as he nudged past her, pulling him close, feeling his warmth against her naked body. She shivered again and turned toward shore. Hal stood on the beach barking, a note of distress in his tone.

Nora released Falstaff and started for the shore, freestyle at first and then flipping over and doing a long, elegant backstroke until she felt her hands starting to hit the bottom. As she carefully hobbled over the rough stones to get to the sand, her eyes caught movement. Two figures were approaching. She thought about retreating back into the water, but it was too late. *Let them see an old woman naked,* she thought as she marched forward. She retrieved her robe and then started rubbing her hair with a towel.

Hal barked and greeted.

"Lovely evening," said the young woman, "hard to believe it's October." She dropped the blanket she was carrying and knelt down to pet Hal. The lanky, bearded young man at her side stood holding a grocery bag with both hands. Nora could see part of a baguette above the top of the bag.

"Warmest I can remember," Nora responded, retrieving her glasses from the pocket of her robe. She pulled the couple into a sharper focus. "Guess the weatherman is making up for the cold July and August." Nora considered making a joke about nuclear testing and the weather, but knew her audience was too young to get the humor.

Falstaff trudged onshore. Starting with his nose and moving to the end of his tail, he shook the water from his heavy coat, repeated the process a second time, and nuzzled his nose under the woman's arm. Nora watched as the woman playfully rubbed the head and ears of the soggy dog, getting several wet kisses in return.

"Come up to see the color?" Nora asked.

"I live here."

"In town?"

"No, I'm a teacher at Leiston School."

"You're so young," laughed Nora. "Hard to imagine you're through college. You a teacher too?" she asked, addressing the young man.

"No, just visiting for the weekend. You live here?"

"Yes," she responded, pointing to her home at the top of the bluff. "Summered here for years. Moved up permanently when we retired." She motioned toward the setting sun, "You kids better get on with your picnic. Not much light left."

"You have a good evening," said the girl, giving each dog a final rub.

Nora stood and watched them recede into soft twilight glow. She felt a pang of jealousy. They had their whole lives before them, all the joys and sorrows that would come with thousands of days.

She slowly climbed the path up to her cottage, Hal in the lead, Falstaff trudging behind with his ball. Her home had once been part of a row of cottages on the shoreline south of the dunes, now only a few remained. And with her death it would disappear, too, all part of the mandate of the National Park Service to return the area to its natural state.

Once inside, the dogs lined up by the microwave as Nora heated two bags of the special food—brown rice and chopped organic chicken—she made for them; she didn't trust commercial dog food.

Once their needs were attended to, she started her evening ritual. She mixed a vodka martini, added a Gorgonzola olive, and splashed in some extra vodka. Settling into a chair on the deck, she sipped the drink and had her second cigarette of the day as she watched the sun slide from view. She had a second martini as the afterglow went from gold to gray.

Mornings and evenings—the edges of the day—were the hard times, the times she felt the most alone, and the saddest. She thought again about the young couple. Were they making love on the beach? If she could only be close to someone again. That's what she missed. Someone to hold onto in the darkness.

Nora woke once in the night, used the bathroom, and returned to bed. She lay half-awake, knowing that she was angry. But what was she angry about, with whom was she angry? Nora had a psychology degree and she was skilled at analyzing her feelings. *You silly old coot*, she finally said. *You had your youth and now they have theirs. You can't be angry because they're young and you're old.* She felt the anger dissolve and soon slid into a deep slumber.

She woke to the sound of wind, thunder, and rain drumming on the roof—crowded in her large bed by Hal and Falstaff, each lying at oblique angles. She got up and started the coffee. The dogs, after stretching and scratching, followed her to the kitchen. She pulled on Hugh's old wax jacket, many sizes too large for her tiny frame, and headed down to the beach. Some mornings they walked south to the stream and back, others they walked north to the base of the dunes and back. This day they headed north.

Nora pulled the hood of the coat up over her head as she followed the dogs, Falstaff charging in and out of the waves, Hal leading the way and then running back to her, trying to get this forced march over so he could have his breakfast and his morning nap. They were at their turnaround point when Hal's frantic barking began. He stood on a small rise near the base of the dunes. His tone was one of alarm. Nora called to him but he stood firm and barked. She climbed the shallow embankment and glimpsed at the cause of his frenzy.

After she looked on the scene, Nora grabbed Hal by his collar and pulled him back toward the shore. She fell to the wet beach and cried. She beat the sand with her fists and screamed hysterically. Finally, exhausted, she staggered back to her feet. The dogs moved at her side, protecting her as she struggled to get back to the cottage.

2

Even with the influx of tourists coming in on weekends to see the brilliant display of colors in the hardwood forests, Sunday mornings in the autumn were quiet in Cedar County, a rural stretch of rolling land that reaches out into northern Lake Michigan. The locals took pride in the fact the county had neither a stoplight nor a McDonald's.

By the end of the Labor Day weekend, the throngs of tourists who crowded the roads, swarmed the beaches, and filled the restaurants and shops were gone. Most of the fudge shops and touristy boutiques were open only on weekends and would close by the end of October.

Sheriff Ray Elkins, determined to get through all the paperwork that had been piling up for weeks, was at his desk before seven o'clock on a Sunday morning. He had just started on the first stack when he was interrupted by a call from central dispatch telling him that a hysterical-sounding woman, Nora Jennings, insisted on talking to him. After accepting the call, it took Ray several minutes to calm her to the point were he could understand what she was saying. Then he put her on hold for a few moments and checked with dispatch to see if there were any units in her area. When he came back on the line he told her to lock her doors, that he would be at her house in less than twenty minutes.

Ray had known Nora and her late husband, Hugh, since he was a teenager. He had done handyman work for them in the summers when he was in high school and college. They had left Grosse Pointe and retired to their summer home on Lake Michigan by the time Ray moved back to the region to look after his mother during her final illness. He and Nora became closer after Hugh's death. He tried to have dinner with her at least once a month and made every effort to check on her when he was in her part of the county.

Ray carefully navigated through the savage fall storm, the wet pavement strewn with leaves and broken branches, impromptu streams and pools forming at low points along the two-lane highway. The gale-force winds stripped the trees of their leaves—swirls of red, yellow, and brown from the maples, poplars, and oaks. He switched off the siren as he turned onto Burnt Mill Trail, a single rutted road that ended at a small park on Lake Michigan. The first half-mile was flat—running through sandy fallow fields of a long-deserted farm. The road turned west as it entered a dense cedar forest and gradually descended into a rain-swelled swamp. Ray slowed, shifted into four-wheel drive, and carefully maneuvered through the deep, water-filled potholes. Near the shore the trail climbed out of the swamp, pine, and hardwoods lining the road. At the entrance to the park, an access to the beach and trailhead for dune walks, Ray turned onto a sand lane that ran parallel to the shore. He followed the narrow two-track another quarter of a mile, pulling off and parking behind a lakefront home.

He had barely come to a stop at the rear of the cottage when Nora came running from her back door. She clung onto Ray as he emerged from his car. He held her, her delicate frame shaking violently as she sobbed. They stood in the heavy rain for several minutes, Ray waiting until she slowly calmed to a gentle weeping. As they reached the cottage door, a second sheriff's vehicle arrived.

Nora briefly disappeared, leaving Ray to greet the dogs,

and reappeared with a stack of towels. Ray was using one of the towels to dry his glasses as Deputy Sue Lawrence came through the back door. Nora pulled a third mug from a hook as he made introductions.

"Tell us exactly what you found," Ray asked.

"I tried to tell you on the phone."

"Yes, but please go through it again, slowly."

"We went down to the beach this morning, as usual. I like to give the boys a good run before we have breakfast. As we were walking up toward the dunes, Hal got excited about something. He wouldn't come when I called, which isn't like him. He's always so good. So I went up to take a look . . ." She started sobbing again.

"It's okay, Nora, take your time."

"There they were."

"Who?"

"The couple, the beautiful young couple I saw last night. They were lying there, naked. I just knew they were dead."

"Yesterday, when did you see them?"

"It was in the evening. The boys and I had gone down for our swim. They came walking along the beach, must have left their car at the park. They caught me skinny dipping."

"About what time?" asked Ray.

"I don't pay much attention to time, Ray. It was near sunset."

"And you're sure that the . . . bodies . . . are the same?"

"I'm sure. We talked for a bit. The girl patted the dogs."

"Besides these two, did you see anyone else?"

"No, they were the only ones. There's hardly been anyone on the beach for more than a month."

"So, where are they? Would you show us?"

"Just where the dune starts. I'll take you, but I don't want to go up there."

"You don't have to," Ray said.

"Does anyone want coffee?" Nora held a carafe near the mugs and looked disappointed by their response.

Ray and Sue retrieved their raincoats and boots and followed Nora up the beach, Hal at her right, Falstaff at her left, both on leads. The waves rolled high on the beach as they struggled into the wind. Yesterday's calm and near-record highs had been replaced by high winds, intense rain, and plummeting temperatures.

"It's just there," Nora said, after they had covered about a quarter of a mile. "Up there on the right side of the trail through the dune grass."

Ray and Sue walked up the path; they paused when bodies came into view, moving forward with great care to get a clear view, but at pains not to disturb the scene. Ray could see two bodies, a woman and a man, both naked. He moved closer for a clearer look. The woman was at the side of the blanket, her eyes were open, a fixed gaze into the falling rain. He could see several puncture wounds in her chest. The man was on his back in the center of the blanket, eyes closed. His throat had been slashed. In the leaden light their skin looked gray and waxy. The driving torrent had washed away most of the blood.

Ray inhaled slowly, trying to fully comprehend the scene. He stood motionless for several minutes, his eyes carefully scanning the site, the position of the bodies, the angle of the limbs, the color and texture of the skin, and the wounds. He looked at the man, lanky and light skinned, bearded, eyes closed, mouth ajar. Then he looked at the female, lean and athletic, her long auburn hair swirled behind her head. He gazed at her lifeless face. Her delicate, classic features were still very much evident, yet her vacant eyes stared into nothingness. Ray shuddered; he had seen this visage before in a painting, or a dream, or perhaps in the distant past.

3

~~~

S ue Lawrence and Ray escorted Nora back to her cottage in silence, the dogs moving with them in a somber procession. Ray called for additional support and the medical examiner. They left Nora's house and returned to the murder site in Sue's Jeep, driving along the beach.

Working together, they laid out the scene, and Sue started carefully photographing the grid, section by section. After completing the photography, she drove back to the park to pick up the county's part-time medical examiner. As she awaited his arrival, she called in the plates from the aged Volvo resting in the parking lot and requested some tarps to protect the crime scene, along with some lights and a generator.

The gruff, curmudgeonly Dr. Dyskin—a semi-retired pathologist who had spent most of his career in Detroit—slid into the parking lot, the sides of his rusting black Lincoln Town Car dripping with mud. Sue was about to ask him to get rid of his cigar when she noticed that it wasn't lit. He tossed a small, worn, black leather bag in the back of her Jeep and pulled his portly body into the passenger seat. The smell of smoke and Old Spice filled her car.

Sue knew that Dyskin had worked thousands of crime scenes during his career, but she had difficulty enduring his blasé reaction to death. She wished he'd at least grimace slightly.

"What do you got?" asked Dyskin.

"Two victims, male and female," Sue responded, partially opening her window.

"Murder-suicide?" he asked, his voice grave.

"Murder."

Sue parked near the shore, and they walked up the small hill. The rain intensified. Dyskin pulled on a pair of rubber gloves and stood for a long moment looking over the fog-shrouded crime scene. Then he moved in to begin his assessment. Sue and Ray held large black umbrellas over Dyskin as he carried out his examination, crouching near the victims, moving from one position to another to get a better view. He studied each body carefully—gently lifting fingertips, measuring wounds, palpating skin—making notes on a small pad with the stub of a pencil. Finally he stood up, brushing sand from dark wet ovals at the knees of his baggy khaki pants.

"It was fast. They were dead before they felt much pain," he explained with great certainty.

"What's your scenario?" asked Ray.

"Don't think there was any struggle. They were occupied." He looked at Ray and Sue and then slowly moved his gaze toward the bodies. "Given the way they're lying, the killer probably came up from the beach, took a few moments to plan his attack, and then moved in. The killer was fast, first the man and then the woman, before she could begin to defend herself. The male victim's head was pulled back, probably by his ponytail, and his throat was cut. He was dead before he knew what happened. The woman would have seen something, perhaps even reached up to defend herself, but she was pierced in the heart. Look at those chest wounds, any one of them would have been fatal. But the killer kept on stabbing her. Bag her hands. Maybe we'll get lucky and find something under her nails. Have you found the weapon?"

"Not yet."

"Well, it shouldn't be hard to spot. You're looking for a big, sharp knife with a wide blade. The neck wound is very clean, almost surgical; there's no tearing." Dyskin stopped and lit the stub end of his cigar with a Zippo lighter, curling his hand around the flame to protect it from the wind.

"Time of death?" asked Ray.

"What's the temperature?"

"Now it's about forty degrees; it's been dropping all night."

"Ten, twelve hours, more or less," Dyskin said, as he gathered up his instruments and tossed them back into the leather bag. "Couldn't have been completely dark yet. The assailant had enough light to see what he was doing. Those wounds in the woman's chest—right on target. He wasn't doing it by Braille."

"Same weapon?" asked Ray.

"Same weapon." Dyskin moved back to her body and pointed to one of the punctures. "Look how clean the entry is here. One sharp edge, with tearing on the opposite side, probably serrated. Maybe a big hunting knife, one of those commando things. And the perp was plenty strong. Someone was very angry." Dyskin peered at them over the top of his glasses. "He wanted them more than dead. There was a lot of rage here. I wonder," he stopped short.

"Wonder what?" asked Ray, peering into Dyskin's protruding eyes.

"Just a passing thought, we'll know a lot more after the autopsy."

Twenty minutes after the phone call from Sheriff Ray Elkins, a dark green Jeep Cherokee with sheriff department banners on the doors came up the drive and stopped at Leiston School's elegant main building. *At least he didn't have his flashers on,* thought Ian Warrington, the school's headmaster, as he pushed through the double doors and ran to the car through the heavy rain. He didn't like being seen getting into a police car, a fact that would undoubtedly be observed by a few and reported to many. But given the circumstances, there was no other way to handle the situation.

Ian Warrington climbed into the passenger seat and gave the young officer at the wheel a curt hello as they headed toward the gated entrance. Once on the highway Ian looked across at the driver again. Warrington was surprised by how young the deputy looked, just about the age of Leiston's seniors. "Have you been doing this long?" he asked, trying to make conversation.

"No sir, I graduated from Wayne State in May. Started working for the department in July."

"Are you from the area?"

"No sir, grew up in Novi. My grandparents have a cottage up here. I've always wanted to live here."

Ian fell silent. He wondered what effect the death of a faculty member would have on the school, what effect it might have on him and his future? It was like waking up to a nightmare. The sheriff hadn't told him much on the phone, just that he was needed to identify the body of Ashleigh Allen. And when Ian asked about where the accident took place, the sheriff responded that it was not an accident. And before Ian could pursue, he was told that a deputy would be coming to pick him up.

"Where are we going, the medical center?" Ian asked the deputy.

"No. We're going to the scene. The bodies will be transported to Grand Rapids."

"Why all the way down there?"

"Forensic pathologists," the young deputy offered, but he didn't bother to explain. Given his demeanor, Ian felt it would be futile to ask. "We're going to meet the sheriff at Burnt Mill Park," the deputy continued. "They have tentative identifications based on items found with the victims, they just want you to confirm."

Ian was silent for the rest of the short trip. The deputy parked at the end of a line of emergency vehicles, their flashing lights pulsating silently in the heavy rain and fog.

"It doesn't appear they're off the beach yet. I'll get you when they're ready," the deputy said as he stepped out of the car.

Ian sat for a few minutes and then followed the deputy's path out to the beach. He could see another cluster of flashing lights several hundred yards north on the shore. He put a cigarette in his mouth and realized how much he was trembling as he attempted to light it. Ian was consumed with a sorrow that was tinged with fear.

Eventually two vehicles headed down the beach, two Jeeps. He saw them approach at what seemed a mournful pace, watched them leave the beach and crawl across the expanse of sand into the park.

"Sir, come with me please," said the young deputy. They walked together toward an ambulance. Ian saw two body bags transferred from the back of the second Jeep into the ambulance. The sheriff was waiting near the rear doors, his yellow raincoat glistening in the beam of a small spotlight mounted above the doors.

"Thank you for coming, Dr. Warrington," Ray said. "I hope this won't be too difficult for you."

Ray opened the ambulance doors, and he and Ian Warrington climbed into the back of the unit and crouched next to the stretchers. Ray slowly unzipped the first black body bag, opening it just enough to reveal the face.

Warrington flinched, a convulsive movement ran through his frame. "Yes," he replied softly. "Ashleigh, yes."

Ray closed the first bag and unzipped the second. "Do you know this person?" he asked.

"Yes, that's Dowd, David Dowd. He's a friend of Ashleigh's; they graduated from Leiston the same year." Ian looked at the sheriff for a long moment and then bolted clumsily out of the ambulance. Ray watched him run across the beach toward the lake. Ray gave Warrington several minutes and then walked to him.

4

~~~~~

It was still raining heavily two hours later when Sheriff Elkins turned off the county road into the entrance of Leiston School. He slowed at the security booth that divided the entrance drive; the attendant on duty waved him through the open gate.

A hundred yards farther up the road he pulled off the blacktop and followed the narrow drive that circled the front of Leiston School's main building, his headlights reflected off the rough surface of the wet granite pavers.

The mansion, built in the Georgian style, had been constructed soon after World War I by a Chicago tycoon, Norton Howard, who had made his fortune in lumber and railroads. The estate, originally known as Forest Glen, was a gift to his English-born wife who had longed for a country house. Ray could remember that when he was young his grandfather and the other old-timers would reminisce about the crew of English masons imported to build the house. How the men cut the ashlars for the exterior walls from large blocks of stone that had been quarried in Wisconsin and carried across Lake Michigan by steamship. A narrow-gauge railroad had been built to haul the stone blocks and other building materials from the Lake Michigan shore to the construction site, and some of the locals had been hired to erect the scaffolding that circled the house when the stone walls were laid.

Ray parked on a small turnout across from the entrance, each of the four spaces marked "Visitors Only." As he approached the double doors at the center of the building, the one on his right opened. A small, attractive woman clad in a black sweater and skirt greeted him.

"Sheriff Elkins?" Ray clasped her extended hand and held it for a long moment as she identified herself. "I'm Sarah James."

He looked at her closely; her facial features were delicate. Redness at the edges of her dark green eyes showed that she had been weeping. Her dark black hair, cut short and carefully styled, was streaked with an occasional gray hair, but her skin was unlined and youthful; he judged her to be in her late thirties or early forties.

"And your position here, Ms. James?" he asked.

"I'm director of administrative services," she offered without further comment. She escorted him down a long hallway to the right and then to a second corridor on the left, leading him into the building's south wing. Halfway down the long hall she stopped, opened the door marked *Headmasters Office*, and waited for Ray to enter. Once inside she said, "Mr. Warrington has shared with me . . . I'm so shocked . . . I can't imagine," she wiped tears away with her left hand. "He'll be with you in a few minutes." She moved away, stopped and looked back at Ray—as if to confirm that this was all real—and then left, closing the heavy oak door quietly behind her.

Ray wandered around the office as he waited. The room had obviously once been the mansion's library. A large black marble fireplace was centered on the west wall. Bookcases ran from each side of the fireplace and also covered most of the east and north walls. The south wall had three sets of French doors that opened onto a brick terrace and overlooked a small lake.

The books were shelved behind doors framed in oak with

tarnished brass-screened center panels. Sets of dusty, leather-bound books, gold on the spines, filled the cases. Ray opened one of the doors and withdrew a volume from a set titled *Famous Women of the French Court.* He paged past the marbleized endpapers searching for a copyright date. Ray decoded the Roman numerals to 1921. As he started to leaf through the book, he noted that the signatures—the large multi-page sheets that were printed and folded to make sections of the book—were uncut. The book had never been read. *So much for the women of the French court,* he thought as he replaced the book.

He moved toward the floor-to-ceiling doors on the south wall. Velour curtains in a faded rose, decades past their prime, framed the spans. A large oriental rug, threadbare on the traffic patterns, covered much of the oak parquet floor. The harsh light from two banks of fluorescent lights suspended from the ceiling violated the tone of the architecture.

"Too bad about those," said Ian Warrington, noting Ray's gaze as he entered the room. "My predecessor had some strange ideas about how to modernize things. I've been trying to rectify and restore things as money allows." He paused; his tone became grave. "But that's a small problem now. I've told Sarah James and my wife, Helen, about Ashleigh." He slid his thin athletic frame into a worn leather chair near one of the windows and gestured for Ray to use the adjoining one. "We are beginning to plan how to present this to the students," he said, a troubled expression on his face. "I've never faced a situation like this." There was a long pause, Warrington lost in thought, his last comment seemed more to himself than to Ray.

"We need to notify Ms. Allen's and David Dowd's next of kin as quickly as possible," said Ray. "Could you help us identify the people who should be contacted?"

"I had anticipated that you would require that. Sarah is working on it, but I'm not sure what she is going to find. Ashleigh didn't have much of a family. Her mother died when Ashleigh was a young teen, breast cancer, I think. She was a student here at

Leiston at the time. Ashleigh was the grandniece of Mrs. Howard, the school's founder. And Mrs. Howard was her legal guardian after her mother's death." His tone changed, "You grew up around here, didn't you, sheriff?"

"Yes."

"Did you know Mrs. Howard?"

"I knew her by sight. I would see her shopping in the village," Ray responded. "She was very hard to miss, an imposing looking woman, drove a large, old, blue sedan, a Jaguar I think. But this place," Ray made a sweeping gesture with his hand, "was always a mysterious enclave: gated, walled, posted. The Howards made it clear they didn't want their privacy intruded upon. They seldom hired locals, brought their own staff from Chicago. Even their year-round caretaker was an outsider." Ray paused briefly. "And it didn't seem to change very much after she started the school."

"Yes, I know," Warrington said as he ran his right hand through his light brown hair. "Another thing I hope to address."

"And her father? Ashleigh's?"

"I don't know the whole history, there are people here at the school, some of the old-timers, who probably know more. The version I've heard is that she was conceived when her mother was a graduate student at Berkeley. The man, perhaps one of her professors, was married. He drifted out of her mother's life before Ashleigh was born. I don't know if Ashleigh ever had contact with him, I'm not sure she even knows his identity," he paused and corrected himself, "even knew his identity."

"Did her mother ever spend time in this area?" Ray asked.

"I really don't know. The fact that Mrs. Howard ended up as Ashleigh's guardian suggests that she was close with the mother, so there's the possibility that she did."

"Other relatives?"

"She had no siblings. Her grandmother, Mrs. Howard's sister, has been dead for years. I don't think there's anyone else. But Sarah is working on it; we'll see what she finds out." Warrington exhaled heavily and sagged into his chair.

"David Dowd, can you give us some help . . . ?"

"Sarah has pulled his records. She has names and addresses for his parents and is checking to see if they are current. They were divorced by the time David was at school here. What else do you need?"

"We need to trace Ashleigh's movements during the last few days. Did she live here at the school?"

"Yes, she resided," Warrington paused for a moment—Ray heard the pain in his voice, "in one of the older faculty lodges, duplexes, actually. They were built as guest cottages in the early years of the estate. Mrs. Howard had some additional ones built in the '60s in the same style as the original ones when she started the school, but the early ones are much nicer. They're built like this place," he gestured to his surroundings, "stone and timber, very solid. They look like something you'd find in the Cotswolds. That's in England," he added.

Ray nodded. "We need to know who saw her yesterday, who she was with, at what time. We also need access to her quarters."

Warrington shook his head back and forth, "You don't suspect that anyone here could have . . ."

"This is the beginning of a homicide investigation. We will be looking at all possibilities. We have to learn as much as we can about the victims and the people with whom they associated. Have you arranged a meeting with the staff?"

"Ms. James is trying to contact everyone. Being the weekend, she's having some difficulty. The staff meeting is tentatively scheduled for five o'clock. Then we have a meeting of the whole school scheduled for six." Warrington paused, pushed his glasses up his long, thin nose and continued. "Our consulting psychologist will be here and two crisis counselors from Detroit are flying in this afternoon. When is the media going to . . ."

"They already know that there has been a double homicide. We've been able to withhold the names and keep them away from the crime scene. I've promised them a press conference after we've notified next of kin."

"How do I keep them off campus?" asked Warrington.

"You won't have much trouble if it's just the local media. If you meet with the reporters and give them some time, I think they will respect the fact that this is a school and they will keep their distance. But if one of the networks jumps on the story, well . . ." He paused and watched the gloom settle on Warrington.

"Anyway, I would like to be at your staff meeting. I'll have Deputy Lawrence with me. And I'll have her available for your community meeting if there are any questions she might be able to help with."

"Is there any way we can keep the students out of this?" Warrington asked.

"I understand your desire to shield them from this horrible crime, but it's possible that one of them might have seen or heard something that will aid our investigation." Ray paused, then looked directly at Warrington, his tone hardened. "Do you know of anyone who might have a motive to do this? Have there been any threats against Ms. Allen?"

"Everyone loved Ashleigh. She was a bright, beautiful young woman. Students adored her, and she was popular with the staff."

"Someone didn't love her," Ray said, his tone flat. "This is one of the most brutal homicides I've ever seen." He waited. Warrington didn't respond. "How long has she been here?"

"As a teacher, three years. This was her fourth. We were fortunate to recruit her back." Warrington brightened for a moment as he remembered that time, then he became solemn again. "I'm in the process of revitalizing the school. It was almost moribund when I arrived. One of my first objectives was to hire young, energetic faculty members as our senior people retired. Ashleigh was the first new hire in more than twenty years. She was going to be an important part of this rebuilding process."

"Three years," Elkins repeated. "Did she have any enemies? Do you know of any threats?"

Warrington peered at the ceiling and rubbed the back of his

neck, he looked back at Ray and said, "No," as he shook his head back and forth.

"What do you know about the second victim, David Dowd.?"

"Not much. He was one of the people she dated. She'd occasionally bring him to school functions when he was visiting. Seemed like a nice enough young man."

"His driver's license gives an Ann Arbor address. Do you know if he was in school?"

"He was a doctoral student, social psychology, I think."

"When did you last see Ashleigh?"

"Let me think about that." He stroked his chin with a thin, bony hand. "I see her every day when school is in session. We all have lunch together, the faculty. People chat in the halls between classes, and they pop in to say hi and ask questions."

"Did you see Ashleigh yesterday, Saturday?"

Warrington moved to and fro in his chair a few moments before he answered. "I don't think so. We had a home soccer game, lots of things going on, parents and visitors on campus. I remember seeing her on Friday, at lunch. Ashleigh was very animated. On Thursday she'd taken her environmental biology class on a field trip to that swampy area near the mouth of Otter Creek. She had a funny story about one of the kids, a rather large girl, wandering away from the group and getting mired in the mud up to her waist. It took the rest of the class to pull her out."

"And David Dowd. When did you last see him?"

"Can't remember for sure. Probably some weeks ago. He occasionally visited her on weekends."

"Was this a serious relationship?"

"I don't know, but I don't think it was exclusive, if that's what you're asking."

Ray noted an edge to Warrington's tone. "Exclusive?"

"Ashleigh was a very attractive, engaging young woman. I don't think she was interested in an exclusive relationship. She wasn't ready to settle down."

"Can you identify any of her other male friends?"

"By sight, possibly. I wasn't always introduced. None of my business, really. Maybe others here can help you. I just know she dated several men."

"Living in this," Ray hesitated as he reached for words, "this almost cloistered community, her dating, was that a problem?"

"No, not really. She was discreet. Not that a few of the students weren't watching; they seem to keep tabs on their favorite teachers." He stopped briefly. "But faculty housing, it's off in its own area. And Ashleigh's cottage is the most remote of the group. I think she could come and go without anyone . . ."

"Didn't you say she lived in a duplex?"

"Yes, Janet Medford lives in the other half. But Medford is in her own world. I doubt she'd have noticed much. She has a drinking problem, after her teaching day is over she disappears into a bottle."

"Might Ashleigh have been involved with one of the students?"

"Impossible," Warrington shot back. "She was a real professional."

"Could one of Ashleigh's students been involved with her, at a fantasy level?"

"It's possible," he responded. "I don't think any of us adults can accurately speculate on what goes on in the heads of teenagers. But Ashleigh would not have reciprocated. Ashleigh was an adult. They're kids. She always made it clear to them that she wasn't one of them. And they knew the difference." Warrington's pitch rose, and he was making a jabbing motion with his forefinger to stress his point.

"Did she date anyone here at the school?"

"Well, no." Warrington moved back in his chair and looked ill at ease.

"Meaning what? Did she or didn't she, Dr. Warrington?"

"There was some speculation that she was involved with

Tony Davis her first year. He had been her mathematics instructor when she was a student here."

"And?"

"And nothing. He was married, and it was getting a bit sticky. Fortunately he decided to go back for his Ph.D. Enrolled at Stanford. Sometimes you get lucky and HR problems go away, far away," he said.

"And this Tony Davis hasn't been in the area?"

"No. Haven't seen him or heard from him in more than a year."

"Here at the school, how do you keep track of the students, how do you know where people are?"

"It's pretty much a closed campus. They can't have cars, and they must be with a responsible adult if they go off campus in a car. During their free time they can sign out to go to the village or ride their bikes through the national park. Everyone has to be in their dorms by ten during the week, midnight on Friday and Saturday. The house parents do an informal check."

"Informal. You often don't know where students are?"

"We do, and we don't," Warrington answered in an irritated tone. "We're not a military school. We don't line them up in formations every hour or two and count heads. One of the goals of Leiston School is to teach personal responsibility. We expect students to follow the rules, they must sign the school's code of conduct when they matriculate."

"And there are few violations of the code of conduct?"

"Very few, very few indeed. Our students quickly realize how special this place is. They don't want to do anything that would hurt the school or get themselves kicked out."

"So, no one is ever asked to leave?" Ray pursued.

"Very seldom, I can think of only one case since I've been here."

"What kind of security measures do you have in place?" Ray asked, taking the conversation in another direction.

"You don't think anyone is in danger, do you?" Warrington asked, a tone of alarm in his voice.

"I'm trying to get a sense of how the school operates."

"Gary Zatanski heads campus security. He's a retired ATF officer. He's got three assistants. His men also do some emergency maintenance. They carry cell phones so we can always reach them. The 11-7 guy stays at the entrance at the main gate. He monitors the security cameras on the perimeters of the dorms and at their entrances and calls the house parents if the natives are getting restless."

"Does that happen often?

"No, perhaps once or twice a year, usually in the spring when the kids are feeling frisky or sometimes the night before a vacation. Like we've had late-night snowball fights before Christmas break. Pretty innocent stuff for the most part. We have quality students here, and we work them very hard. By ten or eleven they're ready to crash." Warrington paused. "But why focus the investigation on Leiston?"

"Simple, Mr. Warrington, victims usually know their killers. This was her home, her community, if you will. So, Leiston will be an important part of our investigation."

"But couldn't it have been some crazed . . . I don't know."

"We will be looking at all possibilities."

There was a break in the conversation. Finally Warrington asked, "How else can I help?"

"I would like to become familiar with the layout of the school. And we will also want to search Ashleigh's apartment. You'll have to sign off on some paperwork."

"I would be happy to, but you can imagine how busy I am. Perhaps Sarah can show you around."

"That would be fine," answered Ray, interested in the way he was being handed off, but glad to have someone else's view of Leiston.

5

~~~~~

On Ray's second trip of the day to Leiston, an anxious Ian Warrington met him soon after he pulled into a parking place near the front of the mansion. Warrington quickly escorted the sheriff to his office.

"I'd appreciate it if you would stay here until we are ready to start," he said. "Otherwise some of our more inquisitive staff members will be demanding to know why you're here. I'll have Sarah fetch you when we're ready to begin."

After offering Ray coffee, Warrington excused himself and slipped out of the office.

Ray began exploring the bookshelves again, opening the doors and searching the shelves for something familiar. He pulled a leather-bound volume of Tennyson from a row of dusty books and held it in his hand, examining the cover. He opened the book, looked for the publication date, and found the string of Roman numerals in an archaic typeface near the bottom on the back of the title page. He paged through the book, pausing to read the beginning of *Ulysses*, lines he had memorized in college. He stopped a second time at the opening lines of a familiar stanza from "In Memorium."

If Sleep and Death be truly one,
And every spirit's folded bloom
Thro' all its intervital gloom
In some long trance should slumber on;

Unconscious of the sliding hour,
Bare of the body, might it last,
And silent traces of the past
Be all the color of the flower:

So then were nothing lost to man;
So that still garden of the souls
In many a figured leaf enrolls
The total world since life began:

And love will last as pure and whole
As when he loved me here in Time,
And at the spiritual prime
Rewaken with the dawning soul.

Ray's attention was pulled from the page by the sound of the office door opening.

"What a perfect place for you, surrounded by books," said Deputy Sue Lawrence, catching Ray lost in a print world. "What are you reading?"

"A poem by Tennyson," Ray responded, "that I haven't read since I was an undergraduate. Makes a lot more sense now than it did then. I probably hadn't lived enough." He closed the book and returned it to the bookcase.

"Amazing," Sue said looking around. "I've only seen rooms like this in movies. The people who built this place must have been serious readers, all these sets of books."

Ray admired Sue's enthusiasm for new experiences. He worried that the brutal side of police work would dull her joie de vivre. "Just decorations, I'm afraid."

"Decorations," she repeated in an incredulous tone.

He pulled several volumes from the case, explaining the printing process and showing her that the signatures were uncut, indicating that the books had never been read. As he closed the door to the case he asked, "Did you find the weapon?"

"No. We've worked the scene, no hint of a knife or anything like that. We've also gone up and down the beach for more than a mile in each direction and checked along the hiking trail that runs above. Nothing. But, you know, it would be so easy to bury it a foot deep in sand. It would only take a couple of minutes." She paused briefly. "Given the rain and wind, I'm not sure there's much left to preserve at the scene, but we've covered the immediate area with tarps. As soon as the weather breaks, I'll go over it again and see if there is anything we've missed."

Ray caught her eyes; she suddenly looked much older than her twenty-four years. "How are you doing?" he asked gently.

"When I'm there working—you know how it is—your mind is engaged. But when I was driving over here, the horror of it all . . ." Her eyes glistened. She looked toward the ceiling and blinked to clear the tears. "She was about my age."

Sue paused, breathed deeply and started again. "We've closed off the access road to the park. And I've got an officer assigned to stay above the scene in case a curious soul decides to hike in over the dunes."

"Let's try to get this completed tomorrow, early in the day if possible," Ray said. "And have someone go over the area with a metal detector."

"I thought you'd be ordering me into the lake," Sue offered with a wry smile.

"That's not a bad idea. Bring your suit."

"Too cold, let the scuba guys do it."

"Nora is still swimming."

"She's a lot tougher than me. The greatest generation and all that," she retorted, her tone lightened momentarily. "One more thing, we've gotten confirmation from the Shaker Heights Police that they met with David Dowd's parents."

Ray nodded, "Always a painful duty."

Sarah James interrupted their conversation. "Mr. Warrington says he is ready to begin." She led them to the school's cafeteria, a large, joyless addition tacked on the back of the mansion. Its terrazzo floors, fluorescent lights, and ceramic tile walls had a cheerless quality. The visual impression was reinforced by the smell of institutional cooking.

The crowd hushed as the two uniformed police officers entered the room. Warrington, looking very strained, stood at a lectern, waiting. Ray and Sue moved to his side. Ray gazed at the faces of the teachers and staff gathered around tables near the lectern; expressions of concern and apprehension met his eyes. The two police vehicles at the entrance had not gone unnoticed.

"I'm afraid I have some very bad news," Warrington started, his voice breaking, "some very bad news, indeed." All eyes were fixed on him. "This morning the bodies of Ashleigh Allen and David Dowd were found on the beach at . . ."

A sorrowful moan reverberated through the room and hung for several long moments.

"Drowned?" came a voice from the group.

"No. They were . . . they . . . were," Warrington struggled to say the word and couldn't. "This is Sheriff Elkins, many of you know him, and Deputy Lawrence. They will tell you more about . . . about the . . . deaths. He is asking for your help. Sheriff." Warrington moved to the side of the lectern.

Elkins looked out at the stunned, lamenting faces. "The bodies of Ms. Ashleigh Allen and Mr. David Dowd were found this morning at a Lake Michigan beach. They had been murdered," he paused to allow his words to sink in. "We are in the early stages of a homicide investigation, and we need your help. Mr. Warrington has given us the use of the staff conference room. We're interested in talking with anyone who saw Ms. Allen or Mr. Dowd yesterday or in the last few days, especially Saturday. Do you know anyone who might want to hurt either one of these individuals? If you have any information, please see us immediately."

"Certainly it must have been a stranger who did this," a frail woman with thin gray hair offered.

"It's too early in the investigation to know," Ray answered. "We will be checking all leads. But again, if you can, help us establish where Allen and Dowd were on Saturday. We're attempting to track their movements, trying to determine who they were with, and who they might have encountered. And we would appreciate hearing anything else you think might be helpful to the investigation."

A tall, sixtyish man in a red cardigan said, "Bob Kamm, sheriff. I'm one of the house parents. You don't think there's any danger to the students, do you?"

"We have no reason to believe they are in danger; but obviously, until we get to the bottom of this, every precaution should be taken."

"How did they die?" asked a solid woman, whose youthful face contrasted with her steel gray hair.

"We should probably follow Bob's example and identify ourselves," said Warrington. "This is Ms. McAndless, an English teacher."

"We're not ready to discuss that yet."

"And there's no possibility that . . ." McAndless stopped.

"Possibility?" Ray prompted her.

". . . that this was an accident?"

"I'm sorry. There is no possibility. Are there other questions?" Ray waited, looking at the stunned gathering.

The teachers and staff members were quiet. Finally McAndless asked, "Could you tell us again where they were found?"

"At South Dune, north of the park."

"That was one of Ashleigh's favorite places," McAndless responded in a soft voice. "She liked to take her students there. She liked to picnic there. Who would have imagined that . . ." Her voice trailed off as she struggled with the information.

"Do any of you remember seeing her yesterday?" Ray asked the crowd.

"Yesterday was a free day," Warrington answered. "We usually have classes on Saturday morning. But because of the home soccer game and other activities, the students were given the morning off. We announced it at dinner on Friday." He looked at Ray as he continued his explanation. "We do this occasionally. It takes the pressure off the kids, I think most of them sleep till noon."

"I warned you," a small man from the back of the room cried out suddenly, his face crimson. All heads turned in his direction. "This tragedy was waiting to happen and none of you knee-jerk liberals could deal with it. We all knew something like this would take place. It's time to face the music."

There was a long silence and an uneasy stirring in the room after the outburst. Finally Warrington addressed the group. "Thank you for being here. The school community will meet at six o'clock. I urge you to attend. The students will need help from all of us to get through this difficult time."

Sue Lawrence and Ray Elkins stood with Sarah James as the faculty and staff wandered out of the room.

"The angry man," said Ray, "what was that all about?"

"That was Alan Quertermous, and it's impossible to say for sure what he was railing about," Sarah said. "There's seldom a logical connection between his outbursts and the facts."

"Give me your best guess."

"He might have been talking about something that happened a few weeks ago. We had a young man working here in the kitchen, a social services client. The poor kid just didn't seem to catch on. When his supervisor told him that he no longer had a job, the kid blew up, yelled something silly like he would come back with a gun and shoot a lot of people and burn the school down. The students who were working in the kitchen saw the confrontation and heard his threats. It was the talk of the school for an hour or two. You know how kids are."

"What is his name, the person who was fired?"

"Arnie Vedder. Do you know him?" Sarah asked.

"Yes," Ray said. "So no one treated Vedder's threat . . ."

"Of course not. He was just an angry, hurt kid. He probably weighs less than ninety pounds, and he's physically and mentally handicapped. What kind of threat is he?"

"So why would this Alan . . ."

"Quertermous."

"Quertermous, thank you. Why would he, according to your theory, bring Arnie Vedder's threat into the discussion?"

"He was just looking for a way to get at Ian Warrington," explained Sarah. "At the time, he said we should have Vedder arrested."

"Did you have any further problems with Arnie?"

"No, I don't think he has ever been seen on school grounds again. But Quertermous, he'll use anything he can to get at Dr. Warrington."

"Why's that?"

"He's one of the old guard. They're all angry about the changes Ian has instituted. But Quertermous is particularly outraged. I think we've all become immune to his attacks." Sarah glanced at her watch. "Sheriff, if you don't have any further questions, I must look after some . . ."

"Yes, of course. Thank you for giving us some background."

Ray and Sue watched her depart. The room was now empty. "What now?" Sue asked.

"I'd like you to stay here for the meeting with the students and handle any questions. Stick around this evening, get a sense of the place. Talk to their security people. Let's plan to meet early tomorrow morning and go over what we have."

"And you?" Sue asked.

"I'm going to stop by Vedder's. He's not a likely suspect, but I'll stop by and see how he and his mother are doing."

6

$\sim$

There were lights on in the trailer when Ray pulled off the road onto the short gravel drive. He parked next to a sagging, purplish-red minivan. He had been here before, the bearer of tragic news. The door opened as he approached, first a tentative fraction, then wider as the woman inside identified her visitor.

"Sheriff, it's about Arnie, isn't it? What's happened?" The woman moved back from the door allowing him to enter. She muted the television, the pulsating flicker from a *M*A*S*H* rerun illuminating part of the room.

"Nothing has happened, Kim. But I am looking for Arnie."

"He didn't come home last night. He hasn't been here today. I was starting to get worried."

Ray looked around. Everything was neat and orderly, but old and worn. The poorly constructed dwelling was years beyond its intended life.

"Sit down, sheriff. I was just heating some water. Want some coffee?"

"Please," he responded.

Ray watched her spoon instant coffee into two mugs and

add boiling water. She placed one in front of him. "You want some sugar or milk?" she asked.

"No, this is fine. Thank you. Kim, we need to talk." She settled across from him at the small Formica table. "What do you mean Arnie wasn't home last night?"

"Well, you know, since the accident," she fished a box of cigarettes from the pocket of her faded, shapeless cardigan, "he just ain't right. He doesn't live like normal people." She lit the cigarette, a slight tremor in her thin, almost frail hands. As Ray looked at her, he ran the math in his head. She couldn't be more than thirty-five or thirty-six, but she looked like she was in her late forties or early fifties. Her face was etched from years of hard work and sorrow. "Days and nights, it just doesn't matter," she said. "He wanders in and out like they don't exist."

"And he didn't come home last night, and you haven't seen him today?"

"I worked today, went to town real early. Ended up subbing for someone after my shift. Got twelve hours." She drooped against the table. "God knows we need the money."

"And you don't think he was here when you were gone?"

"No. He would have left a trail—dirty dishes on the counter, clothes thrown here and there. Didn't raise him up like that, and he wasn't like that before the accident." She looked across at Ray, her tone became more apprehensive. "Why are you here?"

"This is just routine, Kim. His name came up in the course of an investigation. We're going to be talking to lots of folks. Tell me about his experience working at Leiston."

"Leiston. Why?" Her tone became bitter, tears swelled in her eyes. "What did they say about him? They've already done enough. They gave him some hope. He told me when he got the job that he thought he could be a little bit like he was before. And they seemed so nice to him at first. They even took him on some of their outings. And then, out of the blue, they fired him. And they didn't give him no reason or nothing." Pain spread across her face.

"He's so weak now, sheriff. Getting fired was sorta the last straw." She started sobbing, wiping away the tears with the back of her hand. She got up, retrieved a box of tissues from a kitchen cabinet, and came back to the table.

"And Arnie has no idea of why he was fired?"

"None that he could think of. We talked about it a long time. And sheriff, he's honest. The accident didn't change that. I came home from work, guess it's been a couple of weeks now, and he was on the couch pulled into a little ball like a baby. I could tell he had been crying. I asked him what was wrong, and he told me he had been sacked. When I asked him why, he said, and I remember this so clearly, he said, 'cause I'm fucking weird, Momma. Fucking weird and everyone knows it.' It just broke my heart. Maybe it woulda been better if he had died in the accident. He shouldn't have to live like this."

"Did you contact Leiston School after he was dismissed?"

"Yeah, I called. Couldn't get anyone who wanted to talk to me at first. Finally the head man called back. He was very nice on the phone, but didn't say anything helpful."

"What did he say? Do you remember?"

"Just that it hadn't worked out, and he was sorry. That's all. I could tell he really didn't want to talk to me; he was just going through the motions."

"Not coming home at night, how often does it happen?"

"This past summer, lots. He'd take his bike down to the sand dunes above the beach. He's got a sleeping bag and this telescope his dad got for him the Christmas he worked at Wal-Mart. I think he watches the stars most of the night and falls asleep at dawn. He'd usually come back here sometime late morning, have some cereal, and sleep a few hours."

"But it's almost winter. He can't be sleeping on the beach now. Especially not last night."

"He's built himself a hut deep in the woods, in that swamp a few a miles back from the lake," she said. "He took me there week before last. He's real proud of it. It's rough, but it's a shelter. I'm surprised he could do that good." Kim smiled sadly. "It's even got a little wood stove, something he found."

"And he stays there?"

"Yeah, two or three nights a week. At first I was worried, but he seemed to be doing fine with it. I figure he knows how to keep dry and warm. Imagine he'll give it up when it really starts getting cold."

"Could you take me there?"

"Now?" she asked incredulously. "It's a dense swamp. I don't think I could find the place in the dark."

"How about tomorrow, mid-morning, say ten o'clock?"

"That'd be okay. I'm off tomorrow."

"I'll either pick you up or send a deputy. Where do we start from?"

"The park at that trailhead near Otter Lake. Make sure you got some tall boots. There's several places where you'll be wading halfway to your knees."

7

It was a few minutes before ten o'clock when Ray arrived at a long-standing dinner invitation. He had called earlier in the day to cancel, as events were unfolding, but his friend Marc had prevailed on him, saying that he and Lisa, his companion, would serve dinner whenever Ray arrived, even if it was two in the morning. So, when Ray had completed his interview with Kim Vedder, he called Marc to say he was finally on his way.

Ray and Marc had been friends since they were boys. Marc had been reared by his grandparents who summered in the area, and Ray was a local kid whose parents had worked for Marc's grandparents.

Marc had continued vacationing in northern Michigan as an adult, eventually inheriting the old clapboard cottage that had been in his family for almost a hundred years. In his late forties Marc had quit a high-pressure Wall Street job and become a full-time resident. He originally intended to continue to work in the investment field as a consultant, but he quickly found he was more interested in rebuilding an old wooden sailboat than working with clients.

The summer of Marc's relocation to Michigan, Lisa was

staying just down the beach at her family's cottage, using an inheritance from her father to take a sabbatical from her public relations career in Detroit. Marc and Lisa had known each other over the years, their friendship starting as a big-brother-kid-sister relationship between summer neighbors. Before the summer was out, they had become a couple.

A thick fog had followed the heavy rain, and Ray slowly maneuvered his way through the dense haze and darkness along the narrow two-track to Marc's house. He parked in the round pool of yellow light emanating from a fixture nailed to a large oak tree near the back of the faded blue cottage. He opened the tailgate of his Jeep, removed a carefully wrapped bottle of Cotes du Rhone wine, and walked to the back door. The door springs squeaked as he entered the kitchen. Inside, Ray saw his friend Marc working at the stove while Lisa cleaned up after him.

"You know, you could change that bulb outside. Mosquito season is over," Ray offered with mild sarcasm.

"Once the snow comes it will give everything a lovely golden tint. And then it will be spring and . . ." Marc raised both arms, hands and fingers opening toward the ceiling, "they'll be back. Besides, if it ain't burned out don't . . ."

"I've always been impressed by how quickly you went native," Ray laughed. "Sorry to be so late, good of you to put up with my schedule."

"A fashionable time for an evening meal, very Continental," Lisa said. "Don't most of you locals have dinner about five?"

"Usually about four-thirty, but now that you two are becoming perma-fudge . . ." Ray peered into the large stockpot Marc was gently stirring with a long wooden spoon.

"One of your favorites, coq au vin," said Marc. "And fortunately for you, it was something I could take off the heat without ruining."

"You do look worn," said Lisa as she pulled a large serrated knife through a baguette. "It was the lead story on the six o'clock news. But you set the rules. We'd be happy not to mention it again and give you some rest. And, Ray, while you're standing around, would you serve the wine? I've made a fresh pot of coffee, knowing you probably won't have wine."

Ray poured two glasses from a bottle of Shiraz standing open on the worn marble counter and got himself a mug of coffee.

Mark put steaming bowls of coq au vin at each place, and Lisa passed the ciabatta as they settled in. The table was covered with a bright yellow cloth of a Provencal design.

"Sure you don't want some, even half a glass?" asked Lisa.

"Okay, a taste," Ray said, "enough to bring up the flavor, not that this wonderful food needs enhancing."

Lisa poured a glass and handed it to Ray. He swirled the wine, inhaled the bouquet, and took a small sip.

"Well?" asked Lisa.

"So, you hold dinner for hours, put a wonderful meal before me, pour me some noble red that you've given an adequate time to breathe, and I show you my appreciation by telling you that the wine is corky. Sorry."

"He's right," said Marc after carefully sampling the wine.

Marc opened another bottle, wrapped a towel around the label, and brought three clean glasses to the table. He poured a splash of wine in Ray's glass. "How's that?"

Ray held the wine glass by the base and gently swirled the wine, observing its dark ruby color and near-perfect clarity; he sniffed it slowly, and then took a small sip. "Very nice."

"Is this the bottle you brought or one of mine?" Marc quizzed.

"One of yours. The one I brought is a bit lighter."

Marc removed the towel, revealing the label, and filled Ray's glass. "Good answer, but I thought I'd go easy on you. The rest of your day has provided enough challenges."

"Make sure I only have one glass," said Ray. "It would be tempting to have more."

There was a lull in the conversation as they settled into the meal.

Ray stopped eating and closely examined the coq au vin. "Wonderful sauce, it's rich. And the color. What's in here?"

"Secret ingredient. This will be a real test of your nose, your taste buds, and your powers of detection."

"I'm afraid my powers of detection have already been overly taxed today."

"Sure you don't want to guess?" pressed Marc.

Ray carefully filled his spoon with the sauce. He focused on it through the bottom lens of his bifocal and set the spoon back in the bowl. He then moved forward and slowly inhaled.

"Well, the wine was all red, you sometimes do a white and red combination. You've thickened the sauce a bit, probably with a little arrowroot; it has a lovely sheen. The mystery ingredient, or should I say ingredients?"

"Ingredient. Give up?"

"I have a sense of it, but I just can't put my finger on . . ."

"Okay, enough pain," said Marc. "Chocolate. Bitter chocolate. Recipe suggests one ounce, I liked it so much I put in two."

"Coq au vin with a Oaxacan twist. It's wonderful."

He looked past Marc and Lisa, out toward the starry northern sky beyond the small-paned windows, and sighed at the emptiness of his own new house, which he'd built after his steady decided to move to Seattle to be nearer to her children. He understood, of course. That was what needed to happen. If he had children, and now perhaps grandchildren, he'd do the same. He'd do whatever it took to be part of their everyday lives. He thought back to the first woman he'd dreamed of having children with, a lovely graduate student with whom he had a brief summer romance. Ray wondered where she was tonight.

Lisa looked over at Marc and winked. "He's a culinary genius." The couple smiled at each other fondly. Ray felt a bittersweet pang as he leaned back in his chair and observed his friends together, looking at each other with that brief, knowing glance that people in love share. A fond complicity. He smiled. He was happy for them, happy that they'd found one another and made a warm home together.

"Ray?" Lisa asked, jarring Ray back to the room.

"Yes?"

"You look like you're far away," Lisa said, refilling her wine glass and looking up with concern. "Are you okay?"

Ray sighed and nodded. "I have a lot on my mind tonight. You know how it goes."

"Can I ask . . . ?" Marc paused.

"Go ahead," said Ray, knowing what was coming.

"So, what happened? Double homicide?"

"I thought we weren't going to mention it," said Lisa.

"It's okay," said Ray. He summarized all the public information about the murders, including the fact that one of the victims was a teacher at Leiston School. And then he said to Lisa, "You went there, didn't you?"

"Yes, ninth and tenth grade. By my junior year, Mother wanted me closer to home and enrolled me at Kingswood."

"Tell me about the place. I just have the bits and pieces I've heard over the years."

"I have bits and pieces, too, but perhaps they're different from yours. My grandmother knew the family, even got invited to tea parties there in the old days." Lisa sipped some wine as she organized her memories. "And Mother knew Gwendolyn Howard, she was the second Mrs. Howard. She started the school in the '60s. I think she was probably thirty years younger than her husband. His parents built the estate as their summer home. Gwendolyn had been a teacher before they married and was very interested in progressive education. Soon after they retired up here he died, heart or something. She was left with that enormous mansion and lots of money. She had been very taken with the educational philosophy of A. S. Neill and the way he ran his school, Summerhill."

"I can remember reading *Summerhill* during my brief excursion into ed courses, when I considered a career as a high school English teacher," said Ray. "Summerhill, let me think, lots of stuff about freedom and kids making their own choices." He paused. "Schools should focus on the psychological health of their students rather than pouring knowledge into them. It was very '60s. Made lots of sense to me at the time," he paused and looked thoughtful. "Actually, it still makes sense."

"Good memory," said Lisa. "Mrs. Howard went to England, studied with Neill, and came back and started the school. She called it Leiston, the name of the village where Neill's school was located. But Leiston was her version, or perhaps vision, of Summerhill. It was just a high school because she didn't like working with younger kids. I think Neill would have argued that high school was too late to start. The kids would have already been ruined by traditional schooling."

"How many students?"

"Ninety-six, twenty-four in each grade. She had an elaborate formula based on groups of six and multiples of six. Six students per class for laboratories, twelve for lectures. Twenty-four students in each house, that's what they call the dorms."

"What's special about six?"

"I have no idea. But I'm sure there was some sort of theoretical basis. Maybe number of lines of communication, that sort of thing."

"Why did your mother send you there?" asked Ray.

"It was during father's first illness. You know about his depression?"

Ray nodded.

"Mother thought it would be best if I didn't have to deal with it. He was no longer working; he was at home then and quickly deteriorating."

"So, was there a Summerhill-like freedom when you were a student?"

"Actually, no. Leiston had started to change a lot before I got there. The school had gotten a reputation for drugs, sex, and rock 'n' roll. They were doing their best to shed that image as quickly as possible. By the time I arrived they were making the place much more structured and academic."

"Any great scandals when you were a student?"

"No, just the usual boarding school stuff. We used to gossip about some of the faculty members, romances, things of that sort. I think most of it was the product of our imagination."

"And the drugs and sex?"

"I was only in ninth and tenth grade; I probably wasn't completely aware of what was going on. But I think things were fairly tame."

"Anything else I should know?"

"I did meet the new headmaster, Warrington, earlier this summer."

"Where?"

"I got invited to an alumni tea. It was sort of a fundraiser and student-recruiting affair. White wine, Brie, cucumber and watercress sandwiches."

"What was your impression of Warrington?"

"He was very gracious, seemed interested in what I had to say without being overly solicitous. But there was something about him." She had a troubled expression.

"What about him?"

"I just had this feeling he was a lech. Don't know why. He wasn't sneaking peeks at my parts or saying anything inappropriate. But something about him made me uncomfortable. He was just a bit oily." She sipped some wine and refilled her glass. "You met with the staff?"

"I did. Telling people about a death is always hard. And this was . . ." His eyes showed the anguish.

"Suspects?" Lisa asked.

"Suspects, not really." Ray paused briefly and then moved to another subject. "Did you have a man by the name of Quertermous as a teacher when you were at Leiston?"

"Quertermous, Alan Quertermous, I had that creep for math," Lisa responded, tossing her long, blond hair. "He'd walk around the room while we were doing our worksheets with a swagger stick tucked under his arm. Why do you ask?"

"He launched into a diatribe at the end of the meeting," explained Ray. "I was wondering about him. I sense you didn't like him."

"You are so fast, Ray," she responded in a mocking tone. "So tell us, what was Quertermous in a tizzy about?"

"He was loudly suggesting that the crime was predictable."

"How so?" Lisa asked.

"We're going to find out," Ray replied.

"A likely suspect?" Marc asked.

"Well, you have to be careful not to dismiss anything too quickly," Ray said, "but I don't think so. Quertermous's outburst might have had more to do with the politics of the place than anything else. I have much to learn about Leiston School."

"After a day like today, do you ever regret leaving college teaching?" asked Marc.

Ray didn't stop to reflect on Marc's question. "We brought the headmaster, Warrington, out to ID the victims. After he saw the bodies he got sick," Ray stopped for a moment. "This is hardly dinner conversation . . ."

"We're with you," said Lisa.

"As a rookie cop, I did the same thing," Ray said, continuing the conversation. "But you get beyond it. You disconnect from the carnage and settle into going through the procedures. Necessary perhaps, but I'm not sure it's a good thing."

"Why not?" Lisa asked.

"I think we get hardened. And every exposure furthers the damage. I escaped into academe to get away from the nasty streets of Detroit. But," Ray chuckled, his tone changing as he finally responded to Marc's question, "the ivory tower is not without its dangers. The battles I saw during my university career were brutal. Fortunately, they were mostly verbal. The backstabbing was metaphorical, although I suspect there were some people who had homicidal fantasies." He paused briefly, "And during my brief tenure as the interim director of the campus police, I had to deal with a sociopathic faculty member who was willing to kill for tenure."

"You've never mentioned that," Marc said.

"It's a piece of history I'd rather forget," he paused and peered off into space. Bringing his focus back to Marc and Lisa, Ray continued, "As I was driving over here, I was reflecting back on my university experience and thinking about the people I met at Leiston today. They seemed sincere and united in their grief and sorrow—with the exception of Alan Quertermous, of course. But I couldn't help wondering about what was really going on."

Lisa refilled wine glasses, her glass and Marc's. She looked over at Ray, holding the neck of the bottle toward his glass. He nodded his assent, making a gesture with his thumb and forefinger to suggest half a glass.

8

E xhausted, but still not ready for bed, Ray stood at his
writing desk, a piece of white oak furniture with simple,
clean lines that he had constructed by a local cabinetmaker
several years before. At that time he had been struggling with back
problems and standing to write had been more comfortable than
sitting. Although the back pain had abated, standing at the desk
had become part of his journal ritual, a routine that he tried to
follow each evening before retiring.

Ray took a sip from a cup of mint tea that he had placed in
easy reach on the right side of the desk. He flipped through his
journal, a worn leather binder filled with lined white paper, which
Ray had used for years.

He read his previous entry, a personal piece about autumn
and his feelings of loss since his romantic interest had decided to
move.

> *Our relationship was not one of great passion, but there was*
> *comfort and companionship. However, when her daughter divorced*
> *and needed help with three young children, it was clear to both*
> *of us that she was needed there. It gave her life a purpose again;*
> *something that I felt had been missing for a long time.*

Ray started to write with his favorite fountain pen, an ancient Pelican with a soft nib, gliding over the lined paper, his impressions of the day unwinding in a graceful stream of blue ink. He had word-processed the official account of the murders before he left the office, and though the basic facts in the journal entry would be the same, he was now free to drop the official tone and guarded empiricism of a police report. In this penned account there was no precise chronology, just impressions and his horror and rage. And then there was speculation, theories about motives, questions about the victims.

> *When we first reached the scene, Sue and I stood a long while and looked at the bodies. In the gray light of the dense overcast, the victims' skin had an unnatural, wax-like appearance. Even several yards away their wounds were apparent, but the heavy rains had washed away the blood, giving them a manikin look and somehow lessening the horror of the crime. The female looked vaguely familiar. Have I seen her before? Or perhaps it was something else. The colors and textures and melancholy nature of the place reminded me of a Pre-Raphaelite painting.*

He wrote about the people whom he had encountered, their actions, words, facial expressions, and body language. Was the murderer in the group? How much was theater? How much was real? He wondered about the reasons for Alan Quertermous' rage and his outburst at the meeting. He noted Ian Warrington's agitation, both at the beach and in their later conversations. *What are Warrington's priorities?* Ray wrote. *Is he trying to protect his position, the students, or both in some sort of complex ratio?*

Ray then moved on to Sarah James:

> *I arrived at the school and was met by one of the administrators, an assistant to Ian Warrington. Her sadness and grief, expressed in body language and tone, seemed sincere. She seemed to be working very hard to keep her emotions in*

check so that she could meet her professional responsibilities.
She had such an air of sadness; I wonder if that is her
normal demeanor or just a response to the unfolding tragedy?

Ray thought again about the appearance of the victims. He could see the dead woman's features again—the delicate blue eyes open to the sky, the thick auburn hair fanned out around the head. The face had a dreamlike quality that belied the violence of the scene. Ray lifted his pen from the paper for several long moments as he thought about the woman's physiognomy. The face seemed familiar, but he couldn't remember seeing her in the recent past. Perhaps it was a vision from some faded memory? Was it a face he'd seen once on a museum wall or in an art book? *Where have I seen her before?* he wrote. *And why can't I remember?*

Ray's focus shifted, he wrote about walking from the crime scene and standing and looking out at the blackened water, the carnage at his back, as the storm surged across the lake, the large rollers, every ninth, tenth, or eleventh wave, pushing high up on the beach. Ray had always loved watching storms blow off the lake in November, the power and majesty of nature. He took rather perverse joy in being reminded of his relative insignificance in the scheme of things. *This place of great beauty has been violated by these barbaric acts,* he wrote.

After filling seven pages, Ray closed the book and placed it in the drawer of his writing desk. He refilled the pen with bottled ink and slid it into a soft leather case next to the journal.

Ray pulled back a denim colored comforter and grabbed a copy of Jim Harrison's newest collection of poetry from a stack on the nightstand. After a few pages of struggling to keep his eyes open, Ray switched off the bedside lamp and fell into an uneasy slumber.

9

At six-thirty the next morning Ray was on the phone to arrange a meeting with Ian Warrington. He wanted some background information on Arnie Vedder's employment at Leiston School. Warrington met Ray an hour later at the school's main entrance.

"The food line is open for another fifteen minutes. Do you want some breakfast?" he asked as he guided Ray toward his office.

"No, thank you. I'm really pressed for time."

"You can get a bagel or an English muffin. We can just pop in and get one and eat in my office."

"Okay," agreed Ray a bit reluctantly.

Warrington led the way. Small groups of students were scattered around the room eating breakfast. They passed a steam table, the congealing scrambled eggs evoking unpleasant memories. Ray couldn't recall if they were from his undergraduate years, the Army, or both.

"Tell me about Arnie. What happened with Arnie Vedder?" Ray asked as they settled into chairs on the opposite sides of Warrington's desk with their bagels and coffee.

"Last summer, a woman from the Department of Social Services contacted us about a possible placement for this young man. We've cooperated with them in the past and usually have had positive experiences." He paused, his tone changed. "And I really like to do these kinds of things. Most of our students come from very fortunate backgrounds; they've had very little exposure to the real world." He lifted his head and looked Ray. "We try to include everyone who works here as part of the community. I thought that this would be good for our students and good for Arnie."

"What went wrong?"

"Lots of things, lots of things. He turned out to be much more damaged than . . . Well, I don't think Sharon was totally open with us. He worked for Tom Bates, our food service manager. Tom is enormously accepting and helpful. Arnie was supposed to work in the dish room. You know, things like loading and unloading racks, stacking dishes, sorting silverware. Arnie's not very strong, and he's uncoordinated. Tom found tasks for Arnie that wouldn't put him under too much time pressure. Early on Tom told me Arnie was having trouble catching on. He spent lots of time with Arnie, but his job performance remained only marginal. We tried to save the situation by moving him to the laundry area. His job performance there wasn't much better. We would have probably tried to live with that, at least for a while. But another problem developed."

"Which was?" Ray asked.

"His general demeanor. He had no affect and was unresponsive when given directions. Tom wondered if he was autistic or something. The girls assigned to the laundry complained about his . . ." Warrington fumbled for words.

"Can you be more specific? What did he do?"

"He did a lot of staring at the girls. They told Tom about it; several complained to me."

"Was there any inappropriate behavior?"

"You mean did he touch people or make improper comments?" Warrington asked.

"Exactly."

"No. It was just the staring. But he looks very strange and some of the girls found him frightening. He would also hang around campus when he wasn't working and watch the students playing tennis or Frisbee. He would just sit and stare. I don't think there was any evil intent on his part, but the students started referring to him as 'the stalker.' He also hung around Ashleigh's cottage. She was very kind to him." Warrington stopped, looked thoughtful, and continued. "That was one of Ashleigh's special qualities. She really reached out to people. I know she would take time to talk to Arnie, and I think he was hanging around because he was hoping to see her." Warrington stopped and sipped his coffee. "But when underwear starting disappearing. . ."

"Underwear?"

"Yes, after he started working in the laundry. Ma, Mrs. French, is very kind and patient. She took Arnie under her wing. But after he had worked there for a few weeks, a number of our female students complained that some of their underwear wasn't coming back from the laundry."

"How does your laundry system work?"

"The student body is divided into four laundry groups, corresponding with the days of the week, Monday through Thursday. Members of each group are to drop off their wash on their assigned day when they come to breakfast. Mrs. French washes and folds the laundry and takes it back to the dorms where the students pick it up."

"The underwear, how many pairs disappeared?"

"Don't know exactly, five, ten pairs."

"And how did you decide it was Arnie?"

"I didn't decide, Tom came to me with the suspicion. He thought that since the problem started after Arnie was moved to the laundry, he was the most likely suspect."

"How about the woman in the laundry, Mrs. French, did you talk to her?"

"I had a short conversation with her."

"Did she think Arnie had taken any underwear?"

"No. But even if she had, she probably wouldn't have said anything. She was very protective of Arnie. Apparently she's known him for years."

"Did you ask her directly if she had seen him take some underwear?"

"Yes, and she said if she had she would have done something about it."

"The clean laundry, where does Mrs. French put it when she takes it back to the dorms?" Ray asked.

"There's a room off the lobby with mailboxes and an area for the laundry."

"Is this a supervised area, a place where someone—the house parents—watches the comings and goings?"

"No," Warrington responded.

"So, it would be possible for another student to snatch some laundry now and then?"

"It's possible, but I really think that Arnie is the most probable suspect. And that was Tom's thinking when he asked me for permission to fire Arnie. There was also the problem that the girls believed it and were refusing to work in the laundry if he was going to be in there with them."

"Were there any other suspects?" Ray asked with mild irritation.

"No, he was the obvious suspect," Warrington said.

"No one else would have had an opportunity to steal these articles?"

"I can tell by your sarcasm that you're not very impressed with . . ."

"I didn't mean to be sarcastic," Ray said, "but isn't the evidence awfully weak?"

"Perhaps it is, but I have a school to run here. I have a million details to see to every day and on some of these things I go with the judgment of my staff. This was a quick fix to a problem. We did everything we could to accommodate Arnie's disabilities. But we're not a social agency, we're a school."

"And if laundry continues to disappear, will Arnie Vedder be called back to work?"

Warrington's anger flashed. "Is there anything else, sheriff?"

10

It was just a few miles from Leiston School to Nora Jennings's home on Lake Michigan's shore, Ray's next destination before he began searching for Arnie Vedder. Ray pulled into Nora's drive. The doors of her detached garage were open, and the tailgate of her Ford Explorer was ajar.

When Ray slammed his door, a cacophony of barking erupted as both dogs ran to the screen door and announced his arrival. They quieted when Nora came to the door. "Going somewhere?" he asked as she unlatched the door for him.

"Just got back," she explained. "Had to get supplies to make these guys some more food."

"Do you think they have any idea how good they have it?" he asked, kneeling and rubbing the dogs, one with each hand. "A special diet—free-range chickens and organic brown rice with assorted vegetables mixed in."

"Just look at them, and you've got your answer," she responded with pride. "They're ten and twelve, Ray. Look at the condition they're in, fit and healthy."

"I had a call early this morning, Nora."

"I bet you did," she responded with a knowing nod. "Jeannie, my daughter, rang you at home I bet, probably before seven."

"She's worried, and I think her concern is justified," observed Ray. "Even if she hadn't phoned, I was planning on coming by and talking to you today. In fact, I almost drove over late last night. I didn't like the idea of you being alone."

"Ray, it's been ten years since Hugh died. Ten years I've been here alone and nothing has ever happened."

"True," agreed Ray. "But there's never been a murder on this beach before. Everything is different now and will be until we find the murderer. "

"I've got protection," Nora said. She crossed the room and pulled a double-barreled shotgun from the top of the mantle. The long, heavy old weapon loomed large against her delicate frame. "It's loaded with buckshot, too."

Ray crossed to her and lifted the unwieldy firearm from her grip. He inspected it carefully, noting the hammers were not cocked; then he opened the breach. Using the nails on his thumb and middle finger, he extracted the two shells and scrutinized them. After setting the cartridges on the table, he pointed the barrel toward a ceiling light in the kitchen and looked at the bore.

Nora stood a few feet away, watching Ray's careful examination. "Well, doctor, how's the patient's health?"

"When was the last time this was fired?" he asked, setting the shotgun on the table.

"Well, it's probably been awhile."

"Nora," he pronounced her name slowly. "How many years?"

"Before Hugh died."

"How long?"

"Well, you know, he was sick for awhile. A few years, I guess."

"So, what do you think, maybe fifteen years?"

"Probably less," Nora answered, her weak smile suggested that it was probably more, and that they both knew it.

"Have you ever fired this?"

"Oh, yes," she affirmed with great certainty. "Many times, many times. Hugh and I used to go duck hunting."

"And you used this shotgun?"

"Well, no; I had my own gun, a twenty-gauge."

Roy closed the breech of the empty gun and handed it back to her. "If you had to fire this antique, what would you do?"

"Easy, I'd cock it, hold it tight to my shoulder, and pull the triggers."

"Show me how you'd cock it," he pursued, handing the shotgun back to her.

She held the heavy gun at waist level. Using her thumb, she struggled to pull the hammer back on the right chamber. The left chamber was even more difficult. Finally, she looked up in defeat. "So what?" she asked.

"My concern is . . ." He stopped. "Let me rephrase that." He measured his words carefully. "Nora, this is a very old gun. It's had a hard life, and it isn't in the best shape. I'm not sure it would even be safe to fire with modern ammunition. It's hard to cock, and it will have an enormous recoil. And there's a good chance that an assailant could grab it away from you. There's a murderer out there. I would feel much better if you were out of the area for a while."

"I don't want to go to Grosse Pointe. Last time I was there Jeannie took me around to several retirement villages. She had this whole speech on how much better it would be for me in one of those places." She walked to the picture window and looked out at the lake, then turned back toward Ray. "I can't imagine leaving this place. This is where I want to die."

Ray looked at her and smiled; he noted the calm determination in her gray eyes. "How about your friend Dottie? You stayed with her for a couple of weeks last year after she came home from the hospital. Can you visit her for a few days? I would feel better if you were down in the village."

"Is that what you want me to do?"

"Just for a while."

They stood in silence for a long moment. Then, without enthusiasm, Nora said, "I'll give her a call. She'd probably be happy to have the company."

"Good. I want this to happen today."

"Okay. Is there anything else?"

"One thing. In your collection of defensive weapons, didn't you once show me a big knife you keep on your nightstand?"

"Yes, the bayonet. Hugh brought it back from the war."

"Can I see it, please?"

"What's this all about?" asked Nora.

"You've told me about it, but I've never seen it. So, while I'm inspecting your cache of weapons, I might as well look at that, too."

Nora disappeared up the stairs toward her bedroom. She returned a few minutes later holding a large knife in a lacquered scabbard. She placed it in Ray's hands. He pulled the knife from the case and examined the expertly chromed blade with rounded, dull edges. He smiled as he looked back at Nora. "Did Hugh bring this back from the army after WWII?" he asked.

"Yes. I found the knife in his old military footlocker when I was going through things after he died. I liked having it near me at night, especially at first when I was scared of being here alone."

"Was Hugh in a drill team or a color guard?" he asked.

"Yes, he was, color guard. Remember how tall and handsome Hugh was? He looked just stunning in his uniform."

Ray handed back the knife, smiling. "Hugh was a wonderful man, Nora." He looked around. "I have a few minutes before my next meeting. Can I help you get packed?"

11

~~~

Ray waited as Nora called her friend Dottie and arranged to stay with her, then he helped her quickly gather her things. Once she and the dogs were loaded and on their way to the village, Ray drove three miles to the trailhead of Otter Lake Pathway, a series of footpaths that ran through thousands of acres of low marshland that included swamps, sinkholes, cedar forests, and one small lake that emptied into Lake Michigan via a long shallow stream.

Ray pulled into the leaf-covered asphalt parking lot near the trailhead. He found Deputy Sue Lawrence and Kim Vedder sitting on the back of Sue's Jeep, pulling on tall rubber boots. After a hurried greeting, he also donned knee boots and a raincoat. The clear blue sky and early morning sunshine had been replaced by dense, leaden clouds blowing down Lake Michigan from the Upper Peninsula. Rain had started to fall again.

"Did you bring a GPS?" Ray asked Sue Lawrence.

"It's here, and I just turned it on," she responded, motioning toward the zippered pocket on her rain jacket.

They crossed the parking lot and a narrow band of dunes at the edge of the marsh, and then Kim led the way. The trio waded the stream, swelled over its banks by two days of near-continuous showers, and followed a muddy path into the cedar swamp. The rain intensified, bands of water were carried almost horizontally by the howling wind. Lightning flashed overhead, and thunder reverberated around them. The trail turned into a muddy stream as they slogged deeper into the swamp. And then the trail disappeared completely in the rising water.

Kim stopped, brushing loose strands of wet hair away from her face. She looked at the two possible paths through the marsh. "I not sure which way, I've only been here once. And with all this water it looks different."

"We'll go with your best guess, Kim," said Ray.

"I just don't know."

Ray moved ahead of Kim and studied the terrain. "Let's go to the right. The terrain looks a bit higher." He sloshed ahead, finding firmer ground as they entered a thick stand of cedar. "Does this look familiar?" he asked.

"I can remember trees like this, we walked along the edge of a swamp." She carefully surveyed the area. "If we can find the little lake, his hut will be off to the side."

They worked their way through the cedar swamp, moving along the small isles of solid ground found at the base of the trees. Eventually they reached the shore of a mud lake, only a few dozen acres in size.

"This is it," said Kim. "It's about halfway around. Over there." She pointed toward a thick stand of second growth pine.

Ray could see little through the fog and rain, but he marched off in that direction. A primitive wood and tarp shelter, thirty yards from the edge of the water near the base of a large pine, came into view. As they approached, Ray could see a metal stovepipe, but no hint of smoke. The frame of the tiny structure was built with small cedar logs. The walls were scraps of rough lumber and driftwood nailed in a haphazard manner to the log frame; the roof was draped with a blue plastic tarp fastened with ropes at the corners. A small wooden door faced the water. Ray pushed the door; it was secured on the inside. He shoved it forcefully, and it fell off its makeshift hinges. He peered into the dark cavity, and then fished for the small flashlight on his belt. In its beam he could see an unmoving body wrapped in a sleeping bag huddled against the back wall. Ray dropped to his knees and crawled through the door to get a better look. Sue crawled in behind him and helped illuminate the scene with her light.

"Is he okay?" Kim asked, looking over them from the outside.

Ray touched the wet clothing. He palpated the cold, clammy skin. He reached for the carotid artery, eventually finding a weak, stringy cadence. He put his light on Arnie's face; his eyes were open but non-reactive to the light. "Arnie," he said softly. He said it a second time, giving him a gentle shake. No response.

"Is he all right?" Kim asked the question again, this time more frantic than the first.

"Sue, do you have a large evidence bag?"

She crawled beside him. His flashlight pointed to a woman's sandal close to Arnie on the floor. She carefully picked it up with a gloved hand and slid it into the bag, placing a second bag around the first.

"What's wrong with him? Is he dead, sheriff?" asked Kim—panic in her voice as she peered over Ray's shoulder.

"Arnie's suffering from hypothermia. He's been cold and wet for a long time. We've got to get him to the hospital. Kim, move outside for a few minutes while I cover him. Then you can sit with him." Ray backed out of the hut. "Sue, see if dispatch can get a Coast Guard chopper in here. Tell them we have a victim in stage-three hypothermia."

Ray took off his raincoat and jacket and climbed back into the shelter. After unwrapping the thin damp sleeping bag from Arnie's upper torso, Ray covered him with his jacket and coat and laid him back down. Ray studied the 5-by-5-foot interior—the tiny sheet-metal stove in the corner with a plastic garbage bag nearby, a dented aluminum pan hanging on a nail at the side, three soggy

People magazines, the wet blue nylon sleeping bag, and a small telescope laying near the stove—its eyepiece extending out from a protective nylon bag, nothing else. Kim crawled next to her son. "You can help him stay warm by holding him close," he said. Kim lay next to Arnie and pulled him to her body.

Ray found dry kindling and matches in the plastic garbage bag. He started a fire in the stove and backed out of the hut.

"You want a space blanket?" Sue asked after he emerged from the hut.

"Sure," he responded. Sue dug through her backpack and handed Ray a small packet. He unwrapped the tightly folded package and pulled the thin sheet of silvery plastic around his shoulders. They stood on the shore and waited for the chopper. At the sound of its approach—the thumping of its blades in the heavy air—Sue fired a flare. The projectile arched out over the lake and fell toward the water. Sue glanced back toward the hut to ensure they were out of earshot.

"Is Arnie going to make it?" she shouted over the roar of the approaching chopper.

"It's a crap shoot," said Ray.

The pilot turned the bright orange helicopter in their direction. They could see him wave through the Plexiglas bubble. As the pilot carefully oriented his ship, Ray and Sue moved out into the clearing near the shore and waited for the rescue basket to descend.

12

As Ray entered the conference room he could see that Deputy Sue Lawrence had covered one side of the table with neat piles of documents, photos, and diagrams. She also had a small array of items—a sandal, a blue beach towel, the photo of Ashleigh and her mother—in evidence bags. Ray placed a stainless steel coffee mug on the table and sat across from her.

"Any word on Vedder?" Sue asked as she sorted some photos.

"I just called. They're trying to stabilize him, doing blood warming." Ray sipped his coffee. "It doesn't sound good."

"Kim?"

"She's there. If he doesn't make it, well." Ray dropped his head toward the table, rubbed his forehead with his forefingers and thumb; a wave of fatigue swept across his body. Looking up, he continued, "That poor woman, her life has been one tragedy after another. I wonder how she'll get through this one."

Sue let his comment hang for a long time, finally saying, "Here is the inventory of clothing for Ashleigh and David. You'll notice that we only found one sandal, a women's size eight Chaco for the left foot."

Ray looked at the list of clothing for each victim, followed by the other items collected at the scene.

"Did you process the shoe we recovered in Arnie's hut?"

"Yes, it appears to be the mate—right foot, same size and model of Chaco with a similar amount of wear. I can take this further if need be," said Sue.

"So, assuming that the sandal is a match, we have evidence that Arnie was probably at the crime scene. Warrington told me Ashleigh was someone who had been kind to Arnie and that he was often seen hanging around near her cottage," Ray paused. "And Kim Vedder talked about Arnie's fascination with the dunes and beach in that area. He would spend nights there, looking at the stars, sleeping, and not coming home until after dawn."

"Any chance Arnie is the killer?" Sue's tone suggested her own doubt.

"Check Arnie's clothes for traces of blood; I think the perp would have been covered with blood." Ray stopped briefly and looked directly at Sue, "Can you imagine him overcoming two physically fit adults?"

"He would have had the element of surprise," she countered.

"True," answered Ray. "But, think about him pulling Dowd's head into that position or overpowering Ashleigh. He has the strength of a child, a fairly fragile child at that."

"Okay," agreed Sue, "not likely. But maybe he saw something, like the killer."

"And I think that's very possible. Here is a scenario. Arnie is up at his perch high on the dunes. He sees Ashleigh and David Dowd coming down the beach. Her long hair is pretty distinctive, and he might have even been using his telescope. According to Nora it was close to dusk when she encountered the couple, so his view would have deteriorated in the fading light. He sees the attack, or he wanders down in the dark and finds them. He might have even come on the scene the next morning."

"How do you explain the sandal?" asked Sue.

"I don't know, perhaps he wasn't even aware of what he was doing, just picked something up and ran." Ray slowed, "Arnie is a fragile kid. Just seeing the bodies would have been enough to put him in a complete panic, and if he saw the attack, well . . ." He remained quiet for a few moments as he visualized Arnie at the scene.

"Why wouldn't he try to get help? That would have been such a natural thing to do."

"He isn't normal. His thinking is confused." Ray looked across at Sue's neatly organized evidence stacks. He gestured with his hand, "So, what else do you have?"

"Here," she slid a drawing across the table, "is the diagram of the crime scene. You can see the position of the bodies, clothes, food, and wine bottle. There was a small pocketknife next to the cheese, one of the Swiss army ones with a corkscrew. Not big enough to be the weapon." She lifted up a plastic bag. "That's about it. We searched the whole grid in that diagram, even raked through the sand on our second go, just some typical beach debris. Then we used a metal detector—can tabs and bottle tops. The hours of heavy rain didn't leave much. The photos," she pushed a stack of 8-by-12-inch glossies in his direction, "are keyed to the numbers on the diagram."

Ray sat silently and studied the diagram, then he carefully looked at the photos, examining the scene again, taking in all the details, attempting to visualize the murderous rage of the perpetrator. He closed his eyes and put himself on the beach. He could smell the damp shore, hear the lulling waves and the lovers breathing, sense the shared pleasure, and then feel the sudden yank, slash, and pain.

"And here," Sue, interrupting his musing, slid a second diagram across the table, "I've placed the scene against the wider area using a geographical survey map as the basis for this diagram. The purpose was to look for possible routes to and from the scene. The most obvious one, of course, is the beach, but there's also this trail." She reached across and traced the path. "It starts here at the parking lot, runs through the woods behind Nora Jennings's cottage and up along the ridgeline. Then it turns and runs back across the dune and into a two-track that winds back to the highway." She hesitated. "But I'm probably telling you something you know."

"This was one of my favorite beaches when I was a kid. I've covered that trail hundreds of times."

"We searched the trail from one end to the other."

"Find anything?"

"Nothing unusual, just ordinary litter left over from the summer. Food wrappers, pop and beer cans, plastic water bottles, discarded clothing, and a few condoms off to the side." Sue had a look of mild disgust on her face. "I'd hoped that our perp might have dropped something, or perhaps we'd even find tire impressions in the protected area in the woods, but nothing. We've checked the beach in both directions for about a mile, and sorted through the trash basket in the park. I don't think there's much," Sue paused, a look of frustration covered her face. "If the perp didn't take the knife with him, it would only take a few minutes to bury it and with miles of beach and dune . . ."

"Or," Ray continued, "he could have thrown the knife out into the waves, or even swam out, past the second bar, and buried it." He looked at Sue. "So, what's your theory? How do you think this was done?"

"I think they were either followed or the perp knew where Ashleigh would probably take someone. The killer could have pursued them up the beach, but I think the trail would have been a better bet."

"But . . ."

"Right, the perp would need some knowledge of the area."

"But probably not too much," said Ray. "If they parked in the lot, the trail is marked with a map posted at the trailhead. Plus, once you get out beyond the forest you can see for miles from the top of the dunes."

"Wait. I'm telling the story," Sue smiled. "I think the perp took the trail. From the top of the dune it's easy to watch someone coming up the beach. He waited until they were engaged, probably slid down one of those gullies, and then crawled up through the dune grass from the lake. Approaching at that angle he wouldn't be spotted until the last second." She pushed over the pile of photos. "Look at the position of the bodies, the assailant would have attacked from this line," she used her finger as a pointer, "slashed victim one, and then stabbed victim two. Just the way Dr. Dyskin described it."

"And how about Arnie?"

"He could have been up there too. There's a lot of real estate. And I doubt if the killer would have been aware of his presence."

Ray was silent as he considered this scenario. Finally he asked, "Ashleigh's car?"

"The Volvo was locked. I assume Ashleigh locked it."

"Because?"

"There was a backpack and some other fairly expensive camping equipment in the rear. I opened it with keys we pulled from her jeans. I've dusted the car, her prints are everywhere. Dowd's are on the passenger's side. There are some others, random, and mostly partial. I don't think the killer touched the car."

"What else?"

"We've checked the other cottages along the ridge, they're all closed for the season. And I talked with Nora again. She's sure she didn't see anyone else that evening. Said there were a few people around earlier, but they were long gone by dusk."

Ray slid down in his chair. "You've been thorough. Damn," he muttered. "There just isn't much here." He paused, removed his glasses, and rubbed his right eye. "If we could find the weapon, that might give us some direction. Let's do a search of the water contiguous with that part of the shore, out to the second bar. And sweep a broader area of the beach with the metal detectors. But . . ."

"But what?"

"The proverbial needle, isn't it?" Ray said. He looked at his watch. "Ready to face the cameras? We've got about fifteen minutes until the news conference," he said, pulling several sheets of paper from his printer tray. "Here's the statement I'm planning on reading. Why don't you give it a quick read and tell me if you think I need to make any changes?"

"This is the part I hate," Sue said.

"It won't be bad," Ray offered reassuringly. "I'll take all the questions. And at this point we don't have much that we can tell them."

13

Ray parked near the entrance of the Last Chance Tavern and moseyed in, past the pool table, empty boots, and jukebox and settled on the black vinyl cushion of a barstool. Jack Grochoski, the bartender and owner, his back turned to the room, was focused on a large television screen mounted on the back wall of the bar, above the neat rows of liquor bottles. On screen, Oprah was chatting with a bald-headed, intense-looking man. Ray, making a coughing sound, cleared his throat. Grochoski, looking startled, turned around.

"Ray. Sorry, I didn't see you come in. I was getting counseled on my love life," Grochoski said laughing, as he picked up a remote and turned down the volume. He reached under the bar to get a coffee cup. "I made this about half an hour ago, it's probably still okay," he said as he filled the large, white ceramic mug. "If it has gone bitter, just say the word, and I'll . . ."

"It's fine, Jack," said Ray after he carefully tested the coffee. He laid two photos on the bar.

Grochoski pulled a pair of glasses out of his shirt pocket, unfolded them, and slid them in place, using his forefinger to adjust them on his nose. "Horrible thing," he said, looking at the pictures.

"We never used to have this kind of stuff. Maybe in Detroit, but not here."

"You're familiar with the people in the photos?"

"Yes, the girl especially, Ashleigh. She was a . . . well, I won't say a regular, but she was in here once or twice a week. She'd have a meal, sometimes pick up a six-pack. She was a real cutie, full of life."

"And the young man?"

"I've only seen him a few times. He was a friend of Ashleigh's. He was always with her when he came in. He wasn't a local. I think I'd only seen him on weekends."

"Were they here on Saturday?"

Jack pulled at his right ear as he thought about it. "Saturday, yes, came in for lunch. Ashleigh loved our hamburgers. She liked to joke that she'd had burgers all over the world and mine were the best."

"What time did they come in?"

"It was early. Noon rush hadn't started yet."

"And they left?"

"Probably one or shortly after. They had some burgers and fries, couple of shells of beer. They were sitting over at that table near the window. Seemed to be having a serious conversation. Ashleigh wasn't her usual self, joking and all. And when they left she didn't come over and say goodbye like she always did. She was always teasing me, calling me Mister Jack." His eyes glazed over, sadness ran across his craggy face. He brightened a bit. "Mr. Jack— the name's sorta caught on. Some of the regulars are calling me that now."

"Did she seem upset?"

"I can't say for sure. We had a lot of lunch trade, locals and color-tour folks. I didn't have much of a chance to see what was going on."

"How long has she been a customer?"

"Well, the news said she'd been at Leiston three years. That seems right. The first year she was probably in here a bit more."

"Men. Did you know people she was dating?"

"Didn't seem to let any grass grow under her feet. She was here with a variety of men, but most weren't from around here. Except for Jason Zelke, of course. I think she was sweet on him for a while. Didn't seem to last, though."

"When was that?"

"Zelke, let me think." Jack started to chuckle. "You know, Ray, they say that your mind is the first thing to go, but hell, I got a lot of other things going, too."

Ray smiled, then returned to the question at hand. "Zelke?" he repeated.

"Pretty sure it was last winter. Might have been winter before that."

"Who else did she come in with?"

"Mostly people from the school. The first year she'd come in with Warrington, the headmaster. All seemed proper and above board. I mean they were usually with other people from the school. They weren't hiding in the corner like some couples, but I sorta wondered. His wife caught them together once; they had a bit of a domestic," he pronounced the word slowly and rolled his eyes, "right over there at the table by the jukebox. I think that she was in her cups when she got here. Did a lot of yelling. He did his best to get her out of here in a hurry."

"Things change after that?"

"Sure did. If there was anything going on, they took it underground. Lots of deserted roads and beaches around here, aren't there?" he said with a grin. "And it ain't too hard to get access to a summer home. No need to be seen in public if you don't want to."

"And Mrs. Warrington?"

"Helen," said Jack.

"Tell me about Helen."

"Nice looking woman," Jack observed. "She was a regular for a time, especially the first year they were at Leiston School. She'd stop by in the late afternoon, have a G and T or two. I always thought she had had a couple before she got here. Then her visits started getting less and less regular. And now I don't think I've seen her for more than a year. I heard she started going to AA."

"Did she meet anyone here?"

"No, she seemed to want to be left alone. Can remember one time when a couple of deer hunters hit on her, didn't catch what she said, but they got the message real fast."

"When she was here, what did she do?"

"She'd talk to me, have her drinks, and smoke. Seemed lonely, you know what I mean?"

"Ever talk about her marriage or anything personal?"

"Never. Just local gossip, news, weather, stuff like that. What was happening on the tube," he gestured over his back toward the TV.

"She never brought anyone with her?" Ray asked, rephrasing an earlier question.

"No," said Jack. He looked across the bar, out toward the picture window on the front wall and then back at Ray. "I think I once heard a rumor that she was seen with someone." Jack looked thoughtful. "Maybe it wasn't her. You hear a lot of stories in this job. They all start running together."

"How about other Leiston employees?" asked Ray.

"How far do you want me to go back?"

"Start at the beginning."

"The founder, Mrs. Howard, Gwendolyn," Jack's voice took on a wistful quality, "she was the genuine article, a real lady. Not like these yuppies that are building the trophy houses around here these days. Million bucks for a hundred feet of frontage. Where the hell does that kind of money come from?

"Gwendolyn was the real thing," Jack continued. "Old money. She was a good person who treated you right. In the early days, after she started the school, she'd be here in the evenings with her teachers. They were all young then—in their twenties. She was probably forty-five, or fifty, still a fine-looking woman. They'd pull together some tables, get a few pitchers of beer, and sorta have meetings. There was a lot of excitement and energy, you know what I mean?"

Ray nodded.

"They were building something. And she'd invite me to the school when they were having a special event, like a play or a concert. But over the years we've seen less and less of the Leiston folks. In the sixties those were their tables," he motioned off to the left. "Most of the original teachers are long gone. Those that replaced them ain't the same. Guess the school ain't the same either. And when they come in now they're sort of snooty, like they're better than the rest of us. My girls don't like them. Say they're too demanding and poor tippers."

"Are any of them regulars?"

"Just one old-timer, the sculptor and painter, Janet Medford, she's in here a lot. Mrs. Howard hired her; she was one of the original teachers. She was a real looker back in the '60s—thin, big tits, pretty ass, and funny in a sarcastic kind of way. Think the cigarettes ruined her face. And she let herself run too fat. Used to come in with the drama teacher, Todd Danforth, he was one of the originals. I didn't know whether they were a couple or just liked to drink together. Serious drinkers, Manhattans, light on the vermouth, extra dash of bitters. Didn't seem to faze them. They used to joke that they hated the drinks but loved the cherries." Jack paused, his voice softened. "He died last year, Danforth did, lung cancer. Janet still comes in the evening. Think she's real lonely."

"Going back to Ashleigh. Did she ever pick up men here?"

"Well, I think most men who saw her woulda liked to get lucky with her. Pretty, hell of a body, bit of a tease. But I don't know. She wasn't giving it away, if that's what you mean. But I didn't get the impression she was doing without. She could pick and choose. And most of the local boys, hell, they knew she was out of their class."

"Did you know if anyone was angry with her? Perhaps someone who hit on her and was put down?"

"No. I'm sure that happened. But Ashleigh had such a nice

way about her. She'd handle that kind of situation without making the person feel stupid. I'm going to miss her. Just looking at her made you feel good, know what I mean?"

Ray nodded in agreement, but he was thinking about someone else.

14

Ray Elkins, with the help of a Leiston student, managed to find Sarah James' office. It was in the same wing of the mansion as Ian Warrington's, but farther back, on the opposite side of the hall. After Sarah and Ray exchanged greetings, she led him through a door on the left side of her office into a large formal room. The walls were paneled in dark oak, and a long walnut table was centered below two banks of fluorescent lights that hung from an ornately plastered ceiling. Eighteen high-backed office chairs in black leather, eight on each side, one at each end, surrounded the table. A tray with a silver carafe of coffee, two mugs, and two bowls—one with sugar packets, the other with small sealed containers of cream—was placed near the head of the table.

Ray walked the perimeter of the room, taking it all in. An elaborately carved sideboard stood along the interior wall; opposite were three sets of French doors that faced a central garden. A travertine fireplace filled much of a third wall. Parquet flooring in a herringbone pattern, similar to the one that Ray had seen in Warrington's office, covered the floor. The furniture and dark wood surfaces seemed to absorb most of the illumination from overhead lights and the garden beyond the French doors, giving the space an aura of gloom.

"So this must have been the formal dining room," Ray observed. "And your office was probably the butler's pantry?"

"Yes," Sarah replied, seemingly intrigued by Ray's interest in the building. "The school library has an archive of pictures taken before the mansion was converted. They're quite fascinating," she continued, warming to the topic. "They are all in black and white, of course, but you can get a pretty good sense of how the place looked in the early years: the furniture, the grounds, family photos, and pictures of parties and gatherings. And lots of animals: dogs, horses, and cattle. It was a different world."

Sarah placed a pile of folders on the table, and they settled into adjoining chairs. "I've pulled all our records on Ashleigh Allen. I'm afraid there isn't much. At a small school like Leiston we don't generate much paper." She pulled the tray close to her. "Coffee?" she asked, starting to fill a mug.

"Yes, please. Black," Ray responded. "I'm trying to understand your function here. You take care of the personnel . . ."

"Human resources. Yes, that's one of my responsibilities. My title is associate director for administration. I do the human resources work and handle most of internal management, plus whatever special projects Mr. Warrington assigns."

"In addition to you and Warrington, how many other people work in management positions?" he asked, observing her closely, watching her eyes. She seemed relaxed and was much more attractive than he remembered from their first encounter; her manner was warm and engaging.

"Thompson, Bob Thompson, he's our financial person, and Ian's wife, Helen, takes care of the development office."

"Development?"

"Yes, that's the current euphemism for fundraising. She also looks after alumni relations; they really dovetail. And then there's food service and security/maintenance. I've been told that when Mrs. Howard was alive and ran the school there was a lot more staff. But we're now trying to make ends meet with tuition and a small endowment."

Ray looked through Ashleigh's small stack of papers: college transcripts, a letter of application, three letters of recommendation, a pre-employment physical and drug screening, the report from a third-party background check, a copy of the letter offering employment, and three yearly evaluations. Ray perused each document carefully and found nothing unusual. The evaluations were written by Warrington and were highly favorable. Ray looked up and caught Sarah watching him.

"You have a background check on all employees?"

"We do now, it's one of the many changes Dr. Warrington instituted."

Ray closed the folder. "You're right. Not much here. But I wasn't expecting a great deal. Tell me, Ms. James, tell me about Ashleigh."

"Would you like me to freshen your coffee, sheriff?"

Ray nodded and held out his cup. "Ashleigh Allen?"

"Ashleigh Allen," she repeated as she pulled her glasses off and set them on the table. "Well, as you can see she came here to teach three years ago. But, as I'm sure you know by now, she was a niece of Mrs. Howard and had been a student here."

"Do you think that was a hiring consideration?" he probed.

"No. I'm sure it could look that way, but no. You saw her grades and read her recommendations. Any school would have been lucky to get her."

"But she did upset people," Elkins said, looking into her soft blue eyes.

"Initially, yes, especially early on. She was so good at everything. And the students and their parents loved her."

"But not every one loved her?"

"No, some of the old-timers disliked her. They thought that Ashleigh had an air of entitlement. She would ask for things that no one else would."

"Are you talking about salary?"

"No, nothing like that. Nothing for herself, ever. She'd ask for equipment for her classroom, or things for her outdoors program: high-tech camping equipment, new sea kayaks, even a climbing wall with all the ropes and paraphernalia. And she'd get them. I think that's what the others resented."

"And who would she ask, Warrington?"

"She'd start with him. If she couldn't get the money from school funds, she'd go after an alum or one of our current parents. Ashleigh was very aggressive and quite persuasive."

"Did this ah . . . entrepreneurial approach, did this offend Mr. Warrington?"

"I don't think anything Ashleigh did offended Ian." Once the words were out of her mouth her expression suggested that she wished she could take them back.

"So, in spite of all these stories of how everyone loved Ashleigh, there were some people who were at least unhappy with her . . ."

"They thought she was self-serving. Other people needed things for their programs as well. The art teacher wanted new computers for digital photography; the French teacher wanted a modern language lab. Last year we had requests for a half million in new equipment, but a budget of less than forty thousand. Ashleigh usually got more than her share, and I would hear about it. When people are angry they come to me. They think it's safer to air their grievances with me than with Dr. Warrington."

"How angry?"

She looked thoughtful and then gave Ray a mocking smile. "Not angry enough to kill her, if that's what you're asking. Just the normal kind of friction you find in any organization. And," she slowed down her speech, giving emphasis to her words, "there's less hostility here than in most places I've worked."

"So, who was especially unhappy with Ashleigh?"

"Probably Janet Medford, the art teacher, was the most vocal. She got quite personal, nasty is perhaps a better word. She kept referring to how the budget decisions were being made based on the T-and-A factor. But then Janet is bitter about most things, and it's only gotten worse since her long-time companion died of lung cancer last fall."

"Who was that?"

"Todd Danforth, he was our drama teacher."

"Tell me about the . . ." Ray caught himself and rephrased the question. "Tell me about the man at the meeting who seemed so angry."

"Alan Quertermous."

"Who is?"

"He's one of the math teachers. And what you saw is typical of his performances at staff meetings. He usually explodes three or four times a year. And he's always right and the rest of us are idiots," she paused. "He refers to any of us who aren't agreeing with him as 'pinheads.'"

"Tell me about Mr. Quertermous."

"He's been here from almost the beginning of the school. But he's quite different from the other teachers, especially the other people Mrs. Howard hired."

"How so?"

"This was a very experimental school, especially in the beginning. It had an extremely liberal staff, people who were open to all kinds of non-traditional approaches to teaching. This man, Quertermous, is really reactionary, and I can't imagine he was much different years ago. The other thing that sets him apart from the rest of the faculty is that Alan clearly has independent means. Rumor has it he inherited millions from his father. He doesn't live on campus. He's got one of those big new houses on the ridgeline overlooking the lake. It's sort of a fortress. The joke around here is that he's a mountain man survivalist who wears Brooks Brothers suits and drinks single-malt whiskey."

"Have you ever been to his house?" Ray asked.

"Yes, I'm probably one of the few people here who has. When I first arrived in the area, he was very nice to my son and me. He gave us a wonderful tour of the area and took us sailing." She looked at Ray, "Nothing romantic, at least in my mind. I thought he was probably gay. Then he invited me to his house. It was pretty scary. Lots of guns. He took pride in showing me this elaborate security system: cameras, motion detectors, and floodlights. The place was just creepy. After that things got rather sticky because he continued to try to do things for us, and I did my best to avoid him. Eventually he got the idea."

"And he didn't like Ashleigh?"

"Oil and water. They were at opposite poles. But then, he's often at odds with everyone on the faculty. I know Ian hopes he can get Quertermous to retire this year. But I think he's going to try to hold on as long as possible."

"What kind of a teacher is he?"

"Well, that's the interesting thing. With his peers and us he's usually sarcastic and angry. And some of the kids really dislike him, but others, especially the poorer math students, say he's kind and patient. Sort of Jekyll and Hyde."

"Were there any recent problems between Ashleigh and . . ."

"No, not that I know of. I just think she represented a world that he finds very threatening." She paused for a minute. "There's one more thing about Alan, I sort of forgot."

"What's that?"

"When I was telling Ashleigh about my experience with him, she said during her first semester here he came on to her in much the same way. She said they had one very uncomfortable encounter."

"Did she elaborate?" asked Ray.

"No. Maybe he did that with all the new women employees."

"Who else had problems with Ashleigh?"

"Helen Warrington. I know she wasn't too happy about Ashleigh's solo fundraising activities, the fact that she would bypass Helen's office completely when she was looking for money." She paused and looked directly into Ray's eyes. "I don't think she ever confronted Ashleigh. But she would tell others that if Ashleigh wanted something so much she should get the money from her own trust fund."

"Ashleigh has . . ."

"I don't know. There were rumors that Ashleigh inherited a good deal of money from her mother and her great-aunt. If she did, she didn't wear it. You seldom saw her in anything but jeans and a T-shirt; she drove that ancient Volvo. She traveled during vacations and all summer, but I think it was mostly backpacking and camping. If she had money, she wasn't spending it."

"Tell me about Helen Warrington," Ray probed. He noticed a look of caution in Sarah's eyes.

"What would you like to know?"

"I've heard there may be some difficulties in their marriage."

"What does anyone know looking into a relationship from the outside?" Sarah avoided the question.

"I've heard that Helen had a very public confrontation with her husband over his relationship with Ashleigh."

"Recently?"

"Several years ago."

"That was probably her first year here," she said knowingly. "Ian was very taken with Ashleigh. He's a lonely man. He's married to a very cold, unpleasant person. It's difficult to be around Helen for any amount of time. But I don't know about any public confrontation."

"Let me be more direct. Was Mr. Warrington romantically involved with Ashleigh? Were they having an affair?"

Sarah looked ill at ease. She took a deep breath before answering. "During the fall or winter of her first year, they were often together. Some things are hard not to notice in a small community like this. There were rumors, and I was in a better position than most to observe what was going on."

"Well, did you see anything that suggested they were?" Ray stopped and waited.

She paused, looking exasperated. "I came back late one

night. I'd mislaid my checkbook and walked over to see if I left it in the office. Must have been around eleven o'clock. As I was coming down the corridor, Ashleigh was slipping out of Ian's office. I remember saying something like 'Working late?' She sort of laughed and said something, I can't remember her exact words, but I sensed a sexual innuendo. Like she wanted me to know . . ." she stopped and looked at Ray.

"Wanted you to know what?" he pressed.

"At the time I felt that it was a power thing. She wanted me to know—perhaps I'm projecting—that they were involved. And she knew that I would be discreet; that I wouldn't say anything."

Ray looked out into the courtyard and then back at Sarah, holding her in his gaze for a long moment. Finally he asked, "Were you still having an affair with Dr. Warrington at the time?"

"What made you . . . ?" Sarah looked embarrassed and vulnerable. She moved uncomfortably in her chair, sliding down a bit. "It was over, not long over, but over. Ian had convinced me that it would never work, and it was best for both of us if . . ." Another long pause.

"And how long had you and Ian been involved?"

"He arrived in July the year before. During those first months we worked very closely. His predecessor, Dr. Hellebore, was a wonderful educator, a fine man, but he had no interest in management or finance. He left things in great disarray. Ian and I often worked ten or twelve hours a day that first summer and fall. It's easy to get involved when you work that intimately with someone, and given his marriage . . ." She laughed nervously. "I hear myself making excuses. I guess the truth is that I was lonely; he was attentive and kind. I was very taken with him and perhaps had some foolish expectations. It was pretty much over by spring, Ashleigh arrived the following fall."

"And his relationship with Ashleigh, how long did that last?"

"Not long, a few months at the most. It was over before the end of the school year. I think she was the one who set the terms. She had moved on."

"To?"

"I don't think you catch my meaning. She had moved beyond the relationship; not that there weren't other men waiting in the wings."

"Such as?"

"The one I liked the best was the hunk who rebuilt one of the school's barns," she said.

"Who was that?" Ray asked.

"Let me think, his name was on the purchase order." Sarah closed her eyes briefly. "Zelke," she said reopening them. "Jason Zelke, Old Oak Timber Frame."

"And Warrington, has he had other relations?"

"There seems to be a pattern, a kind of serial monogamy," she said coyly. "Well, that's not quite the case. In addition to his wife, he practices serial monogamy."

"And who's he involved with now?"

Sarah hesitated, picked her glasses off the table and adjusted them on her face. "The chair of our board."

"Wouldn't that be quite dangerous?"

"Yes, dangerous to his position if he falls into disfavor with her. But safe in most other ways . . . quite safe. She's a successful lawyer who's wedded to a much older man. Ian meets her in Chicago every three or four weeks to . . . to discuss school business. Most of the board meetings are held in Chicago, easier travel for the members."

"How old is Dr. Warrington?" Ray asked.

"He's forty-six. His birthday is in January."

"And his wife?"

"She doesn't look it, but she's much younger. Thirty-six or thirty-seven."

"Tell me, Ms. James . . ."

"Sarah. Please call me Sarah, sheriff."

"Sarah, what brought you to Leiston?"

"I was looking for a school for my son, Eric. He wasn't doing well in public school. He was bright enough and all, but he wasn't motivated and lacked confidence. And it only got worse when his father and I divorced. I heard about the school from a friend. We came up one beautiful weekend in late spring. Leiston seemed a good place, but money was a bit of a problem. My ex would have paid, but I didn't want to take anything from him. Then I found out that they had an opening that I was qualified for, and tuition is an employee benefit. I left a good job in Detroit, but I think we both needed to get away. And it has worked out for both of us. Eric has graduated; he's at Columbia now, on full scholarship, and doing very well. I should probably move on, also. But I like it here. It's a good place, I love the area, and I've made a life." She paused, and then asked, "Do you still want a tour of the school grounds?"

"Yes, please."

They walked around the grounds in the late fall afternoon. The winds had subsided and the sun was starting to break through. A brilliant carpet of leaves covered the lawns, their oranges and yellows softened by the warm tones of the autumn sun. Following a long circular path—the older part in red brick pavers, the newer sections in asphalt—Sarah identified the different buildings and campus areas. They lingered outside of the art building, an old rural schoolhouse that had been moved to the estate in the early years. Sarah explained that art classes were now held in the modern addition at the rear that followed the lines of the original building, and the old school housed much of the school's permanent art collection.

They stood for a few minutes and watched the women's soccer team practice. On an adjacent field a group of students, more than a dozen, a few more boys than girls, were having a spirited game of Frisbee. The sounds of basketballs being dribbled drew them to the open door of the large barn near the playing fields.

"Isn't this a wonderful building?" said Sarah, looking up at the curved rafters. "They say it's built like an old wooden boat turned upside down. This was the main barn on the estate. Locker rooms were added," she pointed to doors at the end of the building, "when they converted the building to a gym."

"And there's a fencing program here?" Ray asked, noting two pistes and an electronic scoring box at the far end of the gym.

"Todd Danforth, our late drama teacher, had been a collegiate champion at Wayne State, and I think he was on the U.S. Olympic team in the '60s. He had a flourishing intramural fencing program. The kids loved it. Sadly, after his death there was no one to continue the program."

"How did you get on with Ashleigh?" Ray asked.

"Initially, I didn't like her much. I thought she was a real opportunist. But by her second year here, we became very good friends. I will miss her terribly. She's had an enormous effect on me."

"How so?"

"She got me involved in all kinds of things. First, she got me into jogging with her in the late afternoon. I lost ten pounds and started feeling so much better about myself. And then she taught me how to ride a mountain bike. I was hopeless at first, but she was so patient and supportive. Ashleigh was a real risk taker, and she had me doing things I never would have done. Eventually she had me rock climbing and kayaking." She paused. "But it's not about sports, sheriff. It's about confidence. It's about pushing your limits. She taught me how to do that. And she did so much for my son, and the same is true of all students with whom she came in contact. She was like no other teacher here, and everyone knew it."

They stopped and looked across a meadow to a line of scarlet maples. Sarah brushed away a tear. "If I had had a friend like Ashleigh when I was twenty, I think I would have lived my life in a very different way."

Ray looked over at her. It wasn't the first time that he'd noticed how attractive she was.

15

Ray could see Ma French's battered Jimmy parked next to the laundry building as he approached. The rear window, or what had been the rear window, was covered by a piece of plastic sheeting secured by duct tape. The tailgate was fastened by two bungee cords running from the roof rack to the bumper in a crisscross pattern. Bungee cords also zigzagged across the passenger door, holding it closed. The vehicle was clearly unsafe, but it was her only source of transportation to a job that she and her family desperately needed. Ma, in her late sixties, supported a mentally disabled child and a husband incapacitated by emphysema. Since the decrepit vehicle was only used to get her from their crumbling farmhouse a few miles away to work and the village for groceries, Ray tried to overlook its dilapidated condition, hoping that nothing would happen that would come back to haunt him.

The noise, humidity, and bleach-tinged odors of a laundry hit him as he pushed his way through the double doors, dual hinged with battered stainless steel kick plates at the bottom. Ma, a big pear-shaped women with salt-and-pepper hair pulled tight in a large bun, stood at the center of a large table, a pile of clean laundry on her left, folded clothes on her right next to a basket.

A mournful country and western song wailed in the background over the machine sounds as she skillfully smoothed wrinkles and folded the wash.

She greeted Ray with a bright smile, brushing a few strands of loose hair from her face with her left hand. "Afternoon, sheriff."

"Hi, Ma. How you doing?"

"Better than she is." She gestured toward the radio, the singer recounting a woeful tale of deception and lost love.

"How are Pa and Bobby?" Ray asked.

"I don't know about Pa," slowly moving her head from side to side. "Since they've put him on oxygen, I think he's going downhill. But he keeps telling me he's feeling fine. He wants to go deer hunting with Junior. Says he'll take the portable tank with him. And the man's so stubborn I'll probably have to let him go." She paused and took a breath, "Bobby, well, he's just the same. But nothing is bothering him none. Never does." She moved a pile of folded wash from the counter to the plastic basket at her right. "Don't imagine you came around to check on the family, sheriff. What can I do for you?"

"Got a couple of questions about Arnie Vedder I was hoping you could help me with."

"Poor Arnie," a look of sorrow spread across her heavy features. "Poor kid never had a chance. I wish I could have done more. I just didn't see it coming."

"What do you mean?"

"All this talk about him taking things and such."

"I've heard about missing articles of clothing. You don't think there's any truth to these stories?"

"No. None. Arnie is good boy. I've known him almost since he was born. I know teenage boys do stuff like that. But I don't think Arnie did."

"Why not?"

"Kids are losing things all the time. Half of 'em would lose their ass if it weren't attached. And when some clothes is lost, they come over here thinking I musta lost it." She waved in the direction of a row of baskets, plastic, identical in shape, size, and color—an institutional gray—standing on a long counter. Each one had a label across the front with a student name and dorm. "The kids bring their baskets over and stack them on that counter. When I put the clothes into a washer, I put the baskets right in front. When the washing is done, it goes in the basket, and I move it to a dryer. Then it's back in the basket and put there," she motioned to a counter on the opposite wall, "till I fold it. Now, tell me sheriff, how can stuff get lost?"

"But you do have student help?"

"Yes, I got a couple of community helpers, that's what they call them. Every student has to do a few hours of 'community work' around the school. They rotate jobs every week. I have them fold washing. Girls fold girls' stuff, boys fold boys' and I make sure there's no fooling around. Some of these kids have never had to fold their own washing, so I show them how to do it and make sure everyone does it the same way. And they're good kids, sheriff. Most of the time I enjoy their company."

"Do the students do anything besides folding?"

"They lend a hand at taking things back to the dorms. And that's a big help to me. I'm having trouble with my feet, bunions. Doctor says I need an operation."

"What did Arnie do?"

Ma looked pained. "Well, it was so much less than I hoped. I thought he could help me with everything, but that just wasn't so. Simple jobs, that's what he could do."

"For example?"

"He'd sweep, and he'd mop. I'd find little things that he could do. But sheriff, I would have to give him so much help. He just couldn't seem to keep focused on a task. He'd get lost. Like if he was sweeping, I'd have to stand right there and supervise. I didn't mind; I've had to do the same thing with Bobby. But it was just so sad to see him that way. He was just such a smart kid before the accident."

"Did you tell anyone about Arnie's limitations?"

"No. I tried to make the best of it. And sheriff, he was beginning to pick things up, if ever so slow. But I think it was the girls complaining that finally did him in."

"Complaining about what?"

"I don't know. At first they were so kind to him, but the way he looks, it kinda got to them. And you know how kids are. First they complained to me, and then they talked to Tom Bates, he supervises this area." She placed the folded clothes in the basket. "The panties was one thing. There was also this talk about him being a stalker. I mean, the kids don't know what that is. It was so silly. But some of them got pretty hysterical, especially the younger ones. Then one day he didn't come in. When I went to ask Tom where Arnie was, he told me he had been sacked. Like they didn't ask me anything or tell me beforehand. It just wasn't right, sheriff, it just wasn't right."

"Faculty, do they ever bring in their laundry?"

"No, if they live on campus they've got machines in their cottages. We don't do their laundry. But sheriff, why all these questions about Arnie? You don't think he's connected in some way to the death of Ashleigh, do you?"

Ray shook his head no. "We're just checking on anyone who might know something." His tone changed. "Tell Pa I hope he gets a buck."

"Just what he needs," she laughed, "encouragement."

16

~~~

Ray Elkins had little more than a nodding acquaintance with Jason Zelke, the local man both Sarah James and Jack Grochoski mentioned as one of Ashleigh Allen's love interests.

However, Ray remembered Jason's mother with great fondness. Jane Peters, that was her maiden name, was the prettiest girl in Ray's high school class at Pioneer Consolidated High. Ray remembered the pert blond with the warm smile and wonderful laugh as being more social than academic. She was the homecoming queen, a cheerleader, but never made the honor society. She married Bob Zelke a few days after graduation and six or seven months later gave birth to her first child, three more would follow in the next few years. Zelke—close to ten years her senior, a mechanic at the farm implement dealer—was a steady, plodding fellow who worked hard to provide for his growing family.

The summer after their fourth child, Jason, was born, Jane was tending her flock on a Lake Michigan beach, and she struck up a conversation with a handsome young man, an engineer from Dearborn. He continued meeting her on the beach daily for the rest of his vacation. He returned a month later, loading Jane and one small suitcase into his silver Mustang convertible.

Bob Zelke returned from work to find a babysitter and a note from Jane saying that she had lost too much of her youth caring for toddlers she didn't love, and she was going to live while there was still time. She ended her note with, "See you later, alligator."

In the eight square blocks that constitute the village of Cedar Bay—even today—all the children are watched over by their neighbors, but the Zelke children received special attention and support. Bob Zelke was active in the PTO at the village elementary school, coached little league teams, and ran the cookie sales when his daughters were Scouts. His family settled back into normalcy when he married Joan Mixer, the third-grade teacher at the school.

Jason, the only boy in the family, was over six feet tall by his freshman year in high school. He had his mother's social skills and her good looks—the freckled face and honey-colored hair. He also had his father's work ethic and sense of duty. He was neither a brilliant student nor a gifted athlete, but he lettered in football, basketball, and track his sophomore, junior, and senior years, and his grade point average—boosted by outstanding work in vocational classes—enabled him to graduate as a member of the National Honor Society. He was voted by his classmates as the "most likely to succeed." The townspeople referred to Jason as a "quality kid" who possessed "all the right stuff."

During his junior year, Jason started working for Old Oak Timber Frame, a one-man operation a couple of miles from the village. For forty years the core of Barney Johnson's sawmill and building company business had been barns and storage buildings. Barney died suddenly of a heart attack the spring that Jason completed his associate's degree at the community college. Barney's widow asked Jason to stay on and complete the work already under contract. She hoped that one of her two sons would move back up north and take over their father's business. When neither showed an interest, she offered to sell Jason the business that consisted of the dilapidated mill, a decade-old flatbed truck, a vintage crane, forty acres—thirty of which were covered with hardwoods—and a rundown farmhouse that stood on the property. She made the terms of sale very reasonable, hoping Jason would carry on her husband's life work. He bought the business, and the direction of his life, at least for the near future, was established.

Ray, after parking in front of the main shed of the sawmill, followed the noise; he found Jason operating a large planer. Jason, noticing Ray's presence, finished guiding a piece of oak through the machine and switched it off.

"Was wondering when you'd get around to talk to me," Jason said, pulling the orange plastic hearing protectors off his ears.

"Why's that?"

"You wouldn't have to ask many people about Ashleigh before my name came up." He hooked his right thumb in the suspender of his tan bib overalls. A black Lab appeared at his side, nuzzling against his leg.

"So, tell me about Ashleigh. When did you see her last?"

"It's been six or eight weeks. Actually, we'd sort of broke things off last spring. Not that there was a lot to break off."

"Do you want to tell me about it?"

"I met her, Ashleigh, a couple of years ago." Jason stretched, raising his long, muscular arms over his head, lifting his cap, and pulling a blond ponytail back as he repositioned the hat. "It was one night at the Last Chance, after softball practice. She was with some of those Leiston people. We talked for a few minutes, nothing more. I met her again a week or two later. I was at the school doing some restoration work on one of their barns, dry rot in some timbers. I was sitting on the tailgate of my truck drinking coffee. She came up and asked me questions about what I was doing. I took her into the building and explained how the framing system worked. She seemed real interested and asked good questions." Jason paused, thinking back to that first encounter. "She was a very pretty woman, know what I'm saying, and I was attracted to her, but I knew she was off limits. You know what I mean? Sort of like the summer people; they can be nice to you, pretend like they're real interested in what you're doing, but there's always that difference." He removed his safety glasses and started to clean the sawdust off them with a red bandana he had pulled from a rear pocket.

"I saw her a couple of weeks later," he continued. "It was pretty late in the evening, probably a Saturday. She'd come into the Last Chance to buy a six-pack, one of those imported beers. I walked out with her. She told me she was going to the shore to watch a meteor shower. I asked if she wanted company. That was the beginning."

"The beginning of what, Jason?"

"Well, our little romance, if you want to call it that." Jason poured some steaming coffee from a battered green Thermos into a blue metal cup. "Want some coffee, sheriff? I can go to the house and get you a mug."

"No thanks," Ray said. "So, tell me about this romance."

"Well, it wasn't really much of anything, at least I don't think it was for her," Jason sipped his coffee. "It was about sex. She was more like a man than a woman, you know what I mean?"

Jason waited. Ray nodded, "I think so, but go ahead and explain."

"She knew what she wanted, she set the terms. It was usually on Wednesday night—she called me her Wednesday night boy."

"Was that to suggest that she had lovers on other nights of the week?"

Jason considered the question a long moment. "I'm sure she had other lovers while we were seeing each other, but that's not what she really meant by her Wednesday night thing. I was just part of her schedule, the Wednesday night entertainment. She had tutorials at school on Tuesday and Thursday evenings, and she was involved in lots of other commitments." He paused and sipped his coffee again. "She made it clear that I shouldn't look on our affair as an exclusive relationship. She had this obsession with being honest; she used that word a lot. I think I would have rather been deceived."

Ray noted the sadness in Jason's voice, the pained eyes in his youthful face. "So, being the Wednesday boy, was that okay with you? Was that enough?"

"At first it was. But then I really fell hard for her. I think the last time I fell in love like that was when I was in ninth grade. I wanted more, a lot more. I thought about things I had never thought about before. I wanted to live with her, marry her, make babies with her, whatever she wanted. But she was honest, told me she really liked . . . sex with me. That she wasn't ready to settle down, and she wasn't into exclusive relationships." He stopped and took a couple of deep breaths. "I was sorta her toy boy, nothing more."

"So, how long did this go on?"

"About two years, off and on. Sometimes I was optimistic, thinking that she was starting to care about me as much as I cared about her. But I was just a fool. She really liked Bo here," he reached down and patted the dog's flank, "more than she liked me."

"So, were you ever a couple?" It looked to Ray as if Jason's youthful frame sagged as he considered the question.

"I think I deluded myself into thinking we were. But now I realize it only had to do with sex. If the weather was good, we'd end up screwing our brains out on some beach; she really got off on that. The rest of the time she'd come over here. She liked to . . ." He stopped and looked at Ray.

"What, Jason?"

"Can't run me in for history, can you?" he asked, giving Ray a weak smile, his tone lightening for the first time since the conversation began.

"Depends on the history, but probably not for what you're going to tell me."

"She liked to smoke, you know, weed. It just made her even crazier," he said. Then he added quickly, "It was her stuff, not mine. She brought it."

"When did you last see her?"

"Like I said, it's been about five or six weeks, maybe more. Ashleigh came around one evening in early September. I was surprised to see her; I thought we had ended it. We drank a couple of beers and talked. She wanted to know if we could get together occasionally. I finally got strong enough to tell her I wasn't into it anymore. I didn't hear from her again."

"And you didn't contact her again?" Ray asked, watching Jason's face closely.

"No," he paused, lifted his gaze, and looked directly at Ray. "I must have reached for the phone a number of times, but I held myself back."

"If it was so painful, why did you hang in there for, what did you say, two years?" Ray asked.

"Yeah, about two." Jason answered. "Truth is, I've never been with anyone like Ashleigh. When she was here, it was like I was the only man on earth. I really loved her and," he looked chagrined, "she was an addiction. The best lay I've ever had. That was enough to keep me around for a long time. In spite of the pain."

"That last evening she was here, did you have an argument that evening?"

"Argument?" Jason asked, his manner suddenly wary.

"It sounds like you were very hurt, Jason. Anger and hurt often keep company."

"Yes, but I was beyond anger by that point. I had accepted the situation." He stopped and looked straight into Ray's eyes. "You can't make someone love you who doesn't." A long pause followed. "I'm sorry she's dead. God, am I sorry." He stopped, looked at the sawdust-covered floor in front of him, and then back up at Ray. "You do believe me, sheriff, don't you?"

"Yes, Jason, I do. But just for the record. Where were you Saturday night?"

"I was over at the house with Bo. We watched some football and the news on CNN and fell asleep thinking how fucked up the world was."

"Anyone with you?"

"No," said Jason sadly, "just us guys. Bo's my alibi."

"Jason, one more thing and I'll let you get back to work. Did Ashleigh say anything to suggest that she thought she might be in some kind of danger?"

"Never. And I don't think she would have kept that kind of thing a secret. She was a very open person."

"If anything comes to mind that you think might be helpful, will you give me a call?" Ray handed Jason a business card.

Jason took it with a gloved hand, looked at it, and slid the card into the breast pocket of his coveralls. "Sure will, sheriff."

17

It was near dusk when Ray Elkins met Sue Lawrence in the small parking area near the duplex where the murder victim, Ashleigh Allen, had lived. Ray helped Sue collect an evidence kit and camera equipment from the back of her Jeep, and they followed the sidewalk toward the stone cottage; the back apartment, Ashleigh's, was dark, but the lights were on in the front unit.

Sue held a flashlight as Ray removed the police seal from Ashleigh's door and unlocked it, using a master key from Gary Zatanski, the director of security. Ray pulled on rubber gloves, and putting two fingers behind the handle and turning it gingerly, opened the door. Sue followed him in.

After finding the switch to the overhead light, Ray stood a long while and surveyed the living room. A mountain bike leaned on the wall near the door, and a kayak was suspended from the ceiling by a system of pulleys and ropes attached to the exposed wood beams and tied off at a cleat near the fireplace. A Zapotec-design rug lay beneath a glass-topped coffee table between the hearth and a white leather couch. Bookcases lined the far wall.

"She was neat," Sue said, looking around. "Everything is in order. But it sort of looks like a guy place—mountain bike in the living room, kayak on the ceiling. It's sort of your approach to decorating, Ray." She paused and took in the room. "Are there specific things you're looking for?"

"Let's be open to everything," he said. "And see if there are any drugs. That's another possible angle."

Ray crossed the room and studied the contents of the bookcase.

"What are you finding?"

"Krakauer, several Stephen Kings, Jack Driscoll, Jim Harrison, Doug Peacock, Peter Matthiessen, and Edward Abbey, lots of environmental writers. And no Jane Addams, no Bronte; the only poetry is a book by Judith Minty. But Updike's last book is here, lots of Elmore Leonard's recent stuff, Tony Hillerman, Dennis Lahane, Larry Beinhart, Carl Hiaasen, and some vintage Chandler. A fairly eclectic collection. She was a reader."

"Things you like?"

"Most of it, yes."

Sue pointed at the kayak. "Same passions. You two could have been pals."

Ray pondered her comment. "I wonder why she kept it in here? It must have been a hassle moving it in and out."

"What an amazing looking boat," Sue said, walking around under the kayak and inspecting it from several angles. "It's like your new boat, isn't it?"

"Same builder," said Ray. "It's a slightly smaller model, the Valkyrie. Would have fit her better."

"It's sort of an art object."

"Beautiful," agreed Ray. He wandered into the kitchen and scanned the area. With the exception of a toaster, coffee machine, and drying rack next to the sink, the tiled counters were empty. Ray opened a white cupboard and peered at the stacks of dishes, bowls, and coffee mugs—simple, elegantly shaped china in white. In another cupboard he found the glasses and stemware, graceful wine glasses—delicate globes on willowy stems: eight for white, eight for red—and seven thin-walled water glasses. Ray looked around the kitchen and spotted the eighth glass in the drying rack.

He opened the pantry and pulled out several shelves. The spices were organized by type and arranged alphabetically, cinnamon, ginger, and nutmeg in a row. Another began with basil and bay leaves and ended with thyme. The Indian-cooking spices were arranged in their own section. Ray thought about his own collection of spices—a random assortment of little bottles, tins, and small plastic bags in a low cardboard box hidden from view on a bottom shelf. He reflected on Ashleigh, and the cognitive style that enabled her to bring such order to her world.

On a low shelf he found raw ingredients organized by type: uncooked pastas together, different types of rice, grain, and flour all neatly stored in plastic containers or Ziploc bags. Vitamins and nutritional supplements were stacked in a small woven basket. Sue peered over his shoulder.

"Wish my kitchen looked like this," said Ray. "It just makes my head hurt to think about keeping this organized."

"Mine too," offered Sue.

Ray opened the refrigerator.

"Gatorade, orange juice," said Sue peering in, "and soy milk, but no Diet Coke."

"Coffee beans, three different kinds of mustard, cornichons," Ray added.

"What?" ask Sue.

"These little French pickles." Ray removed the bottle and held it in front of her. And then continued to explore. "Some wonderful cheeses, mango chutney. Interesting ingredients. Looks like she did lots of ethnic dishes."

"How about the freezer? Does she have a stash on ice?" Sue asked.

"No, just some Healthy Choices, ice cubes, and yogurt bars."

"You're a trip Ray. Good thing you bring me along."

"How's that?"

"First you check her bookcases, and then you assess her pantry and refrigerator. Good thing I'm here to remind you of the purpose for our visit."

"I'm just trying to get a sense of the person."

"And your sense of people always starts with what they read and what they eat," she kidded as she pushed open the door of the utility room. A wood rack stood on the floor with panties and bras. "Hand wash," she said. "Guess she liked black."

"It's a great color," said Ray.

"Men," responded Sue, shaking her head.

Ray peered into the room: washer and dryer—liquid soap and bleach on a shelf above the machines, broom, mop and pail in the corner. In the cabinet on the opposite wall he found camping equipment, a backpack, two sleeping bags, a small tent, stainless pans, a backpack stove, and a red aluminum gas bottle. He shook the bottle; it was partially filled.

They next moved to the bedroom and bath. "I'll check the medicine chest. Will you do the dresser?" Ray asked.

David Dowd's shaving kit, a worn brown leather bag, rested atop the toilet tank. Ray unzipped the bag and removed the contents into the sink bowl: toothpaste, brush, comb, a small can of shaving cream, and a disposable razor. At the bottom was a small plastic prescription bottle. Ray studied the label: Dowd's name, the doctor's name, University of Michigan Medical Center, and the drug—a highly advertised anti-anxiety medication. Ray checked the two side pockets, one empty, the second pocket contained two prophylactics in sealed wrappers. He carefully returned the contents to the bag. Ray lifted the top off the toilet and peered into the tank. Nothing.

In the medicine chest, it was unnecessary to remove anything from its carefully ordered interior; everything was clearly visible. His eyes ran along the shelves: a modest collection of cosmetics, dental-care products, and medications—an antibiotic prescribed the previous February, and a wheel of birth control pills, one side of the circle intact.

He looked through the vanity: cleaning products, toilet paper, and Tampax.

Ray walked into the bedroom. "Anything interesting?" he asked.

"Not really. She had a small wardrobe of quality clothing. One very nice suit, a few dresses, blouses, and sweaters, but it looks like she mostly wore jeans and work shirts. And lots of fleece—jackets, vests, pants."

"Anything unusual?"

"She didn't have . . . well, I don't know what she would have worn to a fancy party or wedding. And there is no perfume, not one bottle."

"Is that unusual?"

"A bit, perhaps. But there are no surprises, no stash of drugs or porn, no whips or rubber suits. Well, that's not quite true. There's a carefully folded wetsuit on a shelf in the closet. That's probably kayak gear," Sue said in a questioning voice as she pointed toward its location in the closet.

Ray walked over and examined the Farmer Jane suit. "Yes, kayaking."

Sue continued her exploration of the dead woman's belongings. She pulled open the top drawer of a long modern dresser and motioned toward neatly folded stacks of panties. "Same size and brand, Victoria's Secret, mostly black, a few white."

"Why would you bother?" Ray asked.

"Bother with what?" she responded.

"Having two colors, if you like black, buy black."

"Black shows through, you can't wear it under some things."

"Oh," he muttered.

"Martian," she responded with a tone of playful scorn. Sue checked the other drawers in the dresser, carefully looking through the contents. "You find anything?"

"No," he responded. Ray slowly looked around the room, four pieces of furniture: a dresser, bed, and two small night tables, one at each side of the bed. An elegant steel reading light stood on the top of each table. The matching pieces of furniture were modern in design, finished in a matte black, and finely constructed. A thick comforter, dark gray with a soft, glossy texture, covered the bed. He pulled back the comforter, looked under the pillows, and then lifted the top sheet. He straightened the sheet and pulled the comforter back over the bed. Getting down on his knees on the off-white Berber carpet, Ray peered under the bed. He walked around and extracted a book.

"What did you find?" asked Sue.

"It's probably the book Dowd was reading in bed, hard to imagine that Ashleigh would stash one under the bed."

"What is it?"

"*Leaves of Grass,* Whitman." He opened the cover and looked through the first few pages. "It's a new edition." He stood and looked at Sue. "These were two very interesting young people." He placed the book on the night table, regretting that he had disturbed the order of the room.

"Let's check her office," he said.

They moved to the last room in the duplex, a room slightly smaller than the one Ashleigh used as a bedroom. A Macintosh computer stood at the center of a simple pine desk, three manila folders were piled to the right of the computer. Ray opened the top folder and peered at the stack of student papers. He showed the papers to Sue, "She was probably going to read these on Sunday night after Dowd left." Ray could see the sadness in Sue's face, an emotion he shared.

"Unfinished work and wasted lives," she said, finally.

"Looks like she was into photography," said Ray, spying a camera on a shelf behind the desk.

"Digital photography," said Sue examining the camera. "This Sony is a very new model. She couldn't have had it more than a few months. We'll take the CD with us and see if there are any pictures of interest on it." She slipped the disk into an evidence bag.

They looked through the desk drawers and the file. Most of the papers seemed school related. A few files contained bank statements, income tax returns, insurance records, and monthly reports from Ashleigh's financial advisor. Ray looked through reports. "Well," he said after reviewing a few pages, "Ashleigh was a very wealthy young woman."

"How wealthy?" Sue asked.

Ray showed her the report, pointing out values of the portfolio at the bottom of the sheet.

"Impressive," said Sue. "But you don't see any evidence of it here. She had nice things, but there's no excess. She had enough of everything, but nothing extra. It looks like she was living on her teacher's salary. Probably even putting money into savings."

Ray pulled a heavy plastic envelope from the rear of the bottom drawer and poured the contents onto the desk. Sue picked up a passport and opened it. "Nice picture," she said, holding it so Ray could see it. "Wish mine looked this good."

Next Sue unfolded an official-looking document.

"What's that?" Ray inquired, looking through Ashleigh's undergraduate transcript.

"Her birth certificate. It has her mother's name, but no father is listed," she paused and carefully studied the document. "Pretty name," she observed as she started to refold the document.

"What's that?"

"Allison. If I ever had a daughter, that would be high on the list of possible names. Allison, it sort of rolls off your tongue."

"Can I see that?" Ray asked. He opened the document, scanned it, his eyes resting on Allison's name. Then he handed it back to Sue. She set it to one side as she looked through the rest of the items. She held out a small, faded color photo to Ray. "That's probably Ashleigh and her mother, there's such a strong resemblance, same facial structure, same hair color."

Ray took the photo from her hand and looked at it closely.

The colors were faded and the print had a grainy quality. A gangly girl and a woman stood side by side with a flower-covered hillside as a backdrop. Their similarity was striking, clearly a mother and daughter. Ray turned the photograph over, looking for a date or any other information on the back; there was none. He returned to the picture. A wave of recognition ran through him as he studied the photo again. "How old do you think they are?" he asked in a low voice, trying to control his emotions.

"Hard to tell," she replied, looking at the photo again. "The daughter might be about eleven or twelve; the mother is no teenager. I'd say somewhere in her mid to late thirties." She gazed at Ray. "You okay? You look sort of strange."

Ray was slow to respond. "Yes," he said and then remained silent.

"I guess I've allowed the enormity of this crime to come through," he said, finally. "Once you get a sense of the people, you can't escape the magnitude of tragedy." They were both still and then Ray, his tone subdued, said, "We'll take the computer. I'd like you to search the hard drive. Also, I'd like you to access her e-mail and voicemail." Ray looked thoughtful. "I'm surprised we didn't find any correspondence. No love letters or cards, not even letters from women friends."

"People do e-mail now. I don't get letters anymore," said Sue.

"But don't you have some . . . some from the past?" he said, thinking about the memento-filled boxes in his spare room. He needed to sort through them.

"No, last time I moved I got rid of that stuff. Bad karma. Do you have any?"

"Well, not for the last few years, but . . ."

"Well, there's your answer," commented Sue.

"Right," Ray said, changing the subject. "So, what did we learn here?"

Sue didn't hesitate. "I think that Ashleigh was exactly the

kind of person people have been telling us she was. So far, no surprises."

"That's my take, too," Ray said.

It took two trips to get the computer, files, camera, and other evidence into Sue's Jeep. Ray came back alone, walked through the apartment one more time, slowly, thinking about the faded photo, the girl and her mother, Ashleigh and Allison, ghosts, both of whom were now his ghosts.

18

~~~~~

S ue stood at the threshold of Ray's office and peered in; the
early morning sun streamed through the thin rectangular
windows that ran across the top of the south wall, bringing
a bit of warmth into an otherwise drab interior—off-white walls
and tan steel furniture. Ray, his back to her, was busily making lists
and adding to a complicated diagram with dry-erase markers on
a large whiteboard mounted below the windows. He was using a
variety of colors, and she could see that he had created a key for
the colors on the right-hand side of the board. She cleared her
throat to announce her presence.

"Morning," said Ray turning in her direction. "I've been
listing the people we need to interview and other tasks. Can you
get the crime scene finished up today?"

"That shouldn't be a problem. I'd like to pull Evans from the
day shift to help me."

"That's okay," Ray said. "Do you need anyone else?"

"Just people to continue to secure the scene until we're done.
I'd like to get the tarps off and go over the area again. We should
vacate the area by this afternoon."

"Good," said Ray. Pointing to a list he said, "You can see the people I'm planning to talk to today. I've keyed my interview notes from yesterday. You need to read them. I talked to Jack Grochoski at the Last Chance and Sarah James—she seems to handle the day-to-day administration at Leiston School. They both identified Jason Zelke as someone who dated Ashleigh in the not-too-distant past. So I visited with him. Do you know him?"

"No," responded Sue. "Anything?"

Ray summarized his conversation with Zelke, concluding with, "Jason is a nice kid with a good reputation, hard to see him as the killer." He paused and looked at Sue, "It would be interesting to talk to other women he's dated. I wonder if there's a violent streak there that we don't know about."

"I'll ask around. Anything else?"

"Warrington, you'll see it in my note. It looks like he might have had a fling with Ashleigh."

"When?" Sue asked.

"It would have been her first year. I wonder if there were things that might have motivated him to commit . . ."

"If there are," interrupted Sue, "he wins the prize for best performance on a beach. He was pretty convincing."

"Yes," Ray agreed. "Before you leave, promise me one thing?"

"What's that?"

"You'll come back with the weapon and a good set of prints."

"That would be nice," she agreed.

The chirping sound from Ray's cell phone interrupted their parting. "Elkins here," he said. He nodded as he listened several minutes. "How's his mother doing?" He listened some more and said, "Thank you for the call, doctor." He slowly closed the phone and set it on the table.

"Bad news?" Sue asked.

"That was one of the ICU doctors," he responded, his eyes filled with sadness. "Arnie coded early this morning. They were able to resuscitate him, but he's in very critical condition."

"What happened? Why did he code?"

"They think it was a pulmonary embolism."

"What are his chances?"

"Gonzales said fewer than 10 percent of those who code in the hospital and are resuscitated survive." He paused, "Kim, that poor woman. She collapsed while they were trying to resuscitate Arnie. So they've admitted her. The doctor says she'll probably be okay by tomorrow."

"Yeah," responded Sue, "the medical definition of okay. Your heart is beating and you're still sucking air."

19

The two-lane drive entering Leiston was divided by a small gatehouse sitting in the middle with wooden barriers on each lane. As Ray entered the drive, he slowed near the building. The man inside, Gary Zatanski, the head of the school's security detail, waved him through. Ray parked his Jeep nearby and walked back to the building.

"Good morning, sheriff," offered Gary, holding the door.

As they shook hands, Ray noted that Gary was about his height, average for their generation. A ring of short gray hair surrounded his round shiny head. Gary's thick neck and heavily muscled chest and arms gave him the appearance of a weightlifter or Greco-Roman wrestler, but an expansive waistline suggested that culinary joys had replaced a passion for fitness.

"Want some coffee?" He pulled a clean cup from under a counter that ran across the front of the building. "It's fresh."

"Sure. Thanks," said Ray.

"Any developments?" Zatanski asked as he poured the coffee, his voice grave.

"We're collecting evidence, doing interviews, but no, we don't have a suspect."

"I'm still in shock. You know bad stuff happens every day, but," he motioned with his two hands, "why here? And why Ashleigh?"

"Wish I had an answer." Ray sipped his coffee. There was a long pause where both men were lost in thought. Then, Ray surveyed the array of monitors suspended from the ceiling. "Looks like you have a very sophisticated security system," he said.

"I've pushed them hard to keep things modern. But in a place like this there is never enough money. That said, we've got better stuff than most places, especially schools."

"And this setup, it's your baby?"

"Yes," Zatanski answered with obvious satisfaction.

"Dr. Warrington mentioned that you have a police background."

"ATF, actually. And after I got tired of busting down crack-house doors in Baltimore, I did corporate security around D.C."

"How did you end up here?"

"My wife, she was a middle school science teacher in Silver Springs. A couple of years ago she took an early out. Man, I don't know how she lasted that long. Anyway, she had inherited this little family farm up here. Me, I'd rather have gone to Florida, but you know how it goes." He lifted both hands, showing his powerful arms, and made a submissive gesture. "And she's pleased as punch. She has started an apple orchard and is growing grapes. And she's doing watercolors, even had a little show at the Wayside Tap last summer. She's got a million activities going in the winter, and in the summer we're carting visiting grandkids all over hell's half-acre. But me, well, how much can you fish and golf? So, when Warrington contacted me to do some consulting on security, I was glad to have the work, but I wasn't looking for a full-time gig. We finally worked out a deal that I'd take over the management of campus security as long as it would only be part-time."

"How many hours do you work?"

"I try to keep it under thirty hours."

"And there's always someone on duty?"

"Yeah, 24/7."

"I imagine most days things are fairly routine."

"Yeah, and we're trying to make sure it stays that way. That's why we got all this." He gestured toward the monitors and other electronic devices. "The year before I was here they had a student abducted by a parent. You know, it was one of those custody things."

"I remember that," said Ray. "We heard about it after the fact, long after the fact."

Zatanski continued on, not responding to Ray's comment. "So, after that incident there was finally an understanding of how easy it was to forcibly pick up a kid without being noticed."

"Yes, incidents like that tend to . . ."

"Well, you don't know the half of it. Warrington wanted a plan to prevent something like that from happening again. So, I drew up a plan for a centralized security system. It was the whole nine yards: improved campus lighting, video cameras at strategic places. When Warrington saw it and the price tag, I thought he was going to shit. He wanted to know why we needed all that stuff, so I walked him about and showed him. Like they thought they were doing good by putting new batteries in the smoke detectors in the dorms every year."

"But I take it, you did get the funds?"

"It wasn't easy. I had to tell him some war stories. You know, it's not like talking to business people. Educators are used to working with such little money."

"How were you able to prevail?"

"Warrington had me speak to the school's governing board. I told them there wasn't even a rudimentary security system. I took them on a tour. I started a fire in a wastebasket right under one of those old smoke detectors. And we waited and waited and waited.

"Hey," he said with a laugh, "there's no business like show business. And after it was clear the device didn't work, I asked them how they'd sleep knowing their kids had this kind of protection. Then I laid on what it would take to bring this place up to industry standards. That's just the way I said it, industry standards. The board is made up mostly of corporate types; they respond more to fear than reason, so I played to their fears." Zatanski chuckled to himself.

"So, you pretty much got what you asked for?"

"Yeah, I did. Several board members have kids here. One has two grandkids enrolled. I didn't have to do much convincing. The former board president came up with the cash, so it didn't have to come out of the current budget. But there was hell to pay."

"How so?" Ray asked.

"The system was installed in the summer when the students and most of the faculty were gone. And I don't think anyone would have noticed, or even objected much if it hadn't been for the lights."

"Lights?"

"There was hardly any exterior lighting, and what there was hadn't been maintained. Most of it didn't work. We put modern perimeter lighting on all the buildings, lights on the main drive and parking areas, and lights along all the footpaths between buildings. We also put security cameras in key locations so one person sitting here could pretty much monitor what was happening anywhere on campus. Well, when we made the system operational this fall the faculty went nuts. We were accused of making the place look like a maximum-security prison. They said we had destroyed the rural nature of the place and petitioned Warrington to have some of the lights turned off."

"How was it resolved?"

"The board president invited the faculty to a board meeting. He went head to head with the most contentious faculty members. His well-reasoned arguments, tied with the fact that the board was considering a new salary schedule, seemed to quiet things down."

Ray took this all in, then turned his attention to the video monitors in the gatehouse. "Is this recorded?"

"Yes. Everything goes on tape. The system recycles every 144 hours."

"How do you monitor the vehicles, the comings and goings?"

"That one," Zatanski pointed to a camera mounted on a steel post in front of the gatehouse, "picks up the vehicle from the rear so we get the license plate. The one mounted over there," he gestured toward a camera on the other side of the drive, "gives us the passenger side. Same is true on the exit lane. Sort of overkill, but I wanted to have capacity if we ever needed it. The person working the desk is supposed to log in and out each license number, then the computer can give you output on what vehicles were here and for how long."

"So, do they do it, log every vehicle?"

"Not really. I had a hell of a time getting the guys to do it consistently. We've come up with a compromise; people we know, staff, faculty, the usual delivery guys get waved through. People we don't know get logged in by hand. By next spring I'll have the software to automate license plate function. A camera and computer will do it, and I won't have to depend on my guys' piss-poor keying."

"And the gates are open all the time?"

"During the day. From six in the evening to six in the morning they're closed both ways." He pulled a clipboard from a hook. "People coming during those times need to check in, they need to have a destination, and the name of the person they're visiting. We call and check before they are allowed through."

"So, for Friday evening you can give me a printout that shows everyone who entered and left the school?"

"Yes, that's assuming that the guy in the booth actually logged the plate number. We may be less than 100 percent. "

"And the destinations, you log that in also?" Ray asked.

"The guys are supposed to."

"So, Ashleigh Allen, anyone log into her place?"

Zatanski looked down at a screen mounted under the counter as he keyed in a series of commands. A printer hummed to life. He pulled a printout from the tray and placed it on the counter.

"Looks like Ashleigh only had one visitor. David Dud—spelled D-U-D. See what I mean about getting people to key things correctly?" Zatanski said, his round faced reddening with irritation. He looked over at Ray and explained, "The guys were all in love with Ashleigh. She was quite a babe." Pointing back to the printout, he continued. "Dowd entered the grounds at 7:13—the computer does the date stamping, so we know that's accurate. He left at 7:46 and returned at 11:46. He and Ashleigh probably went to dinner."

"How about Saturday?"

"Saturday is a problem. We had a big crowd here—parents up for the weekend, the soccer game, fans from the other school. Most of the day we just had to wave people through. It's a situation that I haven't figured out how to fix."

"So there's no log of who . . ."

"Correct, from about nine in the morning until seven or eight in the evening. Sorry."

"But, you can give me tapes from these cameras for Thursday through Saturday?"

"No prob. And I'll print up the plate logs, such as they are. What else?"

"Tell me about Ashleigh?" Ray asked.

"We all liked her; she was beautiful and funny. And she always had a smile and something clever to say when she came through. She'd take the time, you know what I mean? She'd stop and roll down her window and chat. Like I said, the guys loved her."

"Arnie Vedder, he used to work here?"

"Yes, I think they let him go a few weeks ago. We all knew little Arnie well. He liked to hang out in the booth and watch the monitors. He thought this place was real neat."

"Do you know why he was fired?"

"I heard he just couldn't do the work."

"No one talked to you about the possibility that Arnie might have been stealing things from the laundry?"

"Oh, the panties. I heard the story, but I didn't think much of it. Anytime you have teenage boys around, panties are going to go missing."

"During your time here, has Dr. Warrington asked you to keep an eye on a specific student?"

"No, I don't think there's ever been a need, and I'm not sure Warrington would use us in that way," Zatanski responded.

Ray looked at his watch. "I have an interview with Helen Warrington scheduled. In an hour or so could you take me on a tour of the place and tell me what you see that the administrators and faculty don't?"

"Happy to. I'll get someone to cover the booth."

20

~~~~

Ray cut across the lawn from the gatehouse to the mansion's main entrance. He walked to the school's offices in the south wing. The door to Helen Warrington's, the first one on the left, was open. Ray tapped gently on the frame, pulling Helen's attention away from a computer screen. She motioned him in. "Have a seat, sheriff. I'm just finishing something up here. Give me a minute."

Ray settled into a chair directly in front of her desk. He had seen Helen before—Ian Warrington had introduced her at the staff meeting—but it wasn't until she was sitting across the desk that he had an opportunity to observe her closely. In spite of her cloying perfume, Ray could smell the cigarette smoke that clung to her, and there was something else, too, a sweet spirituous odor. *And only a little after ten*, Ray thought as he glanced at his watch. *Must be having some brandy with her coffee.* He looked at the covered, stainless steel travel cup on her desk and wondered what it really contained.

Ray examined her profile, everything perfectly proportioned —delicate and feminine. Incipient creases and wrinkles were softened by skillfully applied makeup. Her thick, shoulder-length blond hair was tied off in back with a black leather wrap, and each ear was adorned with a delicate gold hoop. Her skirt and blouse, neatly pressed, were classically casual. Ray noted that everything about her dress and grooming was flawless, perhaps too flawless. She radiated a brittle tension.

As she worked, her delicate fingers flew across the keys. With the exception of the keyboard and flat-screen display, her desk's surface was clear, as was the top of the bird's-eye maple credenza behind her. Ray looked around the office; the furniture was Bauhaus and classic modern in design, new and obviously expensive, but there was nothing of her in the room, nothing personal, not a knickknack, or a photo, or a college diploma. Ray thought it looked like a newly created space, a flawless movie set waiting for characters.

"Sorry for the delay, sheriff," she finally said, making eye contact. "I was responding to a rather frantic e-mail from some parents living abroad. One of their friends e-mailed them a news report about Ashleigh's death. It wasn't supposed to work that way, but we had difficulty reaching them."

"You have a plan for . . ."

"Yes, that was one of the first things Ian did after he arrived. The previous administration had never developed contingency plans for any kind of emergencies. We've tried to identify various kinds of disasters we might have, like a fire, or an accident involving a school vehicle, or even something like food poisoning. And then we developed a response plan, identifying the resources that would be needed and who would be responsible. Getting information to the parents, hopefully before they heard from the media, was a basic part of this planning."

Ray noted how carefully she articulated each word; every sentence was precisely formed, and she maintained eye contact with him as she delivered her lines.

"How did you first learn about Ms. Allen's death?" he asked.

"Ian told me what happened as soon as he returned from

the beach, and I started drafting a phone script. Right after the meeting with faculty and staff, the people who are part of the phone fan-out started making calls to parents. Everyone read from the same prepared script. We gave the parents the facts as we knew them, made it clear that the deaths took place away from campus, and assured them that their children were in no danger."

"And who did the calling?"

"Our dorm parents, Sarah James, myself, and several faculty members who are part of this team."

"What about Dr. Warrington?"

"We didn't want him tied up with this because we knew that a number of parents would want to talk directly with him after they heard the news." Helen looked at Ray with tired eyes. "And they did, many more than we had anticipated."

"And the e-mail?"

"We have a number of parents who live abroad; most of them work for American or multinational corporations, and there are a few people who are with the State Department or NGOs. We used e-mail for this group, backed by phone calls. The parents I was just responding to," she motioned toward the computer screen, "are in Kazakhstan, ExxonMobil Oil. They had some real concerns about their daughter's safety. I was reassuring them that she is in no danger."

She looked at Ray. "That's true, isn't it sheriff?"

Ray ignored her almost-accusatorial tone. "Tell me, Mrs. Warrington, when did you last see Ashleigh Allen?"

"I saw her every day, or almost every day when school was in session. She was part of the environment; I can't say when I last saw her, sometime last week I imagine."

"On a normal school day, when would you see her?"

She pondered the question. "Noon, lunch. She was usually having lunch with her students. Most of the faculty sits together, but not Ashleigh. She liked to be surrounded by her students. It was a sign of her insecurity."

Ray listened intently, showing no emotion. He noted her

patronizing tone and wondered why she was taking the conversation in this direction.

"Insecurity, how so?" he asked.

"Some of the kids doted on her, and she needed that. She couldn't even take time out and have lunch with the adults. And she made a big thing out of it, like she cared more about the students than the rest of us."

"I sense you felt that . . ."

"Sheriff, there are two worlds here—the adolescents and the adults. And it's wonderful when members of the faculty and staff are close to the students. I mean, that's what we're about. But the faculty, the adults, aren't one with the students. They're responsible for the students' education. Ashleigh crossed the line. She used her relationship with her students to take care of her own psychological needs. And in the process she manipulated the kids to get their affection."

Ray held her gaze and didn't respond.

"Sheriff, I have a Ph.D. in clinical psychology," she continued in an authoritative tone. "I am well-versed in these matters. Ashleigh's behavior was probably damaging to some of the more fragile students, especially some of the boys. She was sending them inappropriate messages, things that they couldn't understand."

"Could you be more specific?" he asked. He noted perspiration was starting to distort her perfectly applied cosmetics and the nonchalant façade she seemed to be trying hard to maintain. Ray wondered what lay beneath Helen's veneer of perfection. Was she aware of Ashleigh's affair with Ian? If she knew, what was just beneath her surface: a roiling anger, or a stoic denial of something so tawdry in her flawless, manicured world?

"Yes. Ashleigh was—what's the term you men use—a tease," Helen said. "The boys didn't have the maturity to understand what was going on."

"Are you suggesting that she might have been involved with some of the boys?" Ray's voice had a tinge of defensiveness in it, he realized, startled. Thankfully, Helen seemed not to notice. He breathed in and regained composure.

"No, no, not at all," Helen said. "What I am saying is that she sent signals that were misinterpreted by some of the more vulnerable boys. She knew what she was doing. Her actions left them confused and sometimes hurt; but kept them as loyal supplicants."

"I sense you didn't like Ashleigh?"

"Sheriff, I neither liked her or disliked her. Actually, I was quite indifferent to her."

Ray sensed disdain in her voice.

"But" she continued, "I was one of the few people around here who saw beyond her attractive veneer; I saw her for what she was, an ambitious, insecure, needy young woman."

"But you didn't judge . . ."

"Sheriff, I don't make judgments; I let others do that, but I'm not afraid to call a spade a spade. That said, I didn't share my view of Ashleigh with the others. I was just responding to your query."

Ray nodded. "When do you think you last saw Ashleigh?"

"I couldn't tell you, probably Friday, but I have no specific memory of seeing her. It could have been any day last week, the days sort of blend together."

"But you did have lunch in the cafeteria?

"Dining hall, it's called the dining hall."

"And you did have lunch in the dining hall on Friday?" Ray watched her closely as she considered the question.

"Friday. I'm not sure. Sometimes, when I'm very busy, I just run in and get a yogurt and eat at my desk." She looked at Ray; her tone hardened. "Why does it matter? My seeing her on Friday wouldn't have prevented these horrible events."

"There's the possibility that Ashleigh might have said something that could provide a link to her killer."

"You're suggesting, sheriff," Helen's tone became argumentative, "that someone here might have threatened Ashleigh?"

"No. We are gathering information, trying to reconstruct the last few days of Ashleigh's life—who she saw, what she said. Saturday, did you see her Saturday?"

"No. That I'm sure of."

"You were here?"

"Yes. We had a home soccer game, and then Ian and I met with some prospective students and their parents. We gave them the Cook's tour of the campus and then hosted a dinner."

"How long did that last?"

"Well into the evening. They had lots of questions. I was just exhausted by the time they left."

"Which was?"

"Must have been after eight."

"Then what did you do?"

"We went back to our cottage. I watched some TV, Ian fell asleep reading. I had to wake him to get him to come to bed." She paused and looked at Ray. "But why are you asking about where we were?"

"I'm trying to find out if she was seen around campus."

"I certainly didn't see her. Is there anything else?" she asked in a dismissive tone.

"Yes, I'm trying to get a sense of how the school operates. What specifically is your job?"

"I have several roles. I handle admissions, alumni affairs, and fundraising. The money generated by tuition and the school's endowment only covers about eighty percent of the school's annual budget. We have to go out and find donors for the rest."

"So, when you came to Leiston, the board gave you and your husband a joint offer?"

"Yes, they did, but not my current job. When Ian was interviewed he made it clear that he would come only if I was also offered employment. We both had jobs in San Francisco and at that point in our careers we weren't going to go to a single income. Given my training, the board created a position for a school psychologist. But a death and two retirements left openings in the administration. Ian asked the board if I could take over those positions."

"The school doesn't need a psychologist?"

"We can contract those services locally."

"So, there was no one here who needed your expertise?"

"Sheriff, I spent years treating people with multiple personalities," she paused, then continued, her tone becoming increasingly sarcastic. "No one here needed my special expertise. In point of fact, we do our best to screen out applicants with personality problems. And our curriculum is designed to strengthen each student's sense of self-esteem."

"During your tenure here, you haven't had any students with . . ." Ray paused as he searched for the appropriate term.

"Sheriff, if you're asking about students who have evidenced violent antisocial tendencies, no, we don't have anyone like that. But we do have teenagers, and adolescence is a state of mild madness, and all our students are afflicted with it some of the time. But, to my knowledge, no one is showing symptoms of anything more than that. Is there anything else, sheriff?"

"No," said Ray. "Thank you for your time. I may need to talk to you again."

"You can always find me here," she said with a note of resignation.

Ray started out down the hall toward the exit. He stopped at the headmaster's door and peered in. "Dr. Warrington, do you have a minute?"

"Yes, sheriff, please come in," Ian Warrington responded, his words and tone appropriate, but with an expression that suggested mild irritation. "I hope you're here to tell me you've caught the murderer."

"I wish that were the case. Unhappily, we're still in the early stages of the investigation."

"Have a seat," Warrington offered, his impeccable manners scarcely hiding his lack of enthusiasm for the encounter.

"Yes, thank you. Just a few quick questions. I know you must be very busy. I'm still trying to get a sense of where everyone was on Saturday." He paused, watching Warrington's face, then went on to explain himself. "I'm still hoping that someone will remember seeing Ms. Allen on Saturday."

"Why's that?"

"I think there is a chance that the murderer was keeping track of her or perhaps David Dowd. If people could remember seeing her, perhaps they could also remember seeing someone in the background. It's that someone we're looking for."

"Well, sheriff, as I told you, I don't think I saw her on Saturday. I'm pretty sure that Friday was the last time I saw her."

"Yes. That was at lunch, wasn't it?"

"Correct."

"The faculty, do they eat together?"

"Usually, there's an alcove just off the main dining area where we usually gather."

"So no one eats with the students?"

"We all eat with the students from time to time, but it's nice to have a meal with your colleagues and have some adult conversation."

"And Ashleigh, did she usually eat lunch with her students or with the other faculty members?"

"Usually with her peers, but why all these questions? I don't see the point of all this," said Warrington, trying to control his annoyance.

"I'm trying to get a sense of the victim, all this helps. Saturday you were busy with a soccer game and parents?"

"Yes, and then I had dinner for some prospective parents and their children. We lingered awhile over dessert, they had many questions. They were here until 7:30 or 8:00."

"Well, sounds like you had a long day. And after they left?"

"I came back here for a while to try to clear up some paperwork."

"And your wife?"

"She was very tired, she went home after dinner."

"I admire your dedication. Doing paperwork on a Saturday night after a long week. How long were you able to stay with it?"

"Not long, I was really exhausted. I was home by ten."

Ray rose from his chair. "I appreciate the time."

"But I thought you had some . . . some more specific questions?" Warrington said, looking surprised by Ray's abrupt departure.

"I did, you answered them," Ray responded from the door, leaving Warrington with a questioning look.

21

~~~

When Ray returned to the gatehouse, he found Gary Zatanski sitting at a desk in the rear of the small building working through a pile of papers. "Is this still a good time for a tour?" Ray asked.

"Couldn't be better," Zatanski replied. "Gives me an excuse to put this off and get some air."

"That's what I like to use when the weather's good." Zatanski said, pointing to a mountain bike leaning against the back of the gatehouse as they climbed into a golf cart. "I'm trying to keep my fat ass from getting any bigger." As they slowly rolled up the long curved road that wandered through the campus Zatanski asked, "What do you want to see?"

"Give me a sense of the school from your view of the world," Ray said. "And I want you to tell me about the students and the staff. Is there anyone I should be especially curious about? I'm not looking for rumors, but I'm sure you see a lot of things in the course of your work that probably most other people here aren't aware of and . . ."

"Don't really want to know," interrupted Zatanski, completing Ray's thought. "Yeah, I can tell you about lots of things about this place that Warrington doesn't want to know," he said in a mocking tone. Then he became somber, "Since it happened, Ashleigh getting killed, me and the boys, well it's all we've talked about. Who could have done it, what possible motive?" Zatanski's face was a study in sorrow. He pulled into a clearing near one of the dorms and parked. "Like I said, she was a real cutie, just full of life. We've seen a number of guys, Ashleigh's boyfriends, come and go."

"And Dowd, he seemed to be the current love interest?" asked Ray.

"He's been around on and off for a couple of years. But sometime late last spring he seemed to become the main man. I don't think she was seeing anyone else. If she was, she wasn't bringing him on campus."

"Are there ways to get a vehicle on campus other than the main gate?"

Zatanski grinned. "You know what I said about show business. We've got one secured entrance, but we're sitting on several square miles of land here."

"Any other roads in?"

"No roads, not even two-tracks. There's this old stone fence around most of the property, but anyone could scramble across that. And there are areas out back where it has completely disappeared; the stone probably ended up in someone's building project. There are lots of footpaths and bike trails the kids use to get to the village or God know where else."

"And they do?" Ray asked.

"They're kids, and the school isn't supposed to be a prison. They're not supposed to leave the grounds without signing out," he laughed, "well, kids are kids and who's to know?"

"Could you access the school grounds with a four-wheel-drive vehicle?"

"With a real off-road vehicle, like a Wrangler, it would be a piece of cake."

"Tell me about the students, what are they like?" Ray asked, taking the conversation a new direction.

"Well, they're not the angels Warrington would have you believe."

"What do you mean?"

"I don't mean anything bad, but, like I said, they're kids. They sign this pledge to uphold the school rules every fall, and I think Warrington believes most of them follow it."

"And they don't?"

"They're kids. I see a few of them off in the woods smoking from time to time. And we find the occasional beer can or wine bottle in one of the old barns or outbuildings. And more than once in the last few years I've stumbled across a spent condom or the remains of a roach. But compared to what most high school kids are doing," he raised both hands, fingers spread, "hey, that's not much. They work 'em real hard in class, and they got lots of other things to keep 'em busy."

"But there must be the occasional bad apple?" Ray probed.

"Yeah," agreed Zatanski, "what do the experts say, five percent of the population is goofy? And we got some of those. But I don't see anyone who's bad goofy, criminal goofy, not since I've been here. Heard stories about the past, the early days, when things got a bit wild. But that was probably true of every high school in America at the time. We don't have much of that now. Just normal teenage stuff. You're not going to find your killer among the students."

"Faculty and students, anything going on there?"

"You mean romances?"

Ray nodded.

"No. Most of the teachers are near retirement. I don't think so."

Ray refocused the conversation. "How about the staff. Anything curious there?"

"Staff, no. Mostly locals, you probably know many of them. Just good, steady people who are happy to have a regular paycheck and health insurance—something that's pretty scarce around here. And I doubt if any of them had much contact with Ashleigh."

"Faculty?" ask Ray.

"A few drunks and oddballs, but most of them seem to be hardworking and dedicated. Can't imagine any homicidal types." Zatanski paused and looked over at Ray. "I've never worked homicide, but I can imagine the dance. I just can't think of anyone capable of doing this," he exhaled heavily, his body sagged in a defeated pose. "I just wish I could give you something useful."

"Tell me about the drunks."

"Well, you probably know about Jessica Medford."

Ray nodded.

"Occasionally we've had to send someone over to the Last Chance and pick her up, especially since Todd Danforth died. When the guys do their nightly rounds, they sorta check on her."

"Why?"

"We found her passed out in a snowbank last winter. She didn't make it from the car to her front door. Wouldn't want anything to happen to her."

"Anyone else, drinking problem?" Ray asked, watching Zatanski closely.

The response was a long time in coming. "No, not really."

"No one?" Ray pushed.

"I thought you didn't want to work at the rumor level," Zatanski retorted.

"Don't think I am," Ray said, holding Zatanski in a hard gaze.

"Helen Warrington, if that's who you're asking about. Yes, she had a bit of a problem. But I think she's got it under control. She's been going to AA for a year or more. Heads out late in the afternoon, must go to town for the meetings. Sort of about the same time she used to go to the bar."

"Every day?"

"Weekdays, mostly. She seems to be pretty religious about it. Not that it's made her any more pleasant."

"How about drugs?"

"Don't know everything that goes on behind closed doors,

but I don't think so. Not this crowd, maybe twenty or thirty years ago, not any more." Zatanski backed up the golf cart and turned onto the main drive. "How about I do a circle of the campus and grounds so you'll know where everything is?"

"That would be very helpful," Ray said, settling back into his seat.

22

Ray pulled onto the long asphalt drive that wound up to a large house overlooking Lake Michigan's shore. Ray had never been up there but had been familiar with the massive building since construction began—it was one of a strain of new mega-homes going up on ridgelines throughout the region, structures that insulted the eye with their intrusive design, inescapable size, and questionable architectural heritage. Newspapers increasingly called them *McMansions*.

Ray parked in front of one of four garage doors, each an elaborate piece of joinery in a dark-stained wood. He followed the brick path to the front of the house, taking in the exterior—a mix of cultured stone, rough-sawn cedar, and stucco. Bright copper sheeting shone from the roof of a tower incongruously grafted to the far end of the house.

Ray pushed the doorbell on the side of the entrance—the double oak doors suspended in a portal formed by a ponderous post and beam frame—and heard a Westminster chime reverberate inside. He stepped back and gazed at the building; the red eye of a surveillance camera blinked at him from under the soffit. He heard two deadbolts, one after another, slide back.

The diminutive Alan Quertermous stood in the doorway, his hand extended, his greeting polite, formal, and stiff. He motioned Ray in with a sweeping gesture of his right hand.

"Welcome to my home."

"Thank you," responded Ray.

Quertermous led him into the great room; oak timbers supported a vaulted ceiling. A prow-shaped, glass-clad wall canti-levered over the lip of a ridge. Ray walked near the windows and watched the whitecaps break on the shore a hundred yards below. Everything smelled new: paint, wood, varnish, and leather.

"If it weren't such a gray afternoon, I could offer you one of the best views of a sunset on this coast of Lake Michigan," said Quertermous, his voice high-pitched and nasal.

"Superb location and this room . . ."

"It is fabulous, isn't it? Just fabulous. The architect and I went around and around about this," he raised his short arms toward the ceiling in a benediction-like gesture. "I had him redraw the plans several times, and we got as far as the framing, and it still didn't feel right—the proportions. I had them tear out most of the framing and do it again, but," he made a broad movement with his right arm from right to left, "the final result was exactly what I had hoped for." He looked at Ray, his tone was triumphant. "It's not often in life that we can get things to turn out exactly as we visualize them." He stood and watched his guest carefully examine the structure.

"It's magnificent," Ray observed. He turned and faced Quertermous, who was standing next to the counter that separated the living room from an adjoining kitchen. He was pouring Scotch into a heavy, purple-tinted tumbler. Ray scanned the room, two display cases and one bookcase had been built into the paneled walls. Several large oil paintings, medieval battle scenes in guided Rococo frames, and one piece of metal sculpture in the style of Calder, were hung at eye level, each carefully illuminated from above by small spotlights. Two large chairs and a matching sofa, all covered in thick, dark leather, and an end table made from the hatch cover of an old sailing ship surrounded a large fieldstone fireplace. Ray could see a collection of guns and knives in display cases. He moved closer. The knives—collector quality, polished blades, handles of exotic wood, stacked leather, and antler— were arranged on crimson velvet. Every space appeared to be filled. He moved on to the lone bookcase, quickly scanning titles by Leo Strauss, Allan Bloom, Ayn Rand, and Friedrich Nietzsche.

"I hope you don't mind, but I always have a Scotch when I get home from work. May I offer you a drink?" asked Quertermous, coming to his side. "I also have a pot of fresh coffee."

"Coffee, please," said Ray as he followed Quertermous to the counter. He picked up the Scotch bottle, examined the label, and set it back on the black granite countertop.

"That's an exceptional single-malt, hard to get that in Michigan," Quertermous commented. "I buy it by the case in Chicago." He poured some coffee into a delicate cup and set it on a tray.

"Are you a Scotch drinker, sheriff?"

"When I was younger, but it doesn't seem to agree with me these days."

"Pity, it's one of life's rare joys. Sugar, cream?"

"Black," Ray responded.

Quertermous carried the tray with the whiskey tumbler and cup over to a table, waved Ray to a chair at one side and settled on the near end of a couch. He ran his hand over his carefully combed hair, reddish on top with gray at the temples. He crossed his legs, left over right, and straightened the crease on his trousers. "Thank you for agreeing to meet me here. I was uncomfortable with the idea of having this interview at school. There's been so much talk since Ashleigh got herself killed. That's all the kids are chatting about. I think when any of us are seen with you or your, that young woman . . ."

"Sue Lawrence."

"Yes, her. I think we immediately become suspects." He took a sip of whiskey. "Silly isn't it, but that's how adolescents think.

This whole sad affair has been so disruptive; it's ruined the fall semester. I don't think we'll get things back to where they should be until after the Christmas break. So tell me, sheriff, what can I help you with?"

"Two things, actually. First, we're trying to piece together the last few days of Ashleigh's life; who she was with and if she said anything to anyone that might suggest she felt she was in danger."

"To answer your first concern, I have no idea who she was with," Quertermous answered in sneering tone. "And if she felt she was in danger, I'm sure I would have been the last person in whom she would have confided." Quertermous left his response hanging for several seconds and then asked, "And the second thing, sheriff?"

"At the staff meeting when Ian announced that Ashleigh had been killed, you reacted rather strongly, suggesting that this was bound to happen. I would like to know what you meant by that."

"Yes, I should have kept my mouth shut, but I was so angry." He took a long sip, his gaze shifting to the gray horizon.

"The cause of your anger?" Ray probed.

"Well, I think my immediate response had to do with her defense of that crippled kid Warrington hired. But it goes deeper than that. Ashleigh has been a pain in the ass since she was hired. No, it even goes back further than that; it goes back to when she was a student here. Mrs. Howard was extremely evenhanded with students. But Ashleigh was treated differently; she was always special. And I think there was always this reckless streak, perhaps something she inherited from her mother."

"Could you elaborate?" Ray asked, the ghost that he had been suppressing since the previous evening suddenly released into the room.

"Ashleigh came to Leiston as a freshman. She was very small for her age and sort of immature. Her mother had just died, and her father, from what I understand, wasn't anything more than a sperm donor," his tone derisive. "Mrs. Howard, being her guardian and all, was overly solicitous and spoiled her rotten. Frankly, I think the other students resented her. But no one said a word. We all respected Mrs. Howard too much." He paused and, getting up, took Ray's coffee cup. "Let me freshen your coffee," he said.

Ray watched him mix a fresh drink before pouring the coffee. After Quertermous was seated again Ray asked, "Are you suggesting that the motive for these murders might be traced back to something that happened when she was a high school student?"

"No," Quertermous cut him off sharply. "At least I don't think so. What I'm saying is that early on she had a sense of entitlement, probably because of her special relationship with Mrs. Howard. That said, she was a good student, naturally gifted, actually. She didn't have to work too hard to do well. She was the salutatorian of her class; with any effort on her part she could have been the valedictorian."

"And socially?"

"Early on she was quite moody and shy. But by the time she was a junior she'd come out of her shell. I think that's about the time she became sexually active." He gave Ray a knowing look. "I got the impression from what some of the boys said that she was quite the hot number."

"And this ties with the recklessness you mentioned?"

"Sex was part of it. She always had a devil-may-care attitude, even as a student. Those days I used to take the students skiing. Ashleigh was impossible. She was always trying to see how fast she could go; she was never quite in control. I always anticipated I'd have to bring her back in a box."

"Did you?"

"No, fortunately," Quertermous responded.

"I think you said at the meeting something to the effect that this was bound to happen and that you'd tried to warn people. That sounds like you have some special knowledge of who might want to harm her," Ray probed.

"I didn't mean that at all," he retorted argumentatively.

"Well, what did you mean, Mr. Quertermous?"

"I was talking about her lifestyle. She was just reckless. And she'd drag all kinds of men home."

"And how do you know that?"

"Janet Medford, she's a good friend. She told me about the way Ashleigh carried on. I guess she was quite the little trollop. And yes, you're going to say she was a consenting adult and all, but . . ."

Ray cut him off sharply. "Mr. Quertermous, I wasn't going to say anything. I'm just listening."

"Well, that's what some of the people at school said, our resident, knee-jerk liberals." Quertermous' face had reddened as his agitation increased. "As if the way someone lives doesn't rub off on their students. We are models of the adult world," he proclaimed, his words filling the vast space. "And Ashleigh, well . . ."

"Well what?"

"There's the sex thing, and I imagine drugs were involved, too. Those people seem to want to heighten every experience."

"Those people?"

"The people like Ashleigh's generation, pleasure seekers."

"And your warning, I'm still unclear about what you said. Why did you anticipate something awful would happen to Ashleigh?"

"Really, sheriff, I don't think you're listening. She was a risk-taker: her rock climbing, her kayaking, all the men and drugs. Things happen. Even up here in paradise."

"So, you have no specific knowledge of anyone who might have wanted to harm Ms. Allen?"

"No," he said, settling his small frame back on the couch. "Just the knowledge that if you play with fire often enough you're going to get burned."

"When did you last see Ms. Allen?"

"Her classroom was in the same wing as mine. I saw her all the time. Just passing, of course. And I would see her at lunch.

That is if she deigned to share her eminence with us. Most of the time she ate with the students."

"And this past week, Wednesday, Thursday, Friday?"

"Quite frankly, I don't remember." He finished his drink.

"And the men she dated, can you give me some names?"

"Sheriff, I don't live on campus. I just heard she had many gentlemen callers. It was also rumored that she had a brief fling with Warrington. Fortunately, he had the good sense to end it."

"And the drugs, you suggested that . . ."

"It's lifestyle, sheriff. It just fits." Quertermous paused and looked over at Ray. "Aren't you going to ask me where I was this weekend? I've heard that's a question you're asking everyone."

"Where were you this weekend, Mr. Quertermous?"

"I was here. Saturday evening Janet Medford was here for dinner. I made a crown roast of lamb. I think it is Janet's favorite meal."

"And about what time did she leave?"

"Janet had a bit too much to drink. I was worried about her driving and insisted that she spend the night." He looked mildly embarrassed. "Not what you're thinking, sheriff, I assure you. She slept in one of the guest rooms."

"Are you a hunter, Mr. Quertermous? I notice you have a collection of weapons."

"My father was a hunter. Big game. He loved going to Africa. That was back in the '40s and '50s before the native poachers ruined it. I've kept a few of his rifles."

"And the shotguns?"

"Those are mine. I used to do a lot of skeet shooting. Haven't done much in recent years."

"You also have some beautiful knives on display with the other weapons, yours or your father's?"

"Those are mine. I started collecting them a few years ago. Each one is handmade. They're art objects more than anything else. Is there anything else, sheriff?"

"This house, when was it built?"

"It was completed a year ago September." Quertermous got up from his seat and walked to window. "I inherited the land from my father. He used to own a big part of this coast, from here all the way down to that point where the river empties into the lake. That's before our wonderful government decided to seize all the land up here. They paid him a fraction of what it was worth." His voice became wistful. "My father was a developer, and he had great plans for this area. He would have built a fantastic resort. Restaurants, hotels, condos, golf courses, and a yacht basin, it would all be here. Everything would have been first-class and filled with the right kind of people, if you know what I mean. And what did we end up with?" He gestured toward the beach. "Sand, pine trees, and a bunch of bare-assed bathers and their scruffy urchins."

23

Ray walked along the narrow lane toward the quaint duplexes designed to look like Cotswold cottages. The walls were clad in a limestone ashlar that matched the stone used in Leiston's main house. The dwellings had originally been built as quarters for the estate staff and accommodations for the Howards' many guests. In the years following Leiston's founding, five more duplexes in the same style were added for faculty and staff. The buildings were in a rolling, heavily wooded area. The separate entrances and small, walled gardens provided residents with a sense of privacy. The heavy, masonry construction prevented the intrusion of noise from neighbors.

Each building was named for an English county. Janet Medford lived in Devonshire Cottage, in the front unit that faced the small lane, and Ashleigh had lived in the back half that faced the woods and the lake.

Ray stood on the porch in the fading light and listened to the music coming from the interior—vintage Brubeck. He knocked politely at first and waited; then knocked a second time with greater force. The volume of the jazz dropped, the porch light—a dull frosted bulb in a jar-like globe, the bottom filled with dead insects—switched on. The door opened the length of the safety chain; a face peered at him.

"Yes," came a tired voice. The smell of tobacco and bourbon hit Ray's nostrils.

"Sheriff Elkins, ma'am. May I come in?"

"What is this about?" Janet Medford asked, not moving from the door, her face wrinkled and weary.

"I have some questions about Ashleigh Allen that perhaps you could help me with."

She slid the chain, opened the door, and moved back reluctantly, allowing Ray to enter. "Can I get you something, sheriff?" she asked, her voice deep and raspy. "I'm having a Manhattan. I've also got beer and Coke. And I can make you a cup of instant coffee."

"Coke will be find, thank you."

He watched her disappear into a kitchen, then looked around the room. The walls were covered with oil paintings of a shared style, minimalist seascapes in bold colors. Ray wondered if they were her work and studied the initials at the bottom left of each canvas. JM was deftly fashioned on each, four strokes of a palette knife in raw umber. Most of the furniture was '50s modern, elegantly designed and carefully crafted pieces in teak whose style had successfully weathered the passage of time. A couch was placed against the longest exterior wall and faced a stone hearth. Two Wassily chairs sat at right angles to the couch and formed a U around a coffee table. Ray walked around and studied the neatly organized bookcases, dominated by art and architecture books, with a small collection of dated fiction and a few volumes of poetry.

Medford returned and handed him a glass with ice and an open bottle of Coke. She set a freshly filled decanter on the coffee table and, after adding a log to the fire and pushing things around with a poker, settled onto the couch. She drew two maraschino cherries from a small jar, dropped them into a heavy-bottomed whiskey tumbler, and poured in some golden liquid from the decanter.

"I used to drink these for the cherries," she said after taking a large sip, her voice deep and raspy.

"What do you drink them for now?"

She looked puzzled, like she hadn't really thought about it. She brightened a bit, and responded, "I like the blurring effect. They blot out the pain and make the evenings endurable. I go to bed and sleep. During the day I'm busy, it's the nights that get to me." She lifted a cherry from the glass, catching a drop of the drink with her tongue before she closed her mouth around it. "But I'm sure you're not here to talk about me, sheriff.

"What can you tell me about Ashleigh Allen?"

"Ashleigh Allen. I'm sure I can tell you lots of things. I've known her for years. But if you'd be more specific, I can save both of us some time."

"What kind of a relationship did you have with her?

Medford sipped her drink and gave Ray a long look. "Quite frankly, we didn't have a relationship. In truth, I rather loathed her. It wasn't her fault, really. She hadn't done anything to me. It was just seeing her so goddamn happy all the time."

"Do you know anyone who would want her dead?"

"Not dead, that's taking it too far. But more than a few of us were pissed that she was the fair haired . . . I guess that doesn't quite work, does it?" she laughed. "You know what I mean. She usually got anything that she wanted for her program, and the rest of us waited in line. But no one is going to commit murder over that."

"Did you see or hear anything unusual in recent weeks?"

"Well, she had a lot of people coming and going, but then she always did."

Ray noted a condemnatory tone in her voice. "Who?"

"Students, for one thing. She did her most of her tutorials at her cottage. The rest of us do them at the academic building. We want to separate our personal space from student space. And it's been sort of the rule since . . ."

"Since when?"

"Since they fired Tyler; he was an English teacher, our poet-in-residence—I still have a couple of volumes of his stuff." She motioned toward a shelf. "He got way too friendly with some of the girls. Might have been going on for years before someone noticed. Quite a scandal. He got one of the sweet young things pregnant." She ground the cigarette out and lit another.

"When was this?"

"Been a while, probably fifteen or twenty years, maybe more." She paused and inhaled. "Moved on to a university job, he did. Word was that he found lots of coeds who wanted to be had by a poet. Won the National Book Award a few years ago." Her tone changed as she returned to the earlier topic. "Since Tyler's time the faculty housing has been mostly off limits to students except for cohort meetings."

"What's that?"

"Groups of students working on special projects. We're supposed to help the students learn to work cooperatively, to be team players, and all that happy horse shit. Part of the team building is that the kids prepare a meal together each week with their faculty mentor. It's all part of Warrington's scheme to prepare students for the," her tone became increasingly sarcastic, "the information economy. Rather high-sounding bullshit, if you ask me. But no one asks us about education any more. It's all the fluff that Ian feeds the board and parents. I don't think the man is capable of speaking normal English. He just spouts the latest buzz words that . . ."

"So, students visited Ashleigh. Who else?"

"Well, I didn't sit around here and watch the comings and goings," she grumped defensively.

"I'm not suggesting you did," Ray said, "but if you did observe others . . ."

"Yes, there are times when it's been unavoidable. Like her first semester Warrington was lurking about a lot. And then students, especially boys, but the girls were drawn to her, too. And then this guy she was found with. He spent the weekend with her . . . let me think . . . probably once a month."

"How long has that been going on?"

"It seems like he's been around from almost the beginning, but he's become more of an item since last spring. They may have gone off together last summer."

"Do you know where they . . ."

"Not Paris, that's for sure. Probably off in a kayak, saving the fucking whales."

"Anyone else?"

"Well," she smiled. "There was that rustic Adonis we had here fixing the barns. We were all envious, but he didn't seem to last long. Pity. I wish she had kept him around. I just liked looking at him." She finished her drink, refilled the glass, and gave Ray a wicked, drunken smile.

"How about women? Any women friends?"

"Not that I saw. I don't think she was interested in women."

"No women friends?"

"Sarah James, they were friends. But she was mostly with men, doing guy things. Ashleigh was very outdoorsy; she seemed addicted to every type of exercise," she said with disdain in her voice.

"Female students? Anyone she was close to?"

"I don't think so."

"How about drugs, drinking?"

"I don't know about any drugs. She was the yogurt and granola type, can't imagine she'd befoul her body with drugs or drink." She raised her glass with an unsteady hand.

"Someone suggested that she used drugs."

"Let me guess," she chuckled drunkenly. "Alan Quertermous is always kidding me about having a crack whore next door. He has a very naughty mouth."

"You had dinner with him on Saturday?"

"No. I didn't get as far as dinner. I think I fell asleep during the hors d'oeuvres. Alan's cocktail hour goes on far too long. He did serve me oysters and rack of lamb for brunch on Sunday.

Quite extraordinary, really," she paused and emptied her glass. "As for drinking, I don't know what or how much Ashleigh drank, but I'm the last person to condemn someone for . . . well . . . as you can see . . . I'm drunk."

"Just one more question, about what time did you fall asleep Saturday night?"

"Well, I got to Alan's around six, we had drinks for several hours. He does make such wonderful hors d'oeuvres, and he never lets your glass get empty."

"Eight, nine?"

"I don't know. I think we were both quite drunk." She looked across at Elkins. "Now, sheriff, if there is nothing more, I would like you to go away so I can go to bed."

Ray placed one of his business cards on the coffee table. "If anything comes to mind that you think might be helpful, please call."

Medford gave him a drunken smile and watched him depart.

Ray followed the winding path toward his Jeep. Before he pulled the door open, he stopped and looked back at Devonshire Cottage. The lights went off as Medford moved from room to room until the building was in complete darkness. Moonlight reflected off the roof, a small coil of smoke rose from the chimney. The air was crisp and scented with the burning oak. He held the beauty of the moment, letting his other thoughts and feelings slip away.

24

Ray awakened at four in the morning and stayed in bed and read until five. Then he got up, made coffee, showered, and consumed a bowl of granola before setting off for the office. Shortly before seven o'clock he completed reviewing the reports of the shift commanders for the previous several days, a part of his daily routine that he had put off because of the demands of the murder investigation. By the time Sue Lawrence had arrived for their scheduled 8:00 a.m. case review, Ray had worked through most of the paper that even the smallest of police agencies generates in a few days.

"Morning," offered Sue, setting her insulated coffee cup on the edge of Ray's desk.

"You look a bit rough this morning," Ray observed.

"You really know how to make a girl feel good," she responded.

"I was showing avuncular concern for an esteemed younger colleague," he explained.

"If truth were known . . ."

Ray cut her off, "I have a sense it soon will be."

"Long after you were home and in your warm bed, I was

still gathering evidence." She paused briefly and yawned. "By the way, you owe me for about a dozen glasses of Pinot Grigio, and you're darn lucky it was ladies night. Maybe you can get the county to reimburse me," she said as she dropped into a gray steel chair near Ray's desk.

"What you talking about?" he asked.

"Yesterday, in passing, you said that you wondered about Jason Zelke's relationship with other women. Last night, off the clock, I did some informal research."

"I am constantly amazed by your dedication," Ray offered in a jocular fashion. "And where did you conduct this study?"

"Well, after yoga the girls usually go to the Beanery, drink herbal tea and talk. I suggested we go to Last Chance instead. I even offered to pick up the first round."

"How did it go?"

"Better than I, or you, could have hoped for. By the time the third round of drinks and potato skins had arrived, the conversation turned to guys. There was a lot of kidding going on. They were going through all the local guys and talking about a couple of new arrivals. I mentioned that I'd seen this guy at the health club pumping iron and described Jason. They all knew who I was talking about instantly." Sue had a self-satisfied smile on her face.

"What did you learn?"

"Well, I'm the only one in the group who isn't native to the area. Several of the women went to elementary school with Jason, they all knew him in middle and high school, and several hung around with him during his community college days and after."

"Did any of them date him?"

"They had all dated him sometime between second grade and last year. According to the women, he's too much like a brother. You can call him at three in the morning, and he'll happily drive his big truck over and pull you out of a ditch—all that good, kind stuff. He loves to drop by your house or apartment and fix things. And he's supposed to be great in the sack but . . ."

"But what?"

"The consensus is that he's sort of boring, and he's totally self-contained. He likes to have a woman around when he wants a woman around, but most of the time he's out fishing or hunting or heading to his cabin in the U.P. You can't get him to go dancing or a movie; no one has ever seen him read a book. And he doesn't like parties. He'll cook you a great meal, but he won't take you to a restaurant. He'll hang out with you for three or four days, and then you won't see him for three weeks. And it's not that he's out with other women, he just gets so close and then he pulls back. No one thinks he'll ever really take the chance on a close relationship, unless you're a black Labrador." She laughed at her own joke.

"How about violence. Any suggestion that . . . ?"

"I probed that very carefully. You've got to remember all these women are long-term friends and occasional loves of Jason. I approached the topic by saying I wouldn't like someone that big getting angry with me." She looked at Ray. "Which is true. But the consensus is that Jason just gets hurt when things aren't going well. And he doesn't have the capacity to talk things out or confront. He just wanders away with his dog. There was a lot of armchair psychology, something about his mother splitting when he was a kid."

"How about Ashleigh, were you able to explore that angle?"

"I got lucky on that one. I was just waiting for someone to suggest that my interest might be something other than . . ."

"Social," Ray interjected.

"Yeah, social," she chuckled. "They wanted to know about Ashleigh, wanted to know, woman to woman, if Jason was a suspect. I felt sort of false when I told them this, but I pretended I was giving them some inside stuff. I said that we'd talked to dozens of people, to everyone Ashleigh had any contact with. Jason was on the list, but not a suspect. They agreed that he couldn't have been involved. And then there was some talk about how Ashleigh was really out of his . . ."

"His what?" Ray probed.

"I was going to say 'class,' but that wasn't it. A couple of them had been acquainted with Ashleigh. She came to yoga classes her first couple of years at Leiston. I think the way they phrased it was that Ashleigh was a bit too exotic for Jason. They thought she'd probably had some good rolls in the hay with him and then got bored. But there was the suggestion that he was upset when it was over."

"How did they know?"

"Hey, in this little burg there's a lot of talk."

"The marijuana use, did you put that out there?"

"I floated that a couple of times, but no one responded. They were a bit wary, me being a cop."

"So, your gut feeling, what about Zelke?"

"I don't think he's our guy."

"You're not going to go out with him, are you?"

"He might be the best thing out there at the moment," she said in a teasing fashion. "But no, probably not. He's not a reader. You'd never approve."

"Thank you," said Ray, "interesting stuff." He got up from his desk and pulled down a large white board from the ceiling. Ray went to the list of interviewees and added a question mark to Zelke's name.

"Not convinced?" said Sue.

"I agree, I think it's highly unlikely. But maybe something in him snapped, and he followed them out there. He knows the terrain; he's big enough and strong enough, and he'd have a hunting knife. His only alibi to his whereabouts on Saturday evening is his dog."

"Too bad dogs don't talk. Bet they'd be a lot more reliable than people," said Sue.

"We should talk to him again in a day or two to let him know we're still interested in him. Both of us this time, good cop and bad cop. Are you finished with the crime scene?"

"Yes. We went over the entire area again and then vacuumed the back of tarps on the off-chance that something was clinging to them."

"And?"

"No new findings at the scene. I'll look over the debris we collected when we vacuumed the tarps. We've canvassed the area; I've talked with the Department of Natural Resources. I was hoping there might have been a game warden in the area that evening. Nothing. And I went back to Arnie's shack. Evans and I did a thorough search of the building and the area. I was hoping I'd see something we missed in the wind and rain. Nada. Anything new on Arnie?"

"Not much, and nothing good," said Ray. "I talked to the trauma doctor and to the cardiologist who's treating him. They think if he survives he'll have a lot more cognitive damage. I think it's doubtful that he'll ever be able to tell us anything. Poor kid. Poor Kim. Either way, it's going to be awful for her." He took a deep breath, slowly exhaling. "How do you feel about a fast trip to Cleveland and Ann Arbor?"

"You want me talk to Dowd's parents?"

"Yes, and perhaps go through his apartment in Ann Arbor. You'll have to do some liaison work before you go. I've always had very good cooperation with other agencies when I've needed to do this."

"I'll get started on it right away. Hopefully I can get out of here before noon. Anything else?"

Ray handed her a grocery list. "If you have time on your way out of Ann Arbor, here's a few things I need from Zingerman's Deli."

"Is this in my job description?" she asked in a mocking tone.

"Consider it a professional development activity," he responded. "Zingerman's is a model of efficiency and good customer service." He paused and smiled, "And you will also have my eternal gratitude."

25

Shortly before ten, Ray pulled into the almost empty parking lot of the Bay Side Family Market. He sat in his car for several minutes trying to remember what he needed, the exhaustion of a long day clouding his thoughts. He pulled a small notebook from his shirt pocket, switched on the map light, and listed the necessities: milk, bananas, coffee, bread. Then he wrote "dinner" followed by a question mark.

Collecting a shopping cart near the front door, Ray picked through a pile of bananas, most overripe, until he found a bunch that was more green than yellow. After picking up a quart of milk and a loaf of whole-wheat bread for toast, he noticed a lone baguette on the display rack of a local baker. He tested the crust; it was still hard. The bread became the determining factor for the choice of other menu items for his late-night supper. He grabbed a bag of golden delicious apples, checking the label to make sure they were from an area orchard. Then he moved to the cheese counter, an oval island between the produce section and the wine, four-fifths displaying domestic varieties, the final wedge covered with imported products, including a small collection of artisan and farmhouse cheeses. In a far corner he unearthed a petite pyramid of Valençay, a rare find so long after the summer people were gone. Holding it up and turning it slowly, he inspected the hard rind of charcoal and mold before putting it in the cart. Then he selected a piece of Brie and looked through the modest offering of Stilton, five small packages, checking the rind. His selection technique didn't go unnoticed. He looked up to find Sarah James watching him with great amusement.

"You do a much better job of shopping than I do," she said good-naturedly, playfully offering him her grocery list. She came around the island and inspected the contents of his cart. "Looks like you're planning a picnic."

"Late dinner, actually. Something that doesn't require any cooking."

"Late," she said glancing at her watch. "Very late. You look like you've had a long day."

Ray just nodded.

"I meant to call you today," Sarah said. "Something occurred to me that might be useful." She looked around after she said it. "I don't think it's real important, but it may be of some interest. But this is hardly the place. I'll call you in the morning?"

"If you have time," Ray offered, "we could get a coffee over at the Beanery. At this time of night, I'm sure we could get a booth at the back where we can talk without an audience."

"Done with your shopping?" she asked.

"Just need to pay. How about you?"

"Same."

They chatted as they waited in line. The lone cashier—a tall, thin teenage girl with pinkish hair and multiple facial piercings—worked through customers in front of them, people on milk, beer, bread, and chips runs. Ray walked Sarah to her car, a Subaru wagon, and then followed her to the center of the village. He was out of his car and halfway to the door before he noticed the lights, with the exception of a red neon tube that spelled BEANERY, were out. He studied the sign on the front door. *Fall Hours Now In Effect.*

Sarah came to his side and looked at the sign. "It's not that important, sheriff. It can wait until tomorrow. Just a couple of things that might be useful."

"Tell you what," he said. "If you don't mind, you can come up to my place." He pointed to the bluff behind the village. "I live up there, it's five blocks."

"I won't be intruding on your . . ."

"No, it will be nice to have someone to talk to over bread and cheese."

Ray opened the packages and arranged cheese on a board while Sarah wandered around the kitchen and living room. He sliced up the baguette, put a clean dishtowel in a basket, dropped in the pieces, and folded the towel over the bread. "What would you like to drink?" he asked. I have Diet Coke, coffee, tea, or I could open a bottle of wine.

"A little wine would be nice, but please don't . . ."

"Good choice," said Ray. He selected a Vouvray from a collection of bottles stored horizontally on the bottom shelf of his refrigerator and retrieved a corkscrew from a drawer.

"What a wonderful home you have here," she said, looking around at the kitchen. She stood for a long moment and examined a bookcase on the side of the kitchen island. "Are all these cookbooks yours?"

"Yes," Ray responded. "I've been collecting them for years, and now I finally have a place for them in the kitchen. That was one of the major design considerations for this room."

"And the work area looks like it was designed for a serious cook," she commented as she continued her inspection of the kitchen. "The place has that new-house smell. How long have you lived here?"

"I was supposed to be in by early April, but there were a number of delays. I was sort of camping out here in May and June, and didn't really start to settle in until July."

"So you have two bedrooms?"

"Three actually. I was going to have two, but my local bank manager encouraged me to add a third. They don't like to write mortgages for two-bedroom homes—something about resale value. So, I had the architect add a third bedroom. It worked out okay. I have one nice-sized bedroom and two small ones. One I'm using as a study, and the other is filled with boxes yet to be unpacked."

Sarah helped him bring the cheese, bread, wine, apples, and a cup of coffee to a small table near the wall of glass at the front of the main room. Ray lit two candles and dimmed the lights so they could enjoy the view of the village and harbor. The glow of the candles reflected off the surface of the simple pine table creating an aura of warmth and intimacy.

"This is fantastic," she said as she gazed at the panorama below. "How did you find the lot?"

"It belonged to friends. They were going to build here at one time. But they went their separate ways, and she ended up with it."

"So how did you . . . ?"

"When she decided to move to Seattle to be closer to her daughter and grandchildren, she made me an offer on the lot I couldn't refuse."

"This person, was she a . . . a romantic interest?" Sarah asked coyly.

"We had been close friends for awhile."

Sarah raised her wine glass. "Well, here's a toast to you and your wonderful home."

Ray looked across the table. He remembered how attractive he had found Sarah the first time he interviewed her. And now, in the golden glow of the candles, she was even more engaging.

"You had something you wanted to tell me," Ray said.

"I'm enjoying everything so much, but yes—two things. First, I was putting updates of the employees' health insurance in the faculty personnel files. Alan Quertermous, the math instructor, has this gigantic folder—he's been at the school from almost the beginning. So, I was looking through his folder to see if there was anything that I could discard, much of the material in these files is years out of date. I don't think anyone has ever cleaned them up. Anyway, I found a copy of the letter where Gwendolyn Howard offered him the position."

"So, it's an interesting piece of history," he offered, taking a sip of wine.

"Well, it's more than that. She mentioned the fact that they were distant cousins and how nice it would be to reconnect with that part of her family. No one has ever mentioned that before, Quertermous being related to Mrs. Howard. I thought Ashleigh was the only member of the family to ever work at Leiston. I still don't know how Quertermous and Mrs. Howard were related, there's no suggestion of that in the letter. And I have no idea whether or not he and Ashleigh might be blood relatives. I just thought you might find that interesting."

"Yes," said Ray. He pondered the information for several moments. "And there was a second . . . ?"

"Yes, I was talking to my son, Eric, on the phone last night. He told me about something that happened his senior year." She raised her eyebrows, "He didn't tell me about the incident at the time, at least not the complete story. And I hesitate here, because it's only a rumor and probably is of no significance . . ."

"Go ahead."

"It was near the end of the spring semester. Ashleigh had taken twelve students on an extended camping trip, the final activity of her wilderness survival class. There were supposed to be two adults guiding the group, but something happened to the other leader, I can't remember if he got sick or what. Anyway, Ashleigh, not wanting to disappoint the kids, took them solo. "

"Where?"

"The plan was to spend about six days paddling, hiking,

and doing zero-impact camping on the Manitou Islands. As I remember, it was a cold spring that year. The first few days the trip went as planned, but then they really got hit, a couple inches of wet snow and high winds. They had to stay on South Manitou an extra day. Eric remembers that Ashleigh was very cautious. She had the group listen to the marine weather report with her before they started the next crossing to North Manitou, the longest piece of open water on the trip. He remembers the forecast was calm winds and small waves. But as they neared their destination, the weather changed, and they got caught in a squall. A couple of boats capsized." Sarah paused, her tone softened. "Eric has nothing but praise for the way Ashleigh handled what might have been a tragic situation. But I'm glad he didn't give me all the gory details at the time," she observed, tearing a piece of bread.

"So what happened?" pressed Ray.

"The kids were in the water. Eric said the boy, Billy, stayed with his kayak, but the girl, Monica, became fairly hysterical. He remembers that she was screaming that she was going to die and that she let her boat drift away. Ashleigh had the other kids stay together and she went after Monica. She muscled the kid onto her deck and paddled her to shore. Then she came back for Billy. He had been in the water too long, and he couldn't help. Eric says he still can't figure out how Ashleigh got him back in his boat, he was a big kid. Eric just remembers she sort of scooped Billy up and put him in his boat. Then she towed the kayak to shore and got the rest of the kids safely landed.

"That's quite a story, but I don't see . . ."

"Patience," she offered with a smile. "I'm just getting to the important part. Billy had been in the water for some time before Ashleigh was able to get him back in the boat. By the time she got him to shore he was shivering uncontrollably and not making much sense. She had the kids build a fire and start heating water, and then, to their amazement, she stripped him out of his wetsuit and got him into a sleeping bag. Then she stripped down to her underwear and got in with him and wrapped herself around him. Eric doesn't remember how long it took before Billy stopped shivering. Eventually they moved to a tent where he was force-fed hot tea and energy bars."

"She certainly seemed to know how to handle the situation."

"Ashleigh was that kind of person. Not embarrassed to do what had to be done." Sarah paused and sipped some wine. "She got the kids to set up camp and make supper. The next morning when they went to pack the boats, Ashleigh's kayak had been vandalized."

"Vandalized? How?"

"Eric said there were a couple of holes in the bottom of the cockpit, like someone had driven a large knife or hatchet through the boat. Eric said that when Ashleigh saw the damage, she carried on like this was part of the experience. She got out a repair kit and showed them how to prepare the surface and put on fiberglass patches. She never mentioned the incident again, but the kids talked about it."

"Did Eric speculate on who might have damaged her boat?"

"I asked him. He thinks that one of the boys must have been very taken with Ashleigh. That her climbing into the sleeping bag with Billy triggered a jealous rage."

"Does he have a likely candidate?"

"No, not really. He said that at the time he wished he had been the one needing help with hypothermia." She chuckled and continued, "I reminded him that's not the kind of thing you tell your mother."

"Does he think Ashleigh might have been involved with a student?"

"No," Sarah firmly answered. "Absolutely not. But Eric said Billy got a lot of teasing from the boys about how lucky he was to have Ashleigh wrapped around him."

"How much of this got back to school? I mean, kids really talk about . . ."

"It was near the end of the year. Other than Billy, they were all seniors. A couple of weeks later they were spread to the winds."

"Does Eric remember anything else?"

"I think that's it. He said he had forgotten all about the damaged kayak. Ashleigh's death brought back the episode."

Ray nodded. "The other kids on the trip, can you get me a list? I'd like to know who they are and if any are in the area."

"Billy is still around, he's a senior. As to the class list, I'll have to do some digging. It wouldn't be on our new system. Eric probably can give me the names from memory."

"How about addresses?"

"I'll ask Helen; she'll be able to pull that info from the alumni database. I've found the incident report that Ashleigh completed at the time. Do you want a copy?"

"Please. What does it contain?"

"About what I've told you. It's got the names of the students involved in the accident, and the date, time, and extent of injuries— the usual bureaucratic questions and answers."

"But no mention of her kayak being damaged?"

"No, that wasn't part of it."

Ray, lost in thought, refilled Sarah's wine glass without asking if she wanted more.

"Ask a woman up to your house and then you try to get her drunk," she kidded.

Ray looked abashed. "Sorry. I was just trying to be a good host. Have some more food, that will help. And I can always give you a Breathalyzer test to make sure you're below the legal limit before I allow you to drive home," he said with a wry smile.

"And I have to stay here until I reach the . . . what a clever man you are." She looked at her watch. "This has been wonderful, thank you. But I really must be going. Ashleigh's funeral is tomorrow, and

I've got a very early morning. Let me help you get things picked up."

"That's no problem, I can take . . ." Ray wasn't able to complete his sentence. Sarah was up and carrying things to the kitchen. Working together they had everything in order in a few minutes.

"Tomorrow, would it be appropriate for me to attend the funeral?" Ray asked.

"No problem," she answered. "But you might want to arrive early. We anticipate quite a crowd."

"What time should I be there?"

"The funeral is scheduled for eleven o'clock. I think you should be there by 10:40."

"Yes, ma'am," responded Ray as he helped Sarah with her coat. He followed her to the door where she started to offer her hand and then gave Ray a quick, tentative hug. "Thank you for the nice evening," she said as she departed. Ray stood at the door and watched her taillights disappear down the drive.

After her departure Ray did a final sweep of the kitchen, wiping the counters and starting the dishwasher, and then went to his study. He retrieved his journal and pen from his desk and stood for a few minutes looking out at the lights of the village.

In the years he had been keeping a journal, he had endeavored to separate his personal life from his professional duties, but that wasn't always possible. And this night his focus was on the murder investigation. After several pages his focus shifted to Sarah James. Had she told him everything about her relationship with Ashleigh and Warrington? He also wondered if there was any possibility that she might be involved in these murders. And finally he noted the perfume she was wearing; he became aware of it during their brief embrace. It was not a scent that he recognized, not that his knowledge of fragrances was particularly extensive. It was very subtle and pleasant. In his last few sentences he wondered if she was the person she represented herself to be.

26

~

The morning of Ashleigh's funeral, Ray found Sarah James standing outside near the front of the chapel. "Looks like you've got a full house," he observed looking at the clumps of people on the sidewalks and lawn. "Who are all these people?"

"The students and staff, many alums and parents. And I think there might be quite a few people from the community. Ashleigh had a lot of friends."

"How are you going to get everyone in?"

"We're not. We can only squeeze in about 200, which is far more than this building was originally intended to hold. We've arranged a second seating area in the Kiva, our auditorium-like building. There's a big screen projection system there. Once the chapel is filled, the overflow will be escorted over. And then we're going to serve a buffet lunch in the dining hall. We have some more tables set up on the lawn. We're lucky it's a beautiful day."

"You did all the organizing?"

"Yes, but I had a lot of help getting things in place. Everyone's making an extra effort." She paused and looked at Ray. "That's one of the special things about working here. With a few exceptions, it's a real community."

"The cost, the school is handling . . . ?"

"Well, we were. But Ashleigh's attorney instructed us to forward all the bills to him; he will take care of them. In fact, he was the one who suggested the lunch, told me to spend as much as necessary to make this a special occasion. He said he planned to attend. I hope he identifies himself."

"What's his name? I would like to talk to him."

"Furman Gellhorn. Would you like his phone number and e-mail address? The firm is in Chicago."

"I'd appreciate that. Tell me about the chapel," Ray said as he studied the exterior.

"It was built soon after the main house. The first Mrs. Howard liked the idea of a family chapel. But I've heard the thing that really pushed the project was the marriage of their only daughter, Consuelo. Wonderful name."

"Yes," agreed Ray. "Good period name."

"The chapel was built large enough for the group they anticipated would come up from Chicago for the wedding. The interior was modeled after a medieval chapel; all the materials were fabricated in England and shipped here for assembly. English masons and carpenters were brought over for the construction. Can you imagine the expense?"

"You certainly are knowledgeable about the school's history."

"I give tours to prospective students and their parents. In order to answer their questions, I've done a lot of research. I've looked at everything in print and talked to the old-timers. I'm a real history buff, so this has been a lot of fun."

"Going back to Consuelo, I thought the couple had only one child. I had never heard of her . . . Consuelo."

"She was the eldest child, seven or eight years older than her brother," continued Sarah, "and she died before her wedding. I've heard the story two ways, one was an auto accident, and the other involved a trolley—a detail I need to research. Happened in Chicago weeks before the wedding. And the story goes that Consuelo's mother never entered the chapel after her daughter's death," she said, motioning toward the lovely Gothic building.

"Sad story. But the building was maintained as a chapel?"

"No. My understanding is that it was used for years as sort of a storage building. Mrs. Howard had the chapel cleaned out and returned to its original condition when she started the school. She was Episcopalian, as was the rest of the Howard family, and had a retired Episcopalian priest in residence here during Leiston's first few years. I think he also taught religious studies. After he left, she started having non-denominational services on Sunday, and that tradition has continued up to the present."

"Is anyone from Ashleigh's family going to be here?" Ray asked.

Sarah's administrative tone faded as a look of sadness washed across her face. "I couldn't find anyone, not anyone. It was a very small family and with Ashleigh's death, well, it's sort of the end of the line." She paused briefly. "I've arranged an Episcopalian service; Ashleigh listed that as her religious preference on her employment application, although I can't remember her ever expressing any interest in religion."

The two heavy oak doors were pushed open from the inside and the crowd started to move forward. Ray followed Sarah into the chapel. She led Ray across the vestibule and through a small, partially hidden doorway in the oak-paneled interior. They climbed a narrow stone stairway spiraled up to the organ loft. A thick rope, suspended in steel loops attached to the masonry, served as the handrail. They emerged in an alcove below the roofline. The organist, a slight wiry man, nodded to them as his fingers and feet produced a complex piece of counterpoint. Ray and Sarah settled on a small wooden bench. Their position afforded an excellent view of most of the chapel.

Sarah watched Ray carefully study the crowd. "What are you looking for?" she asked.

Ray brought his hands in front of him in a prayerful gesture, fingertips touching, indicating a consideration of her question rather than an act of religiosity. "I don't know," he admitted. "It would be nice to see something that might serve as a clue to finding the murderer. But maybe I just need to be here; I need to keep the human aspects of this crime at the forefront of my thinking."

Ray surveyed the people filing into the church, filling the dark-oak pews: teenagers, some accompanied by adults; faculty and staff members; people from the community. He studied their faces as they turned from the aisles and moved into the pews. The sorrow and loss he observed, especially on the faces of the Leiston students, was palpable.

The service started, high Episcopalian, replete with incense, a sanctus bell, and the kissing of the Bible. It reminded Ray of the time he was in London and slipped into a funeral at St. Paul's in an attempt to get the full effect of a Christopher Wren church.

Before beginning the service the celebrant—a tall man with a deep resonant voice who identified himself to the mourners as Father Murphy—spoke to the congregation.

His comments were brief and instructional in tone, clearly crafted to help the students through this ordeal. He explained that funeral rites and traditions had evolved to comfort the living, to help them accept the mystery of death, and to give them a way to express their sorrow. Next he talked about the importance of making a final farewell and giving thanks for a person's life.

And then he began: "O God of grace and glory, we remember before you this day our sister Ashleigh. We thank you for giving her to us, to her students and friends, to know and to love as a companion on our earthly pilgrimage. In your boundless compassion, console us who mourn. Give us faith to see in death the gate of eternal life, so that in quiet confidence we may continue our course on earth, until, by your call, we are reunited with those who have gone before; through Jesus Christ our Lord. Amen."

From time to time, as the service moved forward, Sarah would hold a hymnal or the Book of Common Prayer between them, turning to the appropriate pages. And, crowded together on the little bench, he became more aware of her, the sound of her voice in song and prayer, her gentle sobbing from time to time, and the subtle scent of her perfume. It was then the ghost reappeared. Ray thought about Ashleigh's mother, Allison, and their brief acquaintance almost thirty years before. If she had lived, he thought, she'd be in this chapel, the central mourner. He was seized by almost overwhelming sadness.

The celebrant continued: "Father of all, we pray to you for Ashleigh and for all those whom we love but see no longer. Grant to them eternal rest. Let light perpetual shine upon them. May his soul and the souls of all the departed, through the mercy of God, rest in peace. Amen."

The Eucharist was celebrated; a small number of students and adults came forward to take communion, and then, one by one, Father Murphy introduced three speakers to pay homage to Ashleigh's life.

Ian Warrington spoke first. He noted the many contributions Ashleigh had made to Leiston School in her short tenure there. Ray thought it was a wonderful chronology of her accomplishments, but he was surprised Warrington didn't comment on Ashleigh as a person.

Warrington was followed by a current Leiston student. She explained, "I first met Ms. Allen three years ago when I was a freshman. I never liked science before I had her, she taught me to love it. But more importantly, she helped me with a lifelong problem. I've always had a bad stutter," she said, beginning to sob. She stood and took several deep breaths. Under control again, she continued, "With great kindness, through countless hours during tutorials, she helped me overcome this problem. Her love and attention changed my life."

An erect, stately woman with salt-and-pepper hair pulled back into a bun followed her to the podium. She began, "I was a student here in the early days of Leiston School. During those years my life was changed, forever made better, by an extraordinary woman and educator, Gwendolyn Howard, Ashleigh Allen's great-aunt. When my son matriculated here in his junior year, I was delighted to learn Mrs. Howard's niece, Ashleigh, had just joined the faculty. My son Jack and I will always give thanks for her enormous kindness and her great skill. She taught Jack how to dream and helped him develop the skills and the confidence he needed to follow his dreams. Talking with other parents over the last few years and again here today, I am reminded how Ashleigh Allen worked her special magic with so many young people. Her loss is beyond comprehension. Our only comfort is in celebrating the special joy she gave to so many, joy that will stay with them throughout their lives."

Father Murphy requested an extended moment of silence, and then invited others to talk about Ashleigh. A mixture of people came forward—students, alumni, and members of the Leiston community—and shared memories about Ashleigh and the special friendship or kindness she had extended to them. Ray felt his eyes well up several times.

Finally, Father Murphy reminded the mourners that a lunch would follow. He gave the benediction, and the service was over. Ray remained seated and watched the mourners leave. Sarah stayed at his side. Finally she rose, saying, "I'd better check on how things are going."

Ray followed her down the stairs. They stood in front of the chapel and watched the crowd move along the path toward the dining hall.

"Lunch?" Sarah asked.

"No, I better get back to the office." He held her hand for a long moment. "Thank you for the help. I'm glad I did this."

Ray stood and watched her move away with the crowd. He thought about this tragedy, about how the justice system can impose vengeance but can never undo effects of great evil.

27

~~~

Ray was lost in thought, still holding Sarah in his gaze, when a resonant male voice called his name, "Sheriff Elkins?" Ray turned. A tall, elderly man, with steel-gray hair was extending his hand.

"Yes," Ray responded, taking the hand. He studied the man closely; he guessed him to be in his middle to late seventies.

"I'm Furman Gellhorn—Ickles, Gellhorn, Jeffers, and Arendt. We're a Chicago firm. I administered Ashleigh Allen's trust fund and now, unhappily, I am the executor of her estate. Could I have a word?" He motioned toward a bench at the side of the walk near the front of the chapel facing the sun. The crowd had moved toward the dining hall and the two men were alone.

"How long did you know Ms. Allen?" Ray asked.

"It's been quite a number of years." Gellhorn removed his gold-rimmed glasses and polished them with a pressed handkerchief. "Her aunt, Gwendolyn Howard, used to bring Ashleigh with her to our offices; she was only a schoolgirl then. I continued to work with Ashleigh after she came of age. She was a bright, charming young woman, but she had little interest in money, so we continued to look after her financial affairs after she came of age."

"When did you last see her?" Ray asked.

"Let me think. It was June, late June after the end of the academic year here at Leiston. Ashleigh was on her way out of the country. She was with David Dowd; that was the first and only time I met the young man. They were on their way to Greenland, of all places, to do some kayaking."

"Was her visit social?" Ray asked.

"Well, it had a social aspect, we always set up our appointments so we could have lunch together. She was such a joy to be with. I'd try to find an interesting restaurant, one she hadn't been to before. This goes way back to the days when she'd accompany Mrs. Howard.

"But our meeting last spring was more than just social. I had been working on putting a new trust in place for Ashleigh. It's very hard to get young people to think about the possibility that they, well, might not live to a ripe old age. And given that Ashleigh had quite a bit of money, I thought it prudent that she have a plan in place just in case the unthinkable happened. This is difficult to do with people in their fifties and sixties, and almost impossible with someone of Ashleigh's age."

"But Ashleigh . . ."

"Yes, she had a good head on her shoulders. She was very clear on how her assets should be disposed of." Gellhorn pointed to a crowd mingling near and moving into the dining hall. "Unfortunately she never signed the papers—we were scheduled to meet again during the holiday break. But in lieu of any legal beneficiaries, we're moving ahead with her wishes for disposal of the estate. The first thing I was supposed to be concerned with was throwing a good party. I'm not sure that feeding people well in a school cafeteria would ever qualify as a good party. But given the time constraints, it's the best I could do."

"And after the party," asked Ray, "who are Ashleigh's beneficiaries?

"A variety of environmental groups, a few women's organizations, and the endowment fund here at the school."

"Any individuals, family members, anything like that?" Ray asked.

"No individual bequeaths, and I knew of no blood relatives," Gellhorn stopped for a second and rethought his statement. "That's not quite true, there might be a father out there somewhere."

"Your tone suggests there is something more to this story."

"Well there is, and that's why I wanted to talk to you." Gellhorn paused and looked at Ray, his manner tentative.

"Go ahead."

"Well, this isn't about the father—Ashleigh was still searching for her biological father," Gellhorn said. "I've been contacted by someone up here, a member of the faculty, who says he's a second cousin of Ashleigh's and is interested in the contents of the will. I don't know whether or not the individual has accurately represented the familial relationship; I have a very skilled woman, one of our junior people, researching his claimed relationship."

"And who, might I ask, is making these inquiries?" asked Ray.

"I've learned that he's a faculty member here, Alan Quertermous. Interestingly enough, years ago we used to look after his father's legal affairs. Are you familiar with Mr. Quertermous?"

"Yes," said Ray without elaboration. "Tell me, Mr. Gellhorn, might Quertermous be able to make a claim against the estate?"

"Well, as you know, anyone can hire an attorney and cause all sorts of mischief. And I suspect, if he really is related to Ms. Allen, that's what he plans on doing. I don't think he'll have any success, but unfortunately assets intended by the decedent for other purposes will have to be expended to defend the estate." Gellhorn sat for a long moment and looked at Ray. "I know, sheriff, this is a rather inappropriate question, but I was wondering if Mr. Quertermous might be a suspect in the case?"

"We are still in the early stages of the investigation," said Ray. "And I appreciate knowing about Mr. Quertermous' interest in Ashleigh's estate. Tell me, Mr. Gellhorn, how much money are we talking about here?"

Gellhorn pondered the question and his response before he spoke. "If you're asking if there's enough money to provide a motive, the answer is yes. It's not a huge fortune by modern standards, but at least four or five million dollars." He looked off toward the dining hall. "Enough of this. I just wanted you to know about Quertermous. Well, sheriff, will you join me for lunch? I understand Ms. James has really knocked herself out pulling this all together."

Ray thought about things he should be doing back at the office, changed his mind about leaving, and said, "Yes, I would be happy to have lunch with you. Perhaps we can talk further about Ashleigh Allen."

28

Ray looked up from his desk as Sue Lawrence entered his office. Her sense of style and her lithe, athletic frame almost made her uniform seem chic. Sue's strawberry-blonde hair, cut short and carefully groomed, and her tan and freckled countenance highlighted her healthy, youthful appearance.

"How was the trip?" Ray asked.

"Long, interesting, and, at times, quite sad—especially the time in Cleveland," she responded, placing a yellow plastic grocery bag, its sides embossed with print, and a cooler on the desk in front of Ray. "But you're a lucky man, Elkins. I got everything on the list. And," she laughed as she handed him the cash register slip, "you owe me most of your next paycheck."

"How was Zingerman's?" he asked, thinking about his favorite Ann Arbor deli.

"Wonderful, expensive, fattening, great aromas. That bread was hot when I picked it up. So was the pastrami sandwich. Smelled wonderful! Boy are you lucky I didn't eat it on the way back." She opened the cooler and placed a bag filled with packages on the desk for Ray's inspection. "I've never spent sixty bucks just on cheese before, and there's not much there. And forty-five dollars for a little bottle of vinegar," she said, her voice tinged with incredulity.

"Thank you for doing this," Ray said without responding to her comments as he looked for the total amount on the statement. He pulled a checkbook from his desk and began writing. "How did things go with David Dowd's parents and the apartment search?"

"I have them written up, I could print you a copy."

"Just give me a quick summary," Ray said, handing over the check. He opened the bag and peered in at the cheese. "I'll read your whole report later."

"Sure you don't want me to go away and leave you with your treasures?" she teased.

Ray closed the sack and placed it on the top of a bookcase behind him. Turning to her he said, "You have my undivided attention."

"I got to Shaker Heights in the middle of the afternoon. Met with Dowd's mother, Grace. Her house was full of people sitting shivah, piles of food, and lots of talk. She's an elementary principal. The crowd was a study in diversity." She paused, her tone intensified. "You could just see how much people value her. I know it sounds sort of corny, but there was so much love there. People helping her and each other with this loss."

"How's she doing?" Ray asked.

"Given the circumstances, quite remarkably. Grace is an amazing woman."

"During my phone conversation with her, I sensed that. She did her best to be helpful, and she was asking all the right questions. Unfortunately, I didn't have any answers," observed Ray.

"I had a similar experience. Like she sensed my discomfort and helped me get through the interview. And then she insisted that I have something to eat before she let me get on the road. She even wanted to make a care package for me."

"What did you learn?

"David was a wonderful son, had a bright future, would have done something useful with his life and made the world a better place. All of the kinds of things you'd expect a mother to say, but in this case it all seems to be true."

"And his relationship with Ashleigh?"

"Grace said she was first introduced to Ashleigh years ago, when David was a student at Leiston. David and Ashleigh were close friends then and had stayed in contact, even though they had gone to different colleges. She thought they had started seeing each other on a more regular basis sometime last winter. She didn't know how serious their relationship was, but thought that they made a good couple."

"Any suggestion that someone might want to . . ."

"No." Sue moved her head from side to side. "She can't imagine that he had any enemies. That wasn't part of his personality." Sue paused and looked directly at Ray. "She really pushed me hard; she desperately wants to know why this happened. And there was nothing I could tell her."

"How about the father?"

"He was there also. I think he and Grace have been divorced for about ten years. He seemed to be her opposite."

"How so?" Ray asked.

"Grace is effusive and magnetic. Saul, well, he's very quiet and introspective. He's a psychiatrist."

"Did you learn anything from him?"

"No, he echoed Grace's remarks. He was really devastated; it was a struggle for him to talk about his son. He was always on the edge of tears, it was very sad. He, too, pressed me for answers. It's so difficult when you don't have anything to tell them. I've keyed a complete transcript of my conversation with each of them." She paused, "Interesting."

"What's that?"

"Grace, she's a woman I'd really like to know; I'm sure I could learn a lot from her about," she paused as she reached for the right words, "about how to live a life. Too bad we had to meet this way. One additional thing, she gave me the names of two of David's friends from undergraduate school. I called them from

Ann Arbor, one lives in California and the other in Connecticut. And they gave me the same story. David was a very sincere, hard working, pleasant kind of guy with a wonderful sense of humor. They had never known him to make an enemy."

"Police records?" Ray asked.

"He ran a stop sign when he was seventeen. That's it."

"So, tell me about Ann Arbor."

"I went through Dowd's apartment. The detectives from the AAPD had all the paperwork taken care of before I arrived; they were great. We met the landlord, who opened the place up for us. They had an evidence team available at the scene if we needed them."

"And?"

"I think the place was just as he left it. The apartment is in one of those old houses on Ann Street just off Ingalls; it's a couple of blocks from Rackham. The apartments are usually total wrecks, but his place was nicely put together." She paused, "And real neat; and no one had been in there rummaging through things. On his desk I found what appeared to be a beginning draft of his dissertation."

Ray saw the sadness in her eyes. "Anything that might help us?" Ray asked hopefully.

"No. Nothing. Books, clothes, papers, and an assortment of well-used sports equipment, like five tennis rackets. No TV, no drugs, no porn, not even a Playboy. The Ann Arbor Police are working with the university to get the contents of his e-mail account, and they'll go through the hard drive of his computer. They've also requested a copy of his phone records. Everything is going to be available to us as soon as they get it, but I don't think there's anything there."

"Damn," said Ray. "I was hoping we'd get some kind of lead." He sat quietly, considering his next question. He knew Sue had recently ended a long-term relationship, one that stretched back to high school. The romance had lasted through college, continued while her love interest, Braeton, attended medical school. But it had finally come to an end as he was completing his residency. She had been very open with Ray about the breakup, and he had done his best to be supportive, often not knowing the best way to respond. "Did you see Braeton?" he finally said.

"I dialed his number twice and hung up before it rang, drove by his apartment to see if his car was in the lot. It wasn't. In the late afternoon I walked down through the Arboretum like we used to. And I sat on *our* bench and watched the river. I wanted so much to see him, but I didn't want to deal with all the things that were wrong with the relationship."

"You haven't quite put him in the past yet."

"I have, on a rational level. There's just some nostalgia that I'm still dealing with. You spend years thinking about a life together and then," she let her words hang. Brightening up she continued, "I think I need to find a man who's more local. Anyway, the two detectives took me to dinner. They wanted to know how many people we had working the case."

"What did you tell them?"

"The truth. They gave me a good razzing. But I reminded them that we don't even have a stoplight in this county, and that we're investing a major part of our resources into this investigation." Sue giggled, "They spent most of the evening trying to convince me that I should apply to their department.

"And after dinner I spent a quiet night at Webber's Inn keying my reports. Got into Zingerman's early, and here I am. Bet you were hoping that Braeton and I would get back together so you could have a regular source again," she pointed at the bag.

"Not necessarily. I value your long-term happiness more than pastrami."

"Great. What a guy. But do you value my happiness more than a good Stilton, one with a firm rind?"

"Now that's a tough one," he responded, giving her a gentle smile.

29

~~~~~

Sue watched as Ray uncoiled the lines and carefully lowered Ashleigh's kayak to her apartment floor. He rolled the boat over and assiduously inspected the hull, running his hand over the glassy surface.

"Well?" asked Sue.

"Couldn't have been this boat. Look at it, there's hardly a scratch on it, let alone a patch. It's almost new. I wonder if she had another boat stored here somewhere? The school is supposed to own a collection of kayaks. I'll make a call."

Ray went into Ashleigh's office, removed the campus directory from under the phone. Sue listened to the conversation, and after he hung up, she asked, "Well?"

"The old horse barn is used to store, among other things, kayaks, canoes, sailboats, and bicycles. Sarah James is going to meet us outside the building; she said she can identify Ashleigh's other kayak."

"How does she know?"

"Turns out she's been using it since Ashleigh bought this one last spring. I told you it was new," Ray said, motioning toward the boat.

"Pretty woman, Sarah James," said Sue as they repositioned the slings under the kayak's bow and stern. Ray pulled the boat back to its place near the ceiling and tied off the lines.

"Interesting decorating," Sue said, looking up at the boat. "I imagine you approve of her approach to interior design."

Ray nodded.

"I'm surprised you don't have a kayak hanging from your ceiling," Sue said.

"I could do that," Ray smiled. "When I lived in the farmhouse I kept kayaks in the living room, even built a couple there."

Sarah was waiting for them at the large center door of the barn. She moved to greet them as they approached. Handing Ray a manila envelope she said, "Here's the list of the students who were on that trip with Ashleigh. Helen Warrington was able to pull them from the alumni database."

"You have addresses for all twelve?"

"Actually, only eleven. One of the students, Denton Freeler, is deceased."

"Really. Do you have any more information?"

"I asked Helen if she knew how or when he died."

"And?"

"She didn't. She just got a note that he had died. His parents live in the Middle East; his father works for an American oil company." Sarah paused. "Helen said that's usually the way it happens; just a note or an e-mail, seldom anything more."

"What do you remember about this person, Denton . . . ?"

"Freeler. He was in my son's class, but I don't recall much about him. He's not someone Eric hung around with." Sarah looked thoughtful. "He was a gangly kid with reddish-brown hair, very quiet, perhaps very shy. If you're interested, I'll see what else I can find."

"Please."

They walked into the cool, dark interior of the barn. Sarah switched on the lights.

"Let's see, where did I put it last time I used it?" Sarah looked along the wall where several dozen kayaks and canoes were suspended on large wooden dowels. "There it is," she pointed to a kayak, its red deck faded in spots, its white hull showing years of hard use. Sue helped Ray carry the boat out to an open area near the center of the barn. With the boat resting on the floor, he pulled the seat loose and inspected the interior of the cockpit, then he rolled the boat over and looked at the hull.

"Finding anything?" Sue asked.

"Look," said Ray, pointing to two areas. The two women crouched on the other side of the boat. "You can see where the boat has been patched. Someone did an excellent job repairing the hull." He rolled the boat over again and pointed to the areas in the cockpit. "The patches on the interior are more obvious and they're mostly hidden under the seat. Looks like she had the boat professionally repaired some time after that camping trip."

"Well, that fits with the story," responded Sarah.

"And you told me one of the kids on the trip is still at Leiston?"

"Yes, Billy Wylder, he's a senior."

"Any possibility of our talking with him a few minutes about this incident?"

"Well, I can't imagine there . . ." she paused. "Perhaps I should check with Ian."

Ray read her caution. "This is just an interview, Sarah. I would welcome either you or Ian or both sitting in while I talk with Billy." She nodded.

"Are you still using this boat?" Ray asked Sarah.

"No, I'm just a warm-weather paddler; I haven't been out since late September."

"I'd like to have this piece of evidence in a secure location."

"I'm not sure our evidence room is designed for eighteen-foot boats," offered Sue. "How about Ashleigh's apartment?" They both looked at Sarah.

"Why not?" she said.

30

Sarah escorted a large, pudgy, red-haired boy into the conference room. Ray stood to greet them. "Sheriff Ray Elkins, I'd like to introduce you to Billy Wylder. Today Billy is celebrating his seventeenth birthday."

"Well, happy birthday, Billy," said Ray, offering his hand as he studied Billy's freckled face.

Billy took Ray's hand, held it limply, and withdrew as quickly as possible. Ray pulled out a chair for Billy at the head of the conference table and took the one immediately to his right. Sarah settled on Billy's left.

"What do you want to talk to me about?" Billy asked as soon as he settled his ungainly body into the chair. His forehead glistened with perspiration. "It's about Ms. Allen, isn't it?" he asked tentatively.

"Yes."

"What do you want to know?" he asked, pushing his glasses back up the bridge of his nose. He looked directly at Ray, his pale blue eyes magnified in the thick, greasy lenses.

"You had her as a teacher, right?"

"Yes," he responded, rocking his body forward.

"Tell me about the classes you took from her."

"I had three," he said, looking around the room.

"And what were the classes, Billy?"

"I had earth science in ninth and biology in tenth."

"That's two, Billy."

"Oh yeah, and my freshman year, I also had wilderness survival. That was a short course, half of a semester."

"So, you had her as a teacher your freshman and sophomore years?"

"Yes."

"And you didn't have her as a teacher last year or this?"

"Yeah. That's right."

"Did you continue to have contact with Ms. Allen?"

"Well yeah, I saw her almost every day in the cafeteria. I really liked her, she was cool. The best teacher in this place." Billy brightened.

"The spring of your freshman year, you went on a camping trip with Ms. Allen?"

"Yes. Actually I've gone on trips with her the last three years. The first one was part of that survival class. And last year and the year before I went on trips with her as part of our spring adventure week."

"Leiston's adventure week," Sarah explained, "replaces the usual spring break with guided learning experiences."

"Yeah," Billy interjected, "like last year we went kayaking in Belize. It was really neat."

"I want to talk about the trip you took your freshman year," Ray said.

"You heard about that?" he muttered, as a sheepish grin crept across his face.

"Tell me what happened, Billy."

"There's not much to tell. We got caught in a blow as we crossed to North Manitou. Like we should have made it to shore with no problem, but this dumb girl capsized, and she flipped me when I tried to do a rescue." He paused, then continued, "Ms. Allen righted her kayak, emptied it, and tried to get Monica back in the boat. But she was freaking out. Instead of helping, she just kept fighting. She managed to capsize Ms. Allen's kayak two or three times. Ms. Allen just rolled on the other side and come back to her. Finally, she gave up on getting Monica back in her boat; she dragged Monica on her deck and took her to shore. Then she came back and got me into my boat. By then I was really cold. Ms. Allen could tell I couldn't paddle, so she attached her rescue line and towed me to shore."

"Then what happened?"

"They got me in a sleeping bag and gave me hot drinks until I stopped shivering."

"Can you give me some more details about what happened when you got on shore?"

"You mean the sleeping bag part?"

"Yes."

"You heard about that, too?" Billy asked, looking rather uncomfortable.

Ray nodded.

"We get to the beach, I'm shivering, like I'm not making much sense." Billy stopped and looked at Ray. "I don't remember most of this, it's what people told me. I guess she tore off my paddling jacket and wetsuit and stuffed me into the sleeping bag. Then she stripped off most of her clothes and got into the sleeping bag with me and wrapped her body around me. I don't know how long it was before I stopped shivering. When I had warmed up, they moved me into a tent and forced me to drink a lot of hot tea. I really hate tea. That's all. Eventually, I got into some dry clothes."

"Then what happened, Billy?" Ray probed.

"The other kids on the trip were seniors, and the boys gave me a lot of shit," his eyes dropped to the table and his voice became little more than a whisper. "They said everyone could see I had a hard-on. It became a big joke; they called me 'Billy hard-on,' even after we got back to school."

"Did that make you angry?"

"I was just a freshman, like I was really embarrassed."

"Anything else happen?"

Billy looked away from Ray, he brought his hands up to his face and cupped them from his nose to chin, and moved them slowly up and down several times. "You know what happened to Ms. Allen's kayak?"

"Yes, but tell us what you remember."

"Well, the next morning after breakfast the weather was clear, and we got ready to make the next leg of the trip. We broke camp and took our stuff to the beach to load the boats. They were turned upside down to keep the rain out. One of the girls noticed it first."

"Noticed what Billy?"

"Ms. Allen's kayak. It had three or four holes hacked in the bottom. Everyone just stood around and looked, finally she said something about it being a perfect time to show us how to do emergency repairs. She mixed up some epoxy and put fiberglass patches on each side."

"How do you think the punctures were made?"

"It looked to me like they were made with a knife."

"Not a hatchet?"

"No, I don't think so. The holes, they weren't that long, you know like the blade of a hatchet." He paused. "But in some ways a hatchet would make sense."

"Why?" Ray asked.

"The holes, they just had that shape."

"So, who had a knife?"

"We all did, it was a required piece of equipment, but they were mostly little, like Swiss Army knives."

"Do you ever remember seeing anyone with a large knife?"

"A couple of the guys had some survival knives, like the kind the Special Forces carry, the ones with black blades. I remember that because we got in trouble with Ms. Allen."

"What kind of trouble?"

"Early in the trip, maybe the first night, some of the guys were having a knife-throwing contest. They were using a tree as a target. And they were using those knives. The big ones."

"So, what was the trouble?"

"When Ms. Allen caught us at it, she pointed out we were hurting the tree. Making it more susceptible to disease."

"The knives, do you remember who had the large knives?"

"Sheriff, that was three years ago. I don't remember. And I didn't really know those guys. They were seniors. They didn't live in my house."

Ray pulled a sheet out of the folder and passed it to Billy. "Look at the list Billy, your name is on it with the rest of the students who were on the trip."

"Yeah," he peerd at the list, "I sorta remember them."

"Which ones?" Ray pressed.

"I think it was these two," he pointed to two names. "Denton Freeler and Jay Hanson. And they were the guys that started the hard-on thing. They said other stuff, too."

"Like?"

Billy stopped and looked over at Sarah James.

"It's okay, Billy, tell the sheriff everything," she said.

"They said it was too bad they weren't in the sleeping bag."

"Anything else?"

"No, I don't think so. I just didn't like those bastards. They were always acting tough and weird. I was sort of afraid of them."

Everyone sat quietly.

"You don't recall anything else?" Ray asked again.

"Not that I can think of."

"Here's my number," said Ray, handing Billy his card. "You can call me or send me an e-mail if something comes to mind that you think I should know."

"Sure," said Billy, picking up the card and studying it carefully. Then he looked up. "Can I go now?"

"Yes," Ray said.

Billy pushed his chair back from the table, pulled himself to his feet, and shuffled to the doorway. He drew the door open a few inches, stopped, and turned toward Ray. "I hope you get the fucker who did this." He closed the door quietly as he departed.

31

I an Warrington confronted Ray and Sarah in the hall as they headed toward the main entrance. Ian opened his office door and directed them in, taking Sarah by the upper arm and pulling her through the door. Ray saw the anger in Warrington's face and Sarah's surprise at being handled in such a rough fashion.

"What the hell were you two doing? I just encountered Billy Wylder," Warrington demanded. Ray noted the normally calm Warrington appeared almost out of control. Ray started to answer, but was cut off by Sarah.

"Don't ever touch me like that again," she said, her voice filled with anger.

Ray stepped between them. "I think we all better sit down and have a talk," he said in a commanding voice as he pulled two other chairs close to the first.

"Well, who goes first?" asked Warrington in a hostile tone.

Ray took the lead, "In the course of our investigation of Ms. Allen's death, an incident that happened three years has come to our attention."

"What incident?" demanded Warrington.

"It has to do with a trip she took with her wilderness adventure class."

"Oh, the sleeping bag thing," Warrington interrupted, "that's old news. I don't see what that would have to do with anything. And to inflict further psychological pain on a child, well that's . . ." He stopped and looked at Ray, his face flushed. "Well, we've been hosts too long to your incompetent investigation. I'm contacting our lawyer. We're going to get you off this campus. And you're not going to talk to anyone here without first talking to our lawyer and jumping all the legal hoops. And," he continued, looking directly at Sarah, "every member of the staff is going to be instructed not to talk to you without first clearing it with me."

Ray sat quietly, considering whether or not he should explain the statues under which his department was operating in the course of this investigation. But, before he could respond, Sarah said, "Ian, you're being silly."

"Silly, hell," he exclaimed. "Among other things, I am responsible for the legal rights of our students, *in loco parentis*. I'm not going to have our students interrogated without proper counsel. And given the fact that this poor child is still a minor . . ."

"Sir, I was talking to Billy because he might have information that might lead us to the person responsible for these murders. This was an interview, not an interrogation. Billy is not suspected of anything. Ms. James' presence provided a non-police adult witness to the conversation, standard procedure when an officer is interviewing a minor. If it had been anything more than that, I assure you I would have been the first one to make sure that Billy's rights were protected."

"And I tried involve you," said Sarah, "but you were nowhere to be found. I was with Billy during this interview and enabling this conversation clearly falls within my administrative responsibilities."

"We'll see about that," Warrington shot back. "In fact, I

think you should leave so I can talk to the sheriff." Sarah looked over at Ray who nodded; she rose and quietly departed.

"Now, tell me exactly what Billy told you," Warrington demanded. "I know you've already asked for the names and addresses of students who were on that trip. Helen told me. At the time I did a complete investigation of that incident to ensure that nothing like it would ever happen again." He paused; his tone became conciliatory. "Right from the beginning of this whole tragic situation, I've given you my complete cooperation and allowed you total access to Leiston. But I feel that you haven't been completely open with me or extended to me the same cooperation I've given you."

Ray said nothing for a long while, as he studied Warrington's face. Then he said, "I need to go over a few things again."

"Like what?" Warrington asked, his anger palpable.

"Ashleigh's kayak. That's what I was asking Billy about."

"What about her kayak?"

"Did you know that it had been vandalized?"

"When?"

"On that trip."

"What do you mean, vandalized?"

"Someone hacked several large holes in the hull. She had to repair the boat before they could continue." Ray watched the anger drain out of Warrington. He looked stunned.

"I never heard that. There was no incident report on that. How do you know this?"

"I heard it from another student on the trip. I was meeting with young Mr. Wylder to confirm the story." A silence followed as Warrington processed this information.

Finally Ray asked, "I would like you to tell me more about your relationship with Ashleigh Allen."

"What more could there be to possibly tell?" Warrington shot back. "She was a wonderful young woman. Her death has left all of us with a profound sense of loss."

"I'm interested in your personal relationship with Ms. Allen."

"Our relationship," he stopped, clearly considering his words before he continued, "our relationship was hardly personal. She was a member of the faculty, and I was her supervisor, nothing more."

Ray waited to respond, holding Warrington in his gaze. "Mr. Warrington, several people have suggested that the two of you may have had something more than the usual relationship that exists between an employee and a supervisor."

"Well, we did," he responded, his tone changing. "Teaching is not a job, it's a profession. My relationships with all the members of the faculty are collegial. We are a team, communication goes both ways. I pride myself on my capacity to share the governance of Leiston with my faculty."

Ray listened attentively, but he didn't respond.

"And in Ms. Allen's case, she was so young, I perhaps mentored her more than other members of the staff. And I know a few of the old-timers felt that she was accorded some special consideration, which is a long way from the truth."

"There's been some suggestion that early on, your association with Ms. Allen exceeded the bounds of a normal professional relationship."

"Oh, so it's that. Not true, just not true." Warrington reddened. "There are a few people around here who have been enormously unhappy with changes I've made. They've been trying to defame me right from the beginning. And since they can't successfully attack my leadership—I've made this school financially viable and saved their jobs—they're going after me personally."

"Organizational politics are always difficult," Ray agreed, his tone softening. "But I didn't just hear this from the inside. You and Ms. Allen were seen in community together and under circumstances that would raise questions about the nature of your relationship."

Warrington pulled off his glasses and, holding them in his

left hand, slowly rubbed his eyes. "Well, yes, we had a very brief affair. It wasn't something I had initiated, not something I ever would have done, but it happened."

"Do you want to tell me about it?"

"There's not much to tell."

"I'm waiting."

"It was little more than a flirtation that went too far."

"When were you two involved, how long did the relationship last, when was it ended, and under what conditions?"

"It was Ashleigh's first year. I was developing new curriculum for the school and Ashleigh played a major role in developing the program. I presented the curriculum to our board at a winter meeting in Chicago. I brought Ashleigh along to help with the presentation. I also wanted board members to meet her because she embodied the future of this school. The program was well received; we were highly complimented on what we had accomplished in a short amount of time. That evening several members of the board took us to dinner: we both had a bit too much wine with dinner. And when we got back to the Palmer House, well, it just happened. A one-night stand."

"But it was more than that, wasn't it?"

"Well, yes, but not much more." He paused, inhaled deeply, and continued. "Helen and I have been together a long time and, sadly, there hasn't been much . . . ardor . . . in recent years. Ashleigh rekindled old feelings." Warrington's gaze wandered for a moment, then he looked back at Ray. "I never thought I'd be in love again. And for that brief moment—it was only a matter of weeks before I had to admit to myself how silly I was being—it was quite wonderful. But once that realization hit, I ended the affair immediately."

"And Ashleigh was okay with that?"

"Yes, she agreed that it was the only possible decision."

"And seeing her with other men, that didn't engender some feelings of jealousy?"

"No, sheriff, I was over her very quickly. And over the next several years I think our relationship had matured nicely to one of admiration and mutual respect."

Ray rose to leave. Warrington came to his feet and extended his hand. "Please forgive my earlier behavior, I don't know what came over me. I thought I had my temper under control."

Ray took his hand briefly.

"I hope we can continue to work cooperatively," offered Warrington.

"That would be good," Ray said.

32

By late afternoon Ray had completed keying his notes from his conversation with Billy Wylder. He saved them in the case file and forwarded a copy to Sue Lawrence with a memo asking her to see what she could find out about Denton Freeler and Jay Hanson.

As he waited for Rod Tessler, Leiston's psychologist, he worked on sorting the papers that had accumulated in his inbox into four piles in order of importance. Ray had known Rod Tessler from the time he was in elementary school. Rod was ten years his senior and his sister, Amy, was in Ray's class. Rod was a source of pride in the village. He was a handsome, affable kid, a brilliant student, and the first all-state Class D quarterback in the history of Pioneer Consolidated High.

Thirty-some years later, when Rod retired to Cedar Bay after spending his professional life as a psychologist in L.A., he moved into the family home, a century-old farmhouse that his great-grandfather built. It had been standing vacant for some years. His younger brother, Todd, who still operated the farm and orchards, had built a new residence at the top of a nearby bluff, a view home overlooking Tessler Orchards and the bay.

"Thank you for coming by," said Ray, feeling the muscular grip of Tessler's hand.

"Happy to help, sheriff," he responded.

Ray guided Tessler into the break room. "Coffee?" he asked.

"Too late in the day. I'll try some of this herbal tea."

Ray poured himself some black coffee and waited as Tesssler added several packages of sugar to his cup and squeezed a tea bag.

"How's Amy doing?" Ray asked after they were settled in his office. "I haven't seen her since our last class reunion."

Tessler sat across from him. "Pretty well. You know she lost her husband last winter, cancer."

"Yes, I heard that," Ray responded.

"She was up here in August. Two kids are in college, the baby is a senior in high school. She's busy with her law practice. And as you probably remember, she's a real strong person, but it will take some time for her to accept Herb's death." He paused briefly, lifted a baseball cap with a maize block M on the front, and ran his hand over a completely bald-head, pulling the hat back into position by the bill. "On the phone you said you wanted to talk about Leiston."

"Yes," said Ray. "I understand you're the school psych-ologist."

"Well, I've been the school's part-time psychologist for the past year or so. I'd really planned to retire, but this came along and I can use the extra cash. Normally I'm there about fifteen hours a week, more if needed. Since the murders, I've been working every day, even Saturdays."

"I imagine this has been very difficult for some of the students," Ray said.

"Yes, terribly difficult. This is the first time most of these kids have ever confronted death, especially the death of someone who is near them in age." He held Ray in his gaze. "You know, it's not like a great-grandmother dying, something natural and expected. And the fact that she was murdered makes it so much worse."

Ray nodded his understanding.

"Many of them, especially the juniors and seniors, have a long history with Ms. Allen. They are just devastated. Some of the students are very open in their grief, some are not. I guess I worry more about the less verbal ones.

"And you know, the grief thing," Tessler continued, "it's not my specialty, I spent most of my career treating adolescent felons. So, I called a former colleague in California, a woman who works exclusively in this area. She gave me some sound advice on how to proceed and e-mailed a stack of articles."

"I thought Warrington brought in some crisis counselors."

"He did. Good people, but they were only here for a few days. Then I became the point man. I've been mostly doing individual sessions, but now I'm going to start doing some groups. Carolyn, my friend in California, walked me through how to do these sessions."

"Ashleigh Allen, were you acquainted with her?" Ray probed.

"Not really; being a part-timer sort of keeps you an outsider. But I did get to know her a bit."

"What did you think of her?" Ray asked.

"She was an impressive young woman. Real bright, you could just see it; you could hear it in her voice. And the way she carried herself, a kind of easy confidence. You just don't find people her age who are so completely integrated. And she was real good with the kids, a role model. What a tragedy."

"Any students ever complain about her?"

"Never. I observed that a few of the older faculty members didn't seem to care for her, but I think they were just envious of her wonderful abilities."

"The kids, the ones you work with," Ray paused a long moment, searching for the right word, "any real . . ."

"Wackos?" interrupted Tessler. "Sociopaths with homicidal

tendencies, people pissed at Ashleigh for giving them a low grade?" Tessler chuckled. "No, we don't have any kids like that. Nothing that interesting."

"Tell me about problems you normally deal with at Leiston School."

"It's all pretty normal adolescent angst—difficulties with parents, or roommates, or love interests, or trying to figure out their sexuality. Occasionally there's a complaint against a teacher." Tessler paused and sipped his tea. "I've heard tell there was a time when Leiston had some unmanageable students. That was after Mrs. Howard died, when the enrollment fell off, and they were admitting anyone with tuition money. That all ended soon after Warrington took over. The question you want to ask is whether one of the students could have committed this crime?"

"I'm trying to look at every possibility," Ray responded.

"You know, I spent a lot of years working with criminal types, males mostly. After a while you can spot them—the way they look, the way they carry themselves, the way they don't quite make eye contact. Before they open their mouths, you know the story they're going to give you." He looked directly at Ray, "The killer isn't at Leiston School, isn't in the student body."

"How about the faculty or staff?"

"You know, there are a few folks a couple of standard deviations out from the norm, but I'd be surprised if you had any killers. They're just run-of-the-mill crackpots."

"Helen Warrington, she preceded you as the school psychologist?"

"Yes, she's a clinical psychologist."

"Did she ever mention any especially disturbed students?"

"She gave me a briefing on the kids that she had seen in the past several years who were still enrolled and would probably need some continued therapy. We're talking about just a handful of students, none of whom are anything more than runny-nose neurotics. For lots of these kids it's sort of fashionable to be in therapy."

"But," said Ray, pursuing his question, "she never talked about working with any . . ."

"No. She did what was necessary to fill me in on the students I would probably be seeing and shared her notes, nothing more." He paused briefly, "I was surprised at her notes. They weren't very professional for someone who reminds you of her credentials in every conversation. And she's not, shall we say, excessively effusive." He chuckled. "Cuddly as a cactus."

"Tell me about the notes, what bothered you?"

"They were sparse and rather naïve, underwritten, like she wasn't giving it enough time. For someone who seems to be so obsessed with having everything perfect; I was surprised by the shoddy nature of her notes and observations."

"Did you ever encounter a student by the name of Denton Freeler?" Ray asked looking at a small notebook.

"No," Tessler responded.

"How about Jay Hanson?"

"No. Might've been before my time, on Helen's watch."

"Alan Quertermous, the math teacher?"

"He's kinda wild, isn't he?"

"How do you mean?"

"I haven't spent a lot of time in his company, but there's one angry little man."

"Angry enough to commit murder?" Ray probed.

"No, I don't think so. Just someone who bitches about everything. It's probably therapeutic; he doesn't hold anything back. He just makes everyone around him crazy. But," he added, changing the tone of his voice, a smile forming over his leathery face, "let me put in a disclaimer. Psychology is an inexact discipline; I've been scammed by bright psychopaths."

Ray walked Tessler out of the office and toward the parking lot, chatting about the latest flap in local politics. Tessler stopped near the rear of a vintage Volvo, deep blue, the top and hood faded from years of sun, tattered stickers for political and environmental causes covering the tailgate.

"Your car?" Ray asked.

"Yes, had it since new. Women come and go, but this Volvo seems to hang on."

"If you're becoming a permanent resident," offered Ray with a grin, "you might consider getting Michigan plates, perhaps even for the current year."

Tessler looked mildly abashed. "You know, I've been meaning to do that. I just really hate to give up my California tags."

Ray walked alone to the far end of the parking lot and peered into the low valley below and the hillside beyond. Patches of scarlet still remained in protected stands of maple. Fall's special musky perfume hung in the air. He was lost in the beauty of the moment, a brief respite from pressures of the murder investigation.

33

A s Ray walked back across the parking lot, he was thinking about his recent encounter with Ian Warrington. Ray had been surprised by Ian Warrington's loss of control and wondered if Warrington was capable of murder. Although he needed to verify it, Ray didn't doubt Warrington's story about the dinner party the night of the murders, but he was uncertain about the veracity of Warrington's account of what happened after the dinner. Yet, if Warrington had stayed at the dinner party close to the time he reported, it would have been impossible for him to commit the murders. The chirping of his cell phone interrupted Ray's musings on the headmaster's alibi.

"Central, sheriff," came a familiar voice. "We've had two 911s from the Last Chance Tavern. The first one was at 5:14, help needed to break up a fight, the second at 5:21, a shooting in the parking lot."

"Anyone on scene?"

"Jamison has just arrived, and Sergeant Reilly is en route. I've got backup coming from the state police. The Lake Township EMT unit is en route."

"I'm on my way," Ray said as he headed toward his car.

Sergeant Reilly had the scene under control when Ray arrived. EMTs were working on the victim and several officers had set up flares on the open field behind the Last Chance to aid the pilot of the incoming helicopter.

Ray looked across the parking lot, a worn perimeter of blacktop with weeds growing in cracks, the sagging tavern at its center. A group of EMTs encircled the victim. Sue Lawrence, peering over the top of the EMTs, noticed Ray standing with Reilly and came across the lot to meet him.

"It's Jason Zelke, Ray. He's been hit at least three times."

"The wounds, serious?"

"Shoulder and leg don't look bad, but the one in the gut probably is. He's conscious and in a lot of pain."

"And the shooter?" Ray asked.

"He had left the scene by the time Jamison arrived," Sergeant Reilly responded.

Jack Grochoski, the bartender, joined the group.

"What happened, Jack?" Ray asked.

"Jason came in a little after five like he does most days. He usually has a shell or two and takes a six-pack with him. I was at the other end of the bar talking to a customer when I heard it getting started."

"What started?"

"There was this guy yelling at Jason, must of come in while I wasn't looking. From what I could hear it was something about his wife. As I walked down there, the guy took a swing at him. Well, you know how big Jason is, he just took the guy's arm and twisted it behind him. I told them to take it outside, and Jason pushed him out the door. Just to be on the safe side I called 911. I looked out of the window and they were just standing by Jason's truck talking, so I thought they were working it out. I went back to the bar, and a couple of minutes later I heard lots of shooting."

"This person who Jason was with, do you know him?" Sue asked.

"Last name's Reesma or something like that. Dutchman I

guess. He and his wife moved here from Grand Rapids, built a big house in that new sub above the village last winter."

"What do you know about him?"

"Not much, hardly ever seen him. Heard tell he was a ship's engineer; he's gone most of the season. Comes home for a few days every now and then."

"So, what's this all about?" asked Ray

Jack looked pained, like he was betraying a professional trust. "Reesma, his wife comes in here quite often. Real pretty woman, name's Sherry. She's a nurse, works in town. I think she and Jason sorta struck up a friendship."

"What sort of a friendship, Jack?"

"Well, Ray, that I wouldn't know." Jack lowered his voice and moved closer to Ray. "But I've noticed that they seemed to be leaving together lately."

"This leaving together, how long has this been going on?"

Jack took a moment to answer, "Most of the summer."

"Interesting," Ray responded, wondering if Sherry Reesma might be able to provide Jason Zelke with an alibi. "Jack, you didn't see the shooting?"

"No, like I said, I was at the bar. But I ran out here as soon as I heard the shots."

"Was Reesma still here?" Ray asked.

"He was driving away. Damn near ran me over as I came across the parking lot. Took off that way," Jack pointed up the road to the left.

"What kind of car?"

"A black SUV of some sort," he paused. "Maybe one of those foreign jobs."

"And the wife?"

"Didn't see her. How's Jason?" asked Jack looking off at the crowd of paramedics surrounding him.

"He's conscious. We'll have him out of here in a few minutes," said Sue. "Jack, we'll want to talk to the people who were here at the time of the argument and shooting. And we want a statement from you. So, ask your customers to sit tight for a bit. We'll get them on their way as quickly as possible."

The percussive thumping of the blades pulled all their attention as the helicopter cleared the ridgeline. Ray watched as the craft briefly hovered and then gently settled on the thistle-covered field. The paramedics moved as a group toward the craft, and lifted the stretcher onto it. In a few minutes the helicopter lifted off again, its strobes pulsating in misty twilight. The pilot turned the craft 180 degrees, and it quickly disappeared from sight.

"Reesma," said Sergeant Reilly, coming up to Ray's side. "The state police got him."

"What happened?" Ray asked.

"A trooper spotted his vehicle on Indian Hill Road and started to pursue. Another trooper was coming from the other direction. He blocked the road at an intersection. Reesma gave himself up without a struggle. They're transporting him."

"How about the wife?" asked Jamison, the department's youngest officer, who had been standing on the edge of the circle.

"We can only hope she's okay. Where's their house?" Ray asked looking at Sergeant Reilly.

Reilly pointed, "That sub on the ridge, you can almost see the place from here. It's supposed to be the only occupied house at the top of the sub."

"Go up there and look around," Ray said. "We'll pull our notes together at the end of the shift."

34

The large figure of John Tyrrell, the Cedar County prosecutor, filled the frame of Ray's open office door. Responding to the scent of Brute tinged with cigar smoke, Ray looked up. "You working Saturdays now?" he asked, gesturing toward two light-tan steel chairs with gray-and-purple fabric-covered cushions. The furniture was purchased a few years before, when all the county offices moved to the new administrative center. At the time Ray had been impressed that the interior decorator—a tall, handsome, Nordic-looking woman who radiated an artsy style—found colors and materials that were in perfect harmony with the banal architecture of the complex.

Tyrrell settled into one of the chairs, his bulk filling it from armrest to armrest. "Yeah, it's a bitch, isn't it? Should be able to sleep in on the weekend. But, the way you keep finding casualties, it makes lots of work for us." He chuckled at his joke and then took a long sip from a clunky glazed mug. "So, tell me what you got."

Ray reviewed the events of the previous evening and the subsequent developments, stressing the actions his department and state police had taken to insure Reesma's rights had been protected.

"Got the weapon?" Tyrrell asked

"The arresting officers found a 9-mm Glock under the passenger's seat. I'm confident that ballistics will establish it was the weapon used in the shooting."

"So, was Ree . . ."

"Reesma."

"Yeah, Reesma. Was he hurt in the fight with Zelke?

"No. The witnesses said there was some pushing and shoving, but it wasn't much of a fight. And then Reesma went to his car, reached in, got the gun, and shot Zelke."

"Have you questioned him?"

"I attempted to, but he made it clear that he wasn't going to say anything without his lawyer present. And he's made his call."

"Who did he ask for, someone from downstate?"

"No, Noah Johnson."

"Johnson, Noah Johnson. He's never tried a criminal case in his life. When he's not defending loons and wetlands, he does real estate and contracts. Why the hell did . . . ?"

"Reesma," offered Ray.

"Why the hell did Reesma want him?"

"From what Reesma said, Johnson had handled the legal work connected with buying his house. He is probably the only lawyer Reesma knows."

"That's pretty damn silly," said Tyrrell. "On the other hand, if Noah chooses to defend this turkey, well, it will be interesting to see how it plays out. He's damn smart, too smart, and very resourceful. But I don't imagine he'll stay on the case very long. This Reesma, do you have any history?"

"No, they seem to be new to the area. This department has never had any contact with him or his wife. And I haven't found any priors."

"And Zelke, how's he doing?"

"His injuries are serious. But his surgeon, I talked to him early this morning, said Jason was lucky as hell. The bullet went through his intestine with some damage, but an inch or two one way or the other, and it could have been fatal. It's going to take some time, but he should make a full recovery."

"And this was all over a woman?" asked Tyrrell in a dismissive tone.

"Yes, that's the way it appears."

"What a dumb shit. Jason should have known better." Tyrrell paused again and sipped some coffee.

"How about the wife? She okay?"

"Yes. We were worried about her, afraid that her husband might have harmed her before he come looking for Jason And it took us awhile to locate her."

"Where did you find her?"

"At Munson Hospital. Sue interviewed her last night. Turns out she's a surgical nurse there. And one of her close friends, aware of the situation, tipped her off when Jason was rushed in for surgery."

"What did Sue learn?"

"The relationship started in early summer and had quickly become serious. Sherry told Sue that she wanted a divorce and was struggling with how to tell her husband. She thinks that he was either tipped off about Jason, or she did something that made him suspicious; for the last few days she thought she was being watched. Sherry said she moved in with a girlfriend last weekend and was going to stay there until he was served with divorce papers, and the whole thing was out in the open."

"So, there was something that made her cautious?" Tyrrell said.

"Yes, her husband had told her that if he ever caught her cheating he would kill her and her lover. She believed him and wanted to protect both herself and Jason."

"Ain't love grand," Tyrrell observed in a cynical tone. "And the other murder investigation?"

Ray's face suggested his frustration, "Nothing solid. We have one less suspect. Jason Zelke was once a love interest of Ashleigh Allen, and he had a rather weak alibi for the night of the murders.

Sherry has provided him with a solid one that has been collaborated by several other witnesses."

"He gave you false alibi to cover his illicit relationship?" chuckled Tyrrell.

"Yes."

"And just when we thought chivalry was dead." He raised his coffee mug. "Here's to Jason, the loyal friend of comely damsels."

Ray did not respond.

"Any other possible suspects?" Tyrrell asked.

"We've got an interesting cast of characters, but no firm leads, not yet."

"How about the Vedder kid, anything more there?"

"He's still in the ICU. He's semi-conscious part of the time and can take some basic instructions, things like squeezing a hand when directed. But there's still no one home; he's not anyone we can question."

"Are you sure, Ray, you didn't discount the possibility that he was your killer too early?"

"No."

"The man who was killed?"

"David Dowd," responded Ray.

"Have you checked on him? Might he have been the target?"

"We've been making inquiries. He was a graduate student at Michigan, and we haven't found anything in his background that might lead to something like this."

"How about the Allen woman?" probed Tyrrell.

"Nothing yet," Ray responded.

"Random event? Some psychopath?"

"Always a possibility," said Ray, doubt in his voice.

"Well, with the Reesma case, keep things tight," said Tyrrell, using his arms to hoist himself out of the chair. "We don't want to give some fucking defense lawyer anything to hit us with." He stooped, picked up his cup, and moved out of the door and down the corridor.

35

The next afternoon, Ray drove up the steep hill and parked on the apron of the four-door garage. Alan Quertermous, in a pair of clean, pressed gray coveralls, was stretched out on a creeper, his upper torso under a small, diesel tractor. He slid out from under the machine, using his right hand for shade as he looked up at his visitor.

"Getting ready for winter?" Ray asked.

"Something I'd been planning to get done for weeks," said Quertermous, getting to his feet. "Time to get the mower deck off and the snow blower on." Using a red rag, he wiped the grease from his hands and extended his right hand to Ray. "I usually do this earlier, but given the unusually late fall, I've kept the mower attached. But it's time. A little more Indian summer, and then the gales of November will blow down from Canada. We always seem to get clobbered by the first snowstorm. And given my drive . . ." Without bothering to complete the sentence, he pointed to the blacktop ribbon that snaked down the hill to the county road. "Wish your county boys would keep that road as clear as I keep this drive."

"Much of a job putting that on?" Ray asked.

"No, damn good engineering on this machine." Quertermous bent over and retrieved the wrench he had been using. "Got to hand it to Kubota; they know how to make these things. It took three men and a boy to install the snow blower on the last tractor I had. I can put this baby on myself in less than fifteen minutes."

"New toy?" asked Ray, pointing to an ATV with a camouflage paint job that stood in the third bay of the garage.

"I've had it about a year."

"How does it do in sand?"

"It's pretty unstoppable. I've been all over the dunes with it, and I've never gotten stuck." He paused. His tone became guarded. "What brings you up here on this beautiful Saturday afternoon?"

"Yes, the third season is magical, isn't it," Ray said. He looked off at the rolling hills, then slowly brought his attention back to Quertermous. "Still some color left—bits of reds and golds mixed in with the conifers. The autumn sun gives it all such a muted effect, doesn't it?"

"Yes, it does," agreed Quertermous, showing some impatience. "But I don't think you came up here to share pastoral pleasantries. What business have you with me, sheriff."

"I met Furman Gellhorn, Ashleigh's lawyer, at the memorial service. He wanted an update on how the investigation was coming along. In passing he mentioned that you've contacted him regarding the estate." Ray watched the anger pulse through Quertermous' body, his face quickly turning crimson.

"Who I talk to is none of your concern. And Gellhorn's telling you about this is clearly some sort of ethics violation." Quertermous waved a wrench in Ray's face, his fist tightly wrapped around the handle. Ray reached down and plucked the tool from his grasp.

"I'm interested, Mr. Quertermous," Ray continued, slowly and calmly, "that you didn't mention to me that you were related to Ashleigh when I interviewed you."

"The topic was never approached, and it wasn't germane to anything we discussed."

"That's where you're wrong." Ray stood and waited, letting his words sink in. "How are you and Ms. Allen related?"

"We are distant cousins," Quertermous answered.

"And why do you think you might have a claim on the estate?"

"Sheriff, I am a very skilled genealogist. I've traced my father's family back to the days of Richard II, my mother's to the early eighteenth-century. In recent times our family has not been prolific, and wars and illness have taken their toll. I don't think there is anyone living who has a better claim than I do. I have been researching this, and I'm fairly certain of my findings. Of course you know she was bastard child; there's still the chance her good-for-nothing father might appear and try to lay claim to the estate." Quertermous paused briefly and took a couple of long breaths, trying to control his agitation. "Sheriff, at this point I'm only looking at the possibility of contesting Ashleigh's will. I've made no final decision."

"It seems you've been talking to a number of lawyers in recent weeks," Ray observed. "You've filed a damage suit against your broker . . ."

"Does the whole world know my private business?" Quertermous yelled, his relative calm sliding into rage.

"Sir, when you file a suit, it's public information. Here's the article from this morning's *Record-Eagle*." Ray pulled a clipping from his shirt pocket and handed it to Quertermous.

"You allege your broker engaged in risky investments and under his guidance the value of your portfolio declined by sixty-some percent," Ray continued as Quertermous perused the piece.

"Sixty-seven. He deceived me, told me to hang with certain investments, that I was in the right position for the next bull market. My savings, my inheritance, much of it is gone. And you probably think it's a frivolous suit?"

"I have no opinion on that. I'm just curious about your possible claim on the Allen estate. And your lack of openness about your familial connection to Ms. Allen."

"I know what you're trying to do," he screamed, small drops of spittle coming in Ray's direction. "I know how you people think! Since I've got money problems, I've got a motive for murder. Well, your silly supposition is dreadfully erroneous. I didn't know that she had any money until after she was dead. And I just did what anyone would do."

"Really?" Ray responded, leaving the word hang.

"Money's not a bad thing," he explained in a righteous tone. "If Ashleigh didn't do thoughtful planning, the funds could go to foolish causes or the government. I can use that money, and I can see to it that anything that's left will go to a good purpose when I die."

"Regarding Ashleigh's estate, how did you know who to contact?"

"The Howard's have always used the same firm. It wasn't hard."

"And you never told her you were a distant relative? Not when she was a student, not later?"

"No." Quertermous folded his arms in front of him, the now-crumpled copy of the article in his right hand.

"Why?"

"When she was a student, it just didn't seem appropriate. I mean, it wasn't as if we were first cousins or anything."

"And when she came back as a faculty member?"

"Well, I didn't like her much. Before the end of that first fall it was clear that she and Warrington were involved in a liaison. I didn't want to be related to her." Quertermous slowed down, his anger fading a bit. "Gwendolyn Howard created a very special place, a place where adolescents learned to control their own destinies; a place where we nurtured their emotional and intellectual development. We put them in control of their lives, taught them to be passionate about anything they pursued. And if you look at our graduates from those early years, well, they're exceptional people, people who have done good things with their lives, people who have made the world a better place. We have produced poets, doctors, teachers, scientists, carpenters, entrepreneurs, you name it. Most of them have excelled at whatever they have pursued.

"And what are we doing with students now?" Quertermous asked, anger returning to his voice. "All this collaboration and cooperating claptrap. We are training them to be followers. We are not training them to aspire to be the best, or to lead, just to be good team members. " He stopped and inhaled deeply. "And Warrington," he gesticulated wildly, "is at the center of this madness, and people like Ashleigh are willing accomplices. I am glad Gwendolyn didn't live long enough to see how they've destroyed her dream, her school. It's too bad." Quertermous stopped, and a malevolent smile spread across his face.

"What's that?" Ray asked.

"Too bad Ashleigh wasn't with Warrington on the beach. We could have been rid of the two of them."

Ray stood for a long moment and looked at Quertermous, handed back the wrench, and walked to his car. When he reached the bottom of the drive, he paused briefly and looked back up the hill. Quertermous was silhouetted against the horizon, just where he had left him, watching his departure.

36

fter his meeting with Quertermous, Ray drove to Leiston School and returned to Ashleigh Allen's unit in Devonshire Cottage. After removing the seal and unlocking the door, he turned on the lights and walked around the apartment again, slowly viewing the interior, imagining the young woman who had inhabited this space. Finally, he walked to the bathroom, opened the medicine chest, and found two toothbrushes and a tube of toothpaste standing in a heavy plastic cup. He lifted David Dowd's shaving kit from the top of the toilet tank and placed it in the sink. He looked through the leather bag and found Dowd's toothbrush in a plastic container. Replacing the bag, his attention returned to the medicine chest. He pulled on a pair of rubber gloves, removed the two toothbrushes and the cup, and placed them in an evidence bag. He also bagged a comb, hairbrush, and ChapStick tube. After slowly looking around the apartment a final time, he turned off the lights, locked the door, and reattached the police seal.

When Ray reached home late that evening, he carried the evidence bags to his study and placed them under the lid of his writing desk, next to a paternity DNA testing kit from Orchid Genescreen. He removed his journal, placed it on the writing surface, and stood for a long time looking at a blank page. Then he returned it to the desk. Ray wasn't ready to write about this yet. There was still too much turmoil, torment, and uncertainty.

It was after midnight when Ray was awakened from an uneasy sleep by a call from central dispatch; a fire had been reported at Leiston School. He quickly dressed and drove toward the scene.

The security booth was empty when Ray entered the school grounds, the gates on both sides of the drive were open. He followed the flashing lights of the fire trucks and other emergency vehicles along the narrow, twisting blacktop road into the oak grove near the faculty lodges. Pulling his vehicle as far off the road as possible, he followed the example of the arriving volunteer firefighters, leaving the path open for the tanker trucks that would be ferrying the thousands of gallons of water needed to battle the fire. Other firefighters came after him, most in pickups, pulling on their equipment and hurrying up the road, encumbered by their heavy coats, pants, and boots, moving toward the blaze.

As soon as Ray was close, he could see that the burning building was Devonshire Cottage, the duplex that housed Janet Medford and the late Ashleigh Allen. *What did we miss?* he thought, speculating that the fire was set to destroy evidence in Allen's apartment. As he got closer he could see the entire building was engulfed in flames.

The chief, Bernie Rathman, the lone paid member of the village's otherwise volunteer fire department, was positioning the pumper/tanker fire truck on the access drive near the burning building. He then started the second diesel engine, the one that powered the impeller water pump.

Ray caught his attention as he swung down from the cab.

"It's a duplex," Ray said, "only this side is occupied."

"How many people?" Bernie asked.

"Just one, a woman."

"Is she there?"

"Don't know."

Ray moved away and let Bernie get his people and equipment

into position. The fill tank, a collapsible reservoir, was deployed behind the pumper. The first tanker truck backed into position and began pouring its contents into the fill tank.

The big diesel engine on the pump labored as it was engaged. Initially the brilliant yellow flames from the fire and the headlights and spots on the pumper illuminated the scene. Firefighters dragged a generator in place and positioned floodlights around the perimeter of the building. The lights were switched on, bathing the structure in light. People shouted commands over the din of machinery and the thunderous howl of fire. Working in groups, firefighters pulled out the carefully folded hoses, locking sections together.

And then the assault began. Three teams of firefighters in succession signaled back to the pumper to charge their lines, their bodies tensing as they prepared to hold the surging hoses. Streams of water exploded through already cracked windows, a violent hissing sound added to the roar of the blaze.

Two firefighters worked to open the front door, first with a long bar and ax, finally with a sledgehammer. They jumped back as the door fell into the room, a yellow tongue of flame exploded outward and began lapping at the roof. Men at the front of the building redirected a hose into this portal. Smoke and steam poured out of the building, the beams from the strobes and flashers on the emergency vehicles pulsated in the rising column of acrid air.

Several firefighters positioned a ladder on the right side of the building. A small, athletic man with the grace of a gymnast scampered up to the ridge; he moved to the center of the roof and, using a chain saw—the whine of its engine almost lost in the cacophony—started cutting a hole. He pulled back quickly as his final incision allowed a large rectangle of the roof to fall into the conflagration. He quickly retraced his steps off the building.

The fire started breaking through the roof along the rafters, tongues of flame working through the shingles near the exterior walls and climbing toward the ridge, the roof boards burning through and falling away, leaving the roof structure outlined in the flaming joists until they, too, collapsed into the interior on both sides of the duplex.

Ray was so transfixed by the activity that he was startled when he realized a crowd had gathered on the perimeter. Sue Lawrence and some other deputies had secured a line on the far side of the service road, keeping spectators at a safe distance. Ray moved along the line, talking to some of his officers. Suddenly, Ian Warrington grabbed his shoulder.

"Medford, is she in there?"

"I don't know. The front door appeared to be locked." Ray watched Warrington's expression go from concern to horror.

"Oh, my God. When will you know?"

"Not for a while. They've got to get the fire under control before they can send anyone in." Warrington disappeared back into the crowd.

Ray dodged an incoming tanker and drifted back toward the blaze. He lost track of time as he watched firefighters battle the flames. Finally, the color of the inferno was changing, the flames becoming less luminous as the water streamed in. And then, suddenly, the building began to darken, the dazzling light from within started to fade.

The line of floodlights illuminated the next stage of the battle. The firefighters continued to pour water into the interior, now in positions close to the building, isolating the remaining hot spots, much of the flammable material now consumed. The masonry structure was little more than a shell.

Ray watched as two firefighters prepared to enter the smoldering building. Weighed down by Scotch air packs—tanks on their backs, elaborate masks covering their faces—and carrying flashlights, they slogged into the ruins. He could see the blade-like beams from their lights move around the dark, murky interior. After several long minutes they emerged, one of the men walking to Bernie's command post near the front of the pumper, pulling off his breathing apparatus as he approached. Ray moved close to hear the conversation.

"One body on the floor in the main room," he shouted over the rumble of the diesel.

"Everything else clear?" Bernie asked.

"Yeah."

Ray crossed the road to where his deputies and some Leiston staff members, including Warrington and Sarah James, kept close watch over a small group of spectators who remained. Most of the students had returned to their rooms, surrendering to the cold and the hour.

Warrington walked to meet Ray as he approached.

"You should get the rest of the kids back to the dorms," Ray said gravely.

"Medford?"

"They've found a body."

Warrington stood looking at Ray, the revolving lights from a rescue truck reflecting in his glasses. Looking overwhelmed, he nodded at Ray and moved toward the crowd. Ray watched as Warrington, Sarah, and the others shepherded the remaining students away.

When Ray returned to the pumper, Bernie was directing the cleanup. The frenzied pace of the assault was now replaced by the somber and quiet collecting, sorting, and stowing of equipment. The firefighters—most had been pulled from their beds—were exhausted from the battle and now moved methodically.

"The arson investigator will be here in the morning," Bernie said.

"Think he'll be able to tell us much about the cause of the fire?" Ray asked.

"You see what's left," Bernie responded, looking weary and worn. "The obvious causes of a fire, like a fuel can or a welding torch, aren't hard to spot, but beyond that it's often a difficult thing to nail down. A frayed extension cord, a cigarette in a couch, how can you tell? And fires in masonry buildings are especially hot. There's not much there but ashes and bits of metal.

"The other half of the duplex," Ray said, putting his hand on the shoulder of Bernie's coat, "that's where the young woman, the murder victim, lived."

Bernie nodded, indicating his comprehension.

"Janet Medford," Ray continued, "assuming it's the body you found here," he paused, suddenly aware of his own exhaustion and his difficulty coherently explaining his concern, "might have had some knowledge important to the case. And any evidence in the murder victim's apartment is now destroyed."

Bernie nodded again. "The autopsy might tell you how the woman died." He gestured toward the shell of the stone cottage, "Finding the cause of the fire might be much more difficult."

37

Ray, weary and dispirited, drifted away from the blackened masonry skeleton of the duplex. His eyes burned and the stench from the blaze hung on his clothing, skin, and hair. He coughed, his throat sore from inhaling the smoke. He walked slowly down the curving drive. A predawn quiet had settled over the school. Walking past the dormitories, dark buildings in pools of soft light, he wondered how the students would handle this newest tragedy. Lost in thought, Ray was caught unaware by the sudden appearance of Sarah James at his side.

"I didn't mean to startle you," said Sarah.

"I was in my own world. I didn't see you," he explained.

"Want some coffee?" she asked.

Ray did not respond right away. Finally he said, "Sure."

They walked to Sarah's cottage in silence. Entering, she switched on the lights and led him into the kitchen. "Decaf or regular?" she asked, turning toward him.

"Regular," he responded. "If that's what you're going to have."

She looked over at the clock. "It's almost morning, might as well."

Ray visually inspected the kitchen and adjoining living room. There was a comfortable feel to the place; the furniture and other interior decorations were harmonious in color and design—lots of wood and earth tones. He brought his attention back to Sarah. She looked tired, worn, and fragile.

He dropped his coat over a kitchen chair and watched in silence as Sarah placed a filter in the machine, scooped coffee from a bag into the filter, and poured water into the reservoir. She touched the on button and moved toward him.

"Tell me about Medford—from your perspective," he asked.

She didn't respond immediately. Finally she said, "I only knew her on the edges; she was a very private person. She was often difficult, reluctant to accept any changes. But she was a terrific artist, and the kids adored her. And this fire . . ." Sarah put her arms around Ray, "Please hold me."

He wrapped his arms around her and felt her puddle into his body. He felt her sob for many minutes, then slowly regain control. He continued to hold her close.

"I'll get us some coffee," she said, sliding from his arms. "Want anything in yours?"

"No."

Sarah poured the steaming mahogany liquid into two delicate cups, and placing them on matching saucers, carried them to a coffee table in front of the couch. She settled next to him, then moved into his arms. Ray held her close and felt her soften. Once again he became aware of his own fatigue. His eyelids were heavy; he'd been awake for almost twenty-four hours.

When he opened his eyes again, he could see daylight at the edges of the blinds. He felt her jump as he moved. She looked up at him and said, "We must have fallen asleep."

She kissed him gently on the lips and slowly stood. "I'll make some fresh coffee," she said. Ray found the bathroom and tried to wash the sleep from his eyes. When he joined Sarah in the kitchen the coffee was brewing and a plate of buttered toast was on the counter. Ray peered out of the kitchen window at the heavy fog and the gray dawn.

"Thank you for staying." She came to his side, setting a cup on the counter next to Ray and sliding her arms around him. He held back briefly and then enfolded her in a tight embrace for a long moment. The chirping of his cell phone intruded into the scene.

"Must you answer?" she asked.

"I better," he responded, letting her slip from his arms. He pulled the phone from his jacket pocket. "Elkins," he said into the mouthpiece.

"Found your car, but I couldn't find you," said Sue Lawrence.

"I'm having coffee," he responded.

"Arson inspector is here, and Dr. Dyskin is on his way. As soon as it gets a little lighter they'll be getting started."

"Good," said Ray. "Let's keep a wide perimeter on the area until the body is removed. I don't want any of the students to see what's happening. There's been enough chaos in their lives already."

"Yes," came the response.

"I'll be there in a few minutes." He closed the phone and picked up the coffee, carefully sipping the steaming brew.

38

~~~

As Ray walked up the road toward Devonshire Cottage, Dr. Dyskin, going in the other direction in his ponderous, rusting Lincoln, slowed to a stop and lowered his window.

"Elkins," he initiated before Ray could say anything, "can't tell you anything. The body is too badly damaged. The autopsy might provide some useful information." He looked over at Ray. "Get some sleep, you look like hell," he added, before continuing on his way.

Mike Ogden, the arson investigator, was standing with Fire Chief Bernie Rathman near the front of the cottage running through incident indicators, a checklist that would help focus the investigation and explore the possibility of arson.

Ogden, thirty-something, was dressed in a dark-blue jumpsuit and heavy boots. Rust-colored sideburns framed his freckled face, and the brim of his hard hat hid most of his forehead. He acknowledged Ray's presence with a handshake and a quick smile and continued with his questions, recording Bernie's responses on a clipboard.

"So, as far as you could tell, were the doors and windows locked when you arrived on the scene?" Ogden asked.

"Yes," Bernie responded. "Front door was locked. We had to knock the front door off its hinges. It musta been solid oak. Same story with the side entrance. I can't tell you about the back unit. Our attention was on the occupied side of the duplex. Things in back were pretty burned away before we got to them."

As the questioning continued, Ray drifted away and slowly circled the perimeter of the burned-out dwelling. The upper portions of the oak trees near the building were charred, leaves and small twigs burned away, only the trunks and primary branches remained. He climbed a small knoll on the north side of the building and looked down on the four exterior walls—black walls faced with cut stone. The acrid smell of death and destruction clung to the air.

As Ray watched, Ogden carefully photographed the building's exterior. Then he moved inside, shooting the interior section-by-section, including the body. Ogden worked the area a second time, collecting and labeling ash samples in small glass containers. At his direction, the corpse was bagged and removed. Ray and Sue, following the protocol that exists between the police and fire personnel, waited as Bernie's crew and the arson investigator completed their work.

Finally Ogden emerged from the building and carried his gear to the back of his vehicle.

"What did you find?" Ray asked, after walking to his side.

"Come and have a look." Ogden led the way. Bernie and Sue joined Ray in the procession.

Although Ray had been in burned-out buildings many times, he was surprised by the extent of the destruction. And since he had recently visited the cottage, the scene was even more startling. Nothing of the interior—save the distorted skeletons of metal objects and some broken crockery and glassware—remained. The art, furniture, and books, all the things that reflected the life of Janet Medford, were in ashes. The temperatures in the masonry-clad building had been particularly intense; the destruction was nearly complete. They moved from room to room, completing the tour in what had once been the small kitchen. Ogden pointed to a frying pan amongst the debris on the floor near the stove, only a bolt remained where a wooden handle was once attached.

"Might have been something as simple as that," said Ogden looking at the pan. "Happens all the time. Someone starts heating some oil in a pan and then gets distracted, the phone rings or they wander off and look at the TV. Before you know it, you've got a grease fire."

"But you'd run out of the building and call 911," offered Ray.

Ogden gave Ray a boyish smile. "True." He pointed to the controls on the soot-blackened stove. The plastic knobs had melted away. "Look at these three," he said, "they're all in the off position. But this last one, one of the back burners, was in an on position. Unless the knob was hit by something falling before it disintegrated, the burner was probably on."

They walked out of the kitchen door and away from the building. Standing on a small rise, the group looked back at the masonry skeleton of the building.

"The frying pan, you think that's the source of the fire?" asked Bernie.

"Might be," said Ogden. "But then, why didn't the victim get out of the building? Did she have a heart attack or stroke?"

"She was a heavy drinker," offered Ray, "perhaps that played a role."

"Was she a smoker?" Ogden probed.

"Yes," responded Ray.

"There's another possibility," said Ogden. "Do you know how many fires are started by drunks that fall asleep with a lit cigarette in their hand? Lots," he said, answering his own question.

"The victim, any chance someone wanted her dead?" asked Ogden.

Ray explained that the woman who occupied the other half

of the duplex, Ashleigh Allen, had recently been murdered. He also told Ogden that some evidence was being stored in her side of the duplex.

"The couple killed on the beach?" Ogden asked.

"Yes," said Ray.

"How does Medford fit with the murder investigation?"

"She's a teacher here at the school, and she shared the building with the victim. I interviewed her a few days ago. I wanted to know if she had seen or heard anything that might be useful."

"Get anything from her?" Ogden asked.

"Not much. And I doubt that she knew anything that would have put her in any danger." Ray hesitated for a long moment and then said, "She did provide a possible suspect with an alibi. Is there anything suspicious here?"

Ogden pulled off his hardhat and ran his hand over his thick brown hair. After repositioning his hat he said, "Well, as you can see, the damage is so complete that the obvious kinds of things we find in many suspicious fires aren't here. I've collected a lot of samples, and we'll test them for traces of accelerants. If we find some, there's a case for arson. But if the fire was started in another way, even if it was a criminal act, I may be hard pressed to prove it. Any of these prep school kids got pyromaniac tendencies?" he asked with a chuckle.

"That one hasn't come up yet," Ray responded with a smile.

Ogden looked at Bernie. "When you arrived on the scene, were both sides of the duplex engaged?"

"Yes. That's the way it looked. I was on this side with the pumper. I didn't really get to the other side until the fire was under control."

The group carefully moved into the area that had been Allen's apartment. Little remained.

After a few minutes Ogden asked, "You were storing some evidence here?"

"Sue Lawrence and I had gone through the murder victim's apartment quite thoroughly," Ray explained, "but it was nice to know that we could come back here again if we thought there was something more to be learned."

"I'm sort of done here," said Ogden as they exited the building. Looking at Ray, he continued. "Last time you dragged me halfway across the state in the wee hours, you took me to some great little bakery for coffee and chocolate croissants."

"Anything for interagency relations," Ray responded. "I trust the pastries will move this investigation to the front of the line."

"Absolutely," agreed Ogden with a bright smile.

Ray looked at the Sue and Bernie. "We'll continue this discussion at *Le Patisserie*. And I'm buying."

39

~~~

The sun was already low on the horizon when Ray pulled off the county road and headed west on Burnt Mill Trail. He pulled the visor down to escape the glare and fished for his sunglasses in the glove box.

Ray felt exhausted and discouraged as he pulled into the parking lot near the Lake Michigan shore. Sand blown off the dunes during the last storm covered much of the blacktop, and piles of damp leaves had collected in low spots at the edges of the pavement. He climbed out of his vehicle and followed the path that led over the dunes to the beach.

For several minutes, he sat on the knoll at the top of the trail and watched the waves, focusing on the water stretching to the horizon, the ominous play of light in the thin clouds as the sun dropped toward the melancholy gray swell, the gulls riding the wind out over the treacherous rollers.

It had been weeks since Ray had been in his kayak on Lake Michigan, the place where he felt most in tune with the natural world and the most at ease. And he had picked this particular strip of sand and water to paddle because it was the area where the murders had been committed. He wanted to see the scene from another perspective: he was hoping that some new insight would put him on the track of the killer.

Ray walked back to his Jeep and changed clothes in the empty lot—shedding his uniform and pulling on paddling shorts, a neoprene Farmer John, and a neoprene top. He added a heavy fleece jacket and a dry-top—a waterproof anorak with rubber gaskets at the neck and wrists. He slipped into a neoprene spray skirt and then zipped on his life jacket. And last he added a thick rubber hood to keep his head warm if he accidentally capsized or decided to practice doing some Eskimo rolls.

After undoing the tie-down straps, Ray lifted his kayak from the rack and carefully set it on a patch of grass. He secured a hydration pack, his cell phone protected in a waterproof pouch, and some neoprene mittens under the bungee cords on top of the deck at the front of the cockpit. Ray looked up at the darkening sky as he carried the boat and paddle to the beach. He checked his watch, noting that little more than an hour of daylight remained.

The rollers were surging high onto the beach as he pushed the bow into the waves. With the stern still resting on the sand, he slid into the snug cockpit and pulled the tight-fitting neoprene spray skirt around the cockpit coaming, checking that it was securely attached. Then he pulled on the thick black neoprene mittens. Ray was now one with the boat, a watertight unit ready for the challenging conditions.

Pushing against the sand with his hands, he lifted the stern and propelled the light craft forward into the breaking waves. Ray fought his way through the surf zone—paddling hard and bracing at times to avoid capsizing—and then headed for deep water. He wanted to get out far enough to view the whole scene, the shoreline, the steep dunes, and the plateau above.

Once he had passed the second sand bar, he paddled parallel to the beach. He could see the bluish-white yard light at Nora Jennings' cottage; the few other houses up on the dunes were dark and empty.

As he paddled, he settled into the rhythm of the waves,

slowly moving through the water, his attention focused on the beach of the murder. Ashleigh's face flashed across his mind; he was sure he had seen her before, perhaps in the IGA, at Art's, or the Friendly Tavern. He mentally reviewed the scene again and the limited evidence they had gathered. He considered the people he and Sue had interviewed: Ian Warrington, his wife Helen, Sarah James, Janet Medford, Kim Vedder, and Alan Quertermous. He considered the possible motives. Then his thoughts drifted to the Medford fire.

Ray paddled farther than he had planned, past the end of the dunes, into the bay beyond. Daylight was fading into a purple-blue dusk as he turned the craft and started back toward the beach. He pointed the craft straight into the wind until he rounded the stark headland and turned south. Nora's light would help him find his way back if necessary. He paddled closer to the beach, his eyes reviewing the murder scene in the reduced light. He held his paddle in a low brace position and rode the waves, thinking, looking for patterns, links in the bits of evidence and information they had gathered. What did they add up to? Who possessed the wrath needed for these crimes?

The brighter stars began to emerge in the twilight. Ray bobbed in his kayak, scanning the sky for Orion's belt.

Suddenly Ray's hydration pack exploded. It took Ray several seconds to comprehend what had happened. He lifted his paddle, and the shaft between his two hands splintered. Instantly he understood. Someone was trying to kill him.

Filling his lungs completely, he rolled the boat to the right, away from the beach, toward the deep water, and capsized. He groped for the loop on the spray skirt in the dark water, finally pulling it free from the coaming. He held the sides of the cockpit and started to slide out of the boat. He felt the concussion of the next shot, and then the burning in his right leg just before he pulled free from the kayak.

Ray stayed below the boat and waited; there were several additional thuds as bullets smashed through the sides of the boat.

He hung below the capsized craft, occasionally pulling his head into the cockpit to get a couple of quick breaths. He expected the shooter to put a few rounds into the bulkheads, the watertight chambers in the bow and stern that kept the kayak afloat, but it never happened. His eyes slowly adjusted to the dull light of the water and the near-blackness of the cockpit.

Ray felt the water seeping into his wetsuit, at first very cold, then slowly warming as it absorbed his body heat. He felt a numbing pain in his leg. He needed to explore the wound, but didn't want to change his grip on the boat. He wanted the shooter to think that he had been hit, mortally wounded, and was hanging inverted in the overturned boat, held in by the spray skirt.

He worked the cell phone free and carefully lifted it up into the blackness of the capsized cockpit. Through the plastic cover he pressed the keypad, hoping for the light to come on. If he could just key 911, they would trace the call's location. He pushed buttons, but the keypad remained dark. He slid his fingers along the case until he found a tear. The bag was flooded. His spirits dropped. His situation was desperate.

Ray tried to calm down, carefully breathing in and telling himself to consider his options. First, how bad was his leg? He hooked the front of the cockpit with his left arm and cautiously explored his right calf below the knee. He felt the gash in the wet suit halfway to his ankle. Pushing a finger into the hole, he felt the sharp·ends of shattered bone.

Stay calm, he told himself. He practice a breathing exercise he had learned in a yoga class. His tibia was shattered, but the bleeding was probably minimal. Cold, that was the real danger. He was just beginning to shiver—the earliest stage of hypothermia. He knew his condition would rapidly deteriorate, both physically and cognitively. *How much time?* he wondered. *How much time? Was he going into shock? Was the shooter waiting? Would he want to see his kill?*

Ray tried to orient himself. How far was he from the shore? If he surfaced the shooter would know he was still alive. *It would be like shooting ducks in a . . .*

How far was he from the shore? Holding onto the cockpit's sides, he extended down and felt for the lake bottom, touching sand with his left foot. He guessed he was inside the second sand bar, less than fifty yards from the shore. Ray pulled his legs close to his chest to conserve body heat and let the boat drift in the wind, bringing his nose and mouth into the cockpit to breathe. He assumed that the boat would weathercock, the bow turning into the westerly wind. Carefully maneuvering, Ray moved so he was facing the stern—the part of the kayak that would drift toward the shore.

What if the shooter was waiting? Ray knew he was becoming hypothermic, and because of the wound, probably unable support his weight. Using his teeth, he worked the neoprene glove off his right hand, unzipped a pocket in his life vest, and removed a rescue knife. He pushed the serrated blade open with his thumb. He checked the water's depth again, less than four feet. Ray dropped his legs to bottom and slowly and carefully positioned the boat parallel to the shore.

He saw the beam of the flashlight reflecting off the sandy bottom as someone waded toward the boat. He pulled his legs close, hoping they would look like his upper torso was hanging lifeless in the capsized kayak.

Ray held the knife at the ready. His timing had to be perfect. He would have only one chance at the shooter.

40

~~~

Ray's memories of what happened next had a dreamlike quality: He lunged toward the light, driving his knife into the dark figure. He thrust a second time, ripping bone and flesh with the serrated blade. He heard a painful scream and then felt a powerful force pushing him backwards—the flashlight dropping into the water; its beam dimming, disappearing into blackness. Two loud explosions, the figure moving away, back onto the shore. And then barking, and a bigger flashlight, and someone was dragging him by a shoulder strap. He was crawling on the sand, and the world was slipping away. And then it came back. He was covered with blankets, and Sue was at his side, asking about the shooting. He told her about the knife, said he had wounded someone.

And then the world went black again. He was aware of sounds, voices, the slapping of helicopter blades, the scream of the jet engine. When he opened his eyes again he was in a treatment room, the green worm of his heartbeat ambling along on a monitor, IV lines attached to his left arm, an oxygen mask covering his face. One of the nurses, a tall, serious looking man in dull-blue scrubs, noticed his eyes were open.

"How you doing, buddy?" he asked. "Sorry we had to cut up your wet suit. Needed to get a better look at that wound. As soon as you're warmed up a bit, we're sending you to surgery. By the time you wake up in the morning, we'll have you all patched together." Ray watched him for a few more minutes and slid back into a dream.

He woke with a start, the late autumn sun flooding into the room, a different room, flowers—yellow mums—on the window sill. A uniformed officer near the door. Then the voice of Saul Feldman, his internist, "I thought you were an early riser."

Ray tried to speak, his throat sore, his voice ragged. "What . . . ?

"Everything is under control," offered Feldman. "I talked to the orthopedist, he's a damn a good surgeon. Everything went well. A very positive prognosis; you'll make a good recovery. You were lucky, Ray. It could have been a lot worse." He moved closer to the bed and dropped his voice to a less professional tone. "When you came in for your flu shot, what was that, two weeks ago, didn't we discuss the danger of late-season kayaking?"

Ray struggled for a retort, but his head throbbed from the post-operative morphine hangover. Sue entered the room and stood at the end of the bed. "Did you lose a knife?" she asked, dangling an evidence bag in her left hand.

"I'm half dead and everyone's a comedian," Ray said hoarsely. He focused on the knife. "I hope you found the person I planted it in."

"No such luck," Sue said. "Not yet. But we did find a bloody glove. He must have dropped it when he was getting in his car."

"Anything else?"

"Brass. We found eight 223-caliber casings."

"Interesting, think I only counted four shots. Where?"

"At the top of the dune. Right above the original crime scene."

"Ten minutes, Ms. Lawrence," said Feldman. "And I'll be back to check," he said as he walked toward the hall.

"Could you recognize him, the shooter?"

"I didn't really see him. I just lunged from under the boat toward the light. The fact that I apparently wounded him was just luck. What else did you find?

"The flashlight and your kayak."

"My boat, how bad?"

"You won't be happy."

"Damn," he was silent for a long moment. "Prints?"

"Some on the brass and some on the flashlight and the batteries. I've sent them for analysis."

"Hospitals?"

"Yes, we've alerted all the hospitals and walk-in clinics in the region to watch for anyone with a knife wound. So far there's been no response. We're getting the blood type and the DNA from the glove."

"At the end I heard shots. Sounded like a cannon."

"Your friend Nora."

"Nora?"

"You're lucky she had stopped home to pick up some things. She heard the rifle shots and called 911. Dispatch told her to lock the doors and stay in the cottage until an officer arrived. When she saw the flashlight on the beach, she grabbed her shotgun and came down to the beach to investigate. She said she wasn't really aiming for your attacker; she was just trying to scare him away."

"She's lucky that old gun didn't blow up," said Ray. "I bet she's got a bruised shoulder." He lay there and tried to visualize Nora firing the shotgun. Then he asked, "Was it Ashleigh's killer?"

"Had to be. He must have been tailing you, waiting for an opportunity to take you out."

"But why? It makes no sense."

"Well, for what it's worth, here's my speculation. You're the *man*. You're the one who talks to the cameras. He sits at home and sees you on the news. He's personalized this; it's a battle between the two of you. He thinks we're getting close."

"Sue, that's not . . ."

"Not what? Not logical, at least not logical to you? But I bet it makes perfect sense to the shooter. And if he'd only been a better shot . . ."

"Better shot!" Ray motioned toward his leg. "He was good enough."

Feldman appeared at the door. "That's it for a while. Let's give him some rest."

"But," protested Ray.

"No buts. For you, visiting hours are over."

She held his hand a brief moment. "I'll be back in a while. There's an armed officer at the door. Don't try to wander off. He's been instructed to shoot first, ask questions later."

Ray watched her leave. He stared at the ceiling tiles a long time. *Who thinks I'm getting too close? Whoever it is has got a nasty knife wound.*

Before he drifted off again, he remembered that he had never found Orion.

41

<hr/>

"I think it's a goddamn conspiracy, not that I mind getting out of here," said Ray in a grumbling tone as he pushed his way up from a wheelchair, grabbing onto the car door, and hopping on his good leg so he could back onto the car seat.

"What's that, the conspiracy?" asked Sue, holding onto the wheelchair with her left hand while steadying the car door.

"The food. One of the nurses told me he's heard that it's hospital policy to make the food almost intolerable to encourage people to leave as soon as they can."

Once he was seated, she pulled his seatbelt out for him and closed the door. She slid into the driver's seat and said, "I thought Marc and Lisa were bringing you dinner last night?"

"They were, they did—a lovely lamb dish, but they were late. And while I was waiting I was served a plate of tuna casserole," Ray repeated it a second time with heightened disdain in his voice. "Tuna casserole, made the old-fashioned way with cream of mushroom soup. The dish that destroyed the palates of millions of Americans and . . ."

"How did you know about the mushroom soup? Do you have a spy in the kitchen?"

"You can tell. It has a certain congealed looked to it. I don't think there's any other way to get that texture and consistency."

"So, why did you eat it?" she asked, as she turned right out of the hospital drive. Cars lined both sides of the narrow street, and she had to carefully navigate between the parked cars and the oncoming traffic.

"I didn't, I just looked at it. That was enough." Ray paused. "They even had faded green beans on the side, and a wedge of iceberg salad with Thousand Island dressing."

"Sounds real retro," Sue said, waiting to make a left turn. "You know what?"

"What?"

"You're real grumpy. It's not like you. Must be the drugs."

Ray looked over at her, "Your hair, I don't remember it being that red."

"Nice recovery. Grumpy, but still observant." She ruffled her hair with her right hand. "I needed a little change."

"Looks good, I like it."

"I hear you did some hospital rounds this morning."

"Yes," he explained. "With my bodyguard following along, one of the young nurses pushed my wheelchair. I thought I'd look around and see if they had admitted anyone with knife wounds."

"And?" Sue baited him.

"Nothing."

"And that's what we've heard from all the area hospitals and clinics. I've visited Leiston School to see if anyone is wearing a sling or has gone missing. Even had a chat with Alan Quertermous. He was most solicitous of your health and sends you his best regards."

"I'll bet," said Ray.

Her tone changed. "How about Jason?"

"I guess he's out of danger. But he's still surrounded by tubes and wires."

"How is he psychologically?" she asked.

"Jason has never shown much affect, so it's hard to tell, but he seems depressed. He's learned firsthand the dangers of playing with fire. So to speak."

"Yes," Sue agreed. "And Arnie?"

"There's still no one home. One of the doctors told me he was less than optimistic about Arnie's recovery."

They rode in silence for several miles, Ray looking out at the bay. Finally he asked, "Do we have the Medford autopsy yet?"

Sue looked across the car and gave Ray a quick smile before her eyes returned to the road. "I was wondering how long it would take you to get back on task."

"Well?"

"I have everything organized for you. After we get you settled at home, I'll go through it with you."

"Just give me a summary," said Ray, a note of irritation in his voice.

"Grump, grump. It's the drugs, isn't it?"

Ray moved in the seat trying to get comfortable. "They do mess with my head. The few times I've had to use them." He paused, "I tried to explain it to Saul, and he thought I was asking for antidepressants. I finally got him to understand what I was trying to tell him. He said some people react that way to opiates. He said I needed to be patient, it would take a number of days to wash all of them from my system."

"And maybe you're just depressed. Getting shot is not an uplifting experience." There was a long silence as they drove north on the highway toward Cedar Bay, two lanes of blacktop that followed the Lake Michigan shoreline.

"I know I'm down," Sue finally offered. "And I didn't catch any lead."

"What are you upset about?"

"Most of the same things you are. We're not getting any closure on this case." She took several deep breaths. "I've had trouble keeping my distance. And it's real easy for me to relate to

Ashleigh." She stopped and waited for a school bus in the opposing lane. Three elementary-age children, two girls and a smaller boy, each lugging a backpack, crossed in front of them, heading for a cottage perched on a small outcropping of land near the water.

"Maybe that's what I should be doing," she said, motioning toward the children.

"Driving a school bus?" asked Ray in a teasing tone.

"You know what I'm talking about. There are other ways to try to help build a better world than just spending your time looking for the bad guys. I was also thinking about going back to graduate school."

"In what?"

"I don't know. I'm just noodling around with possibilities. Like I used to play flute in the high school orchestra. I was very good, and it made me happy. And I took a lot of art courses in college before I became practical and settled on criminal justice. Maybe I could become an art or music teacher." There was another long pause. "Or maybe I could meet a nice guy and start a family."

"There's always that possibility."

"But I'm not finding many here. I've already scouted out the possibilities around Cedar Bay." She looked over at Ray. "Too bad you're old enough to be my father."

"Why's that?"

"You have most of the things I look for in a man."

Ray chuckled, "I can give you the names of women who would be more than happy to enumerate on my many flaws."

"You probably met the wrong women." Sue said with some tenderness. "How about Sarah James? She's sort of a babe. Have you gone out with her?"

"No."

"Think you might?" she asked, bringing the car to a complete stop, waiting for another school bus to make a left turn.

Ray looked across the bay. There were still a few flashes of color on Old Mission Peninsula. Occasional columns of sunshine shot through the heavy gray overcast, illuminating areas of water and land like a spotlight panning across the horizon.

"Perhaps."

"I saw her at the hospital. Did she visit you more than once?

"Yes."

"We've never considered her as a possible suspect, have we?"

"It did cross my mind." He felt a wave of discomfort run through his frame. "What would be her motive?"

"Jealousy, or . . ."

"Seems like you're making a long reach here."

"I am. I've been going over and over the possibilities the last several days, trying to see if there is anything we've missed."

"And Sarah?"

"We never clearly established her whereabouts on the night of Ashleigh's death, and I just wasn't sure that we'd looked at her as a possible suspect. You were the one who had most of the contact with her."

"And you were wondering, to use your language, if the 'babe' factor protected her from close scrutiny?"

"It was just a thought," responded Sue.

"Well, then I think you should be the one who takes a second look at Sarah James," Ray said. "So, tell me about the Janet Medford postmortem."

"It's just a preliminary report, some of the more exotic toxicology will take a few weeks."

"Give me a summary," asked Ray.

"She died of smoke inhalation. Her blood alcohol was over 0.20—something like 0.23 or 0.24. As I'm sure you remember too vividly, the body was in less than perfect shape, but there was no evidence of trauma. I called the pathologist after I got the report. I had a couple of things I needed clarified. He had some interesting observations that I hadn't quite picked up on in his more clinical statements."

"Like?"

"He said that years of heavy drinking and smoking had taken their toll. Her lungs were severely damaged. And if she hadn't died of smoke inhalation, it seems she would have eventually suffocated from emphysema. And he said that she had a badly diseased heart."

"I wonder if she knew?"

"I was curious about that," said Sue. "Found out she was a patient at the Cedar Bay Clinic, had a conversation with Cornelia Johnson, her internist. Johnson said she last saw Medford during the summer for a routine physical. They had discussed lifestyle issues many times, but she could tell Medford was not about to change her ways."

"So, her visit was just routine or did Johnson give her any bad news?"

"No, just the usual report, 'If you don't stop doing what you're doing you're going to an early grave.'"

"How about the arson investigator, Ogden?" Ray asked.

"One interesting finding, Ogden found some traces of Coleman fuel in Ashleigh's laundry room. He thinks it was just part of her camping supplies and not the initial cause of the fire. It just exploded in the course of the blaze. He said that the source of the fire would be listed as undetermined. Interesting word, isn't it? He went on to say that he thinks it started with a grease fire. She left a pan on the stove, wandered away, fell asleep or passed out."

"So, it might have been an accident?" Ray paused. "Or maybe she just wanted to leave the world rather than suffer alone with a bad heart and broken-down lungs?"

"Maybe," said Sue. "One more thing. You asked me about two former students, Jay Hanson and Denton Freeler."

"Oh, yes," responded Ray. "I'd almost forgotten about them."

"Jay Hanson is studying in Italy this year, according to his mother. He left in August. And Denton Freeler, well, I've had no luck running down his parents. Remember, Helen Warrington said that his death had been reported to the Leiston School alumni office? But I can't find any record of his passing. But, if they are still living abroad, I guess he could have died abroad. Anyway, neither seems to have ever had any problems with the police. My full notes are in a folder with a filename Hanson/Freeler."

She turned left up Ray's long, steep drive. Shooting him a quick glance she said, "You're going to have fun plowing this."

42

Sue helped Ray out of the car and tried to get him to sit in the wheelchair. He insisted on hobbling into his house on crutches. He was happy to be in his own place. As if on cue, the sun poured through the skylights above the kitchen, brightening the airy interior.

She followed him with the wheelchair and finally settled him into it, carefully elevating the leg with the heavy cast.

"Where did the table come from?" Ray asked, looking at a long, folding table covered with neat stacks of papers and folders standing next to the far wall.

"It's mine," said Sue. "I bought it at a garage sale last year. I needed a place where I could organize materials. You don't have enough flat surfaces, just that little table you eat at. That and your kitchen counter and I knew better than to stack anything there. I organize in piles, you organize in," she paused momentarily, choosing her words carefully, "more non-linear ways. Like swirls, maybe." She gave Ray a wry smile. "The exception is your kitchen, where everything has a place."

"Okay," he said, glancing at the neatly organized materials on the aluminum table. "Tell me what I'm looking at."

"It's just the next iteration of what I had set up in the office. Everything is in categories, starting with the murder scene, then everything we've collected on Allen and Dowd. Vedder is here," she pointed to another stack. "Then there are print copies of the notes and related materials from each person we've interviewed. Also, the material from the Medford fire."

"What's all this fanfold?" Ray asked, pointing to a stack of green and white computer paper near the end of the table.

"That's the output of plate numbers from Leiston's security booth. The start date is three days before Ashleigh's death and the end date is yesterday. The data has been exported to a spreadsheet. Using the videotapes from the security booth, Gary Zatanski had his men correct omissions and errors in the original log."

Ray fanned the tall stack of papers, useless information until plate numbers were connected to vehicles and drivers. "So, what's happening with this?"

"I've got Veitch working on this. Good thing we hired a geek deputy. He's checking the accuracy of the faculty and staff list we got from Zatanski. Then he's going to do a first run on those plates. We'll see if anything interesting pops up. I'm having him organize this data with a timeline showing Ashleigh's murder and the Medford fire. After he gets done with the first set of plates, he'll broaden the analysis, looking at the other plate numbers, but then it gets real complicated. There are hundreds of additional numbers."

"When is this all going to be done?"

"He should have the first piece completed this afternoon. The next part will take a lot of time. He's got to retrieve the info on each plate number and then key into his database the vehicle type and owner."

"And we have no way of knowing who actually was driving the car," Ray said.

"There's that," answered Sue, giving him a knowing smile. "Sort of like going to the casino."

"But even there you hit occasionally."

"True," she agreed. "Other than this plate thing, I've looked through everything several times. I've carefully reviewed the notes from each interview, the autopsy reports, and all the crime scene material. I keep expecting that something is going to jump off the page, that I'm going to make this gigantic cognitive leap and identify the killer."

Noticing that Ray was starting to nod off, she said, "You look like you need a nap."

"I'm okay."

"No, you're almost asleep in the chair. We'll get you in bed, and I'll run out to find you something interesting for dinner."

43

Ray was floating in a dream just below consciousness; it was an opium delusion. In waking moments he had been thinking about his dreams, how they differed as his system absorbed different opiates. The drugs took the edge off the pain and made it tolerable, but the relief came with a price. The drug dreams were bizarre, sometimes frightening, like a remote area of his brain had been opened, unleashing unknown demons.

In the dream Ashleigh was in a kayak on his right. They were paddling toward South Manitou Island. He was listening to her, having difficulty hearing her over the din of the wind and waves, but catching her meaning from her tone. Her conversation was punctuated with laughter, which had a joyful, musical quality. Ray glanced over at her, her auburn hair highlighted by the sun.

They neared the island and paddled along the steep rocky shore, looking for a place to land. They found a ribbon of sand in a protected cove and turned their boats toward the beach. Ray released his spray skirt, positioned his paddle on deck behind him, and prepared to pull himself out of the cockpit. As his bow hit the beach, he came out of the boat, sitting on the deck, one leg in the shallow water touching the bottom, the other resting in the boat.

As he looked over at Ashleigh, the world went gray—they were cloaked in dense, cold miasma. As she disappeared from his view, he could hear the panic in her voice. He jumped from his kayak and moved in her direction, splashing through the shallow water, but he couldn't find her. Ray stopped and listened, he could still hear her, there was fear in her voice, she was calling to him for help. He thought she said "father." Then there was only silence. He stood helplessly, staring into the gloom.

He woke with a start.

"Didn't mean to wake you," said Sue, peering into his bedroom from the open door, amused by the pile of books on his nightstand—a worn copy of Boswell's *Life of Johnson*, an early Michael Connelly mystery, a collection of Judith Minty's poetry, Jim Harrison's newest novel, and a book on Inuit kayaks. "I was checking on you."

He looked at his watch. "I didn't plan on going to sleep; I was trying to read. Must be the drugs."

"The drugs, the trauma, the kind of non-sleep you get in the hospital where people are messing with your body at all hours of the day and night. As I remember them, Dr. Feldman's instructions were to take it easy, keep your leg up, listen to some good music, read, and not think about work for several weeks."

"You did get my dinner?"

"Yes," she responded. "Portobello mushrooms with goat cheese and roasted red peppers on a freshly baked sourdough roll."

"And tea?"

"Yes, chamomile with honey, lemon, and some chopped ginger. Michelle knows how you like it. Do you want me to bring you a tray, or do you want sit at the table?"

Ray sat up and slowly slid his legs over the side of the bed. "I've been here long enough, I'll come to the table. Give me a few minutes."

By the time Ray emerged from his bedroom, Sue had the

food set out on the table, a simple rectangle of solid black walnut supported by an elegant central base. She helped him into his chair and took the crutches.

"What's that?" he asked pointing to her plate.

"That's a cheeseburger with gorgonzola and bacon, cottage fries, and a Diet Coke. I made two stops."

Ray gave her a look and moved his head from side to side. "You won't always have that load of hormones to protect you."

"But I do now, so I might as well enjoy it."

"Anything happen while I was unconscious?"

"I've got the first run from the plate numbers."

"Anything interesting?"

"Haven't looked at them. It's our first task to enjoy dinner; then we will look at plate numbers."

Ray watched Sue inhale her cheeseburger with great enthusiasm.

"Is your sandwich okay?" she asked, noticing that Ray was picking at his food.

"Nothing tastes quite right. I don't know if it's my sense of smell or taste—or both."

"You've been under anesthesia, and you're on pain pills. It will take a while to wash all the chemicals out of your system." She finished her dinner and waited patiently as Ray sipped his tea. "Are you done?" she finally asked.

"Yes. I want to look through the material you brought."

"Ray, we can do this tomorrow," said Sue as she rose to clear away the remains of dinner.

"Let's do it now." Ray pulled himself up and stood in the background, rocking back and forth on his crutches as he watched her sort through the pile of folders on the aluminum table. She identified and removed two folders from the stack, and laid out the pages from each one sequentially.

The photo of Ashleigh and her mother slid out of one of the other folders. Ray picked it up and looked at it carefully. He quietly put it back in the folder, hoping that Sue wouldn't comment. Although they were close friends and colleagues, he wasn't ready to talk to her about this. Not yet.

"This is what we have," she said, turning toward Ray. "Here," she pointed to six sheets on the left, "are the plate numbers recorded from the day and evening that Ashleigh and David were killed. In this column you'll see the name of the person to whom the vehicle is titled."

Ray moved to her side. He pulled a pair of reading glasses from the pocket of his robe and looked at the columns of fine print. "Only a few of these are identified by owner."

"Remember, I told you that we're starting with Leiston employees first, then adding the others later."

"Anything interesting?"

"I just had a few minutes to skim through these. Look at the names. Most of these are staff people who are coming to or leaving work. Remember, there were lots of parents visiting and a soccer game that Saturday, which probably accounts for the enormous number of unidentified plates. As you can see, this will take time, and I'm not sure it will yield anything."

"And this other pile?"

"That's from the night of the Medford fire. Six in the evening till six in the morning."

They both scrutinized the two sheets. "Lot of action between seven and seven-thirty," said Sue.

"Probably the kitchen staff was going home," said Ray. He pointed to a name, "Who's that?"

Sue ran her finger down a list of names. "That's McAndless, the English teacher. Left at nine, back at nine forty-five. Looks like a milk run." Sue scanned the bottom of the list. "The Warrington's Toyota left the school about . . ."

Ray, following her finger, completed her sentence, "Five in the morning."

"When did it return?" Sue asked

"Don't see it," said Ray.

"No, it's not there," she agreed. She ran a pencil carefully down the page.

"But Warrington was at the fire. I saw him, I talked with him. I wonder where he was going at that time?"

"Maybe it was his wife. That's something I'll follow up on tomorrow," Sue replied.

44

~~~~

A security detail under Sue's direction watched the exterior of Ray's house; Sue also organized Ray's colleagues and friends to be around the first few days after he came home from the hospital. Nora Jennings, now ensconced in the village with her friend Dottie, was two minutes from his hilltop home. With her dogs Falstaff and Prince Hal in tow, Nora was a frequent visitor in the late morning and early afternoon. Her main responsibility was to see to his lunch.

A volunteer at the village library, Nora filled part of her time organizing and shelving Ray's large collection of books, many still in boxes from his move the previous summer.

Ray was drinking tea in the late morning when Nora came to his side with a copy of Joyce's *Ulysses*. "Ray," she said in a tentative tone as she placed the book in front of him, "This photo fell out when I was shelving this book. I hope it wasn't being used as a bookmark."

Ray took the photo from her hand and looked at it carefully. The color was faded, like a half-forgotten dream, but the subject of the photo and the place were instantly recognizable. A young woman in a black two-piece bathing suit was in profile, the expanse of Lake Michigan and the Empire dune the backdrop. He remembered the day, he remembered walking the beach with her, their picnic on a ridge overlooking Otter Creek. Holding the photo closer, he looked at her face for a long time. A tremor ran through his body, he could hardly breathe. He had first seen Allison's photo when he and Sue searched Ashleigh's apartment. That photo was of a slightly older Allison, a woman with an almost adolescent child. The photo in his hand was of the person he had known for a few fleeting days one August.

"Are you okay, Ray?" Nora asked, sensing that something was horribly wrong, fearing that he was having a stroke or a heart attack.

"Yes," he finally responded.

"Can I get you something, some more tea, perhaps?"

"I'm fine," he responded in a thin voice.

"May I?" she asked, lifting the photo from his hand and slipping her glasses on. "I remember her, she was a friend of our daughter."

"Tell me about her."

"Oh, Ray, that was a long time ago. She was one of Jeannie's up north friends, not someone from home." She paused a long moment. "Her last name was, let me think, Ashton. Yes, Ashton. I met her mother a few times at parties. She was a niece of Mrs. Howard; they stayed with her. They lived out west somewhere, Oregon or Washington.

"Her name?"

"Which one, the mother or the daughter?"

"The daughter?"

"Her first name, she went by a nickname, something with a 'y' ending. Buffy or Taffy or . . ."

"Allie," suggested Ray.

"Allie, yes, that's it. Her given name would have probably been Allison or Alicia, maybe Alice. But I can't remember anyone ever calling her anything but Allie. The picture, Ray, why do you have her picture?"

Ray hesitated as he considered what he wanted to divulge. "I met her one summer. We dated for a few weeks. She was in graduate school at Berkeley. She gave me that book, and I must have put her picture there. But that was so many years ago."

"You gave me start a moment ago," Nora said. "You looked so strange."

"It's the medicine," said Ray. "It makes me feel queasy."

While Ray had welcomed Nora's company, now he wanted her gone. He needed some time to think, to gather things, to search for answers. He had been blocking his memories of Allison, not wanting to deal with the emotions the memories might evoke.

"Nora, I'm exhausted. Maybe you and the guys could leave me for a while. It's hard for me to sleep when anyone is here."

"Are you sure you are okay?"

"Yes. I couldn't sleep last night, and I think I've finally crashed."

"How about lunch, Ray? It's almost time. I've brought fixings for Welsh rarebit and a Caesar salad."

"Maybe if you came back in a couple of hours."

"My guys were hoping for leftovers, but we'll do that."

Ray waited a few minutes after Nora left, then rolled his wheelchair into the third bedroom. One side of the floor was littered with boxes containing personal things—notes, correspondence, and memorabilia—from the last thirty years, most untouched since the move. As he looked at the clutter he remembered there was no apparent order. The more recent accumulations were stored in computer paper boxes, regular shapes and sizes, the tops neatly sealed with transparent packing tape. The things from his twenties were in a motley collection of cardboard containers, deepening shades of brown suggesting relative antiquity.

Handicapped by his lack of mobility, Ray struggled to see the contents of the boxes from the confines of his wheelchair. Finally, in frustration, he set the brakes on the chair and carefully slid to the floor. Scooting in a crayfish-like manner, dragging the heavy cast behind, he moved from box to box, tearing open the flaps, leafing through the detritus of decades long past: graduate school notes, snapshots, brochures, prints, and maps from his travels around Europe and England.

Finally, he found what he was looking for, a small paper carton. He carefully removed the contents: letters and cards from the years he served in the military and later when he was in graduate school. He laid these out on the floor around him, stopping to examine and read some of them. Then it surfaced, a small envelope addressed in a delicate hand. There was no return address, just a faded California postmark.

He removed a single page of stationery.

> *Dear Ray, Thank you for a very special time. Perhaps we will meet again in the future. Enjoy your last year in Europe.*
> *Love, Allison*

Ray piled the rest of the letters and cards in the box. He put the letter back in the envelope and slid it into the pocket of his robe. He struggled into the wheelchair. Once back in the kitchen, he abandoned the chair for a pair of crutches. From Sue's carefully arranged table of documents, he retrieved a copy of Ashleigh Allen's birth certificate. Ray checked the mother's name, Allison Ashton. "Allison," he said softly. No father was listed.

Ray hobbled into his study and slipped into the chair next to his computer, waited impatiently for the computer to boot, then opened a calendar program. He clicked on the "view date" icon, entered Ashleigh's birth date, and printed the calendar for that month and the preceding ten months. He carried the papers to the kitchen and laid them out on the counter.

Ray looked at the date of the postmark, September 4, a few weeks after she had left, and did the math. He closed his eyes and let the memories come streaming back.

They had met the third week of August on the beach. He was home from Europe, on a month-long furlough, before he went back to serve the last year of his enlistment. Through an unexplained twist of fate, he had been assigned to a military police unit in Germany; most of the people he had trained with had gone to Vietnam.

Allison told him she was visiting relatives in the area. Ray remembered her deep tan, rich blue eyes, and the swirl of her long auburn hair. When he first met her, there was an unopened copy of Joyce's *Ulysses* on the sand next to her towel. He used his limited knowledge of Joyce as a gambit to start a conversation. He learned that she was staying with her aunt and that she had gone to Sarah Lawrence and was now a graduate student in English at Berkeley.

Now, as he stood at the kitchen counter, memories came flowing back: Allison's gorgeous smile; her warm laugh; her lovely, resonant voice. And there was also a hint of sadness that he never quite understood.

For the next two weeks they met almost daily. He was the tour guide, taking her to all his favorite beaches from Arcadia to Northport. They climbed the dunes, walked the sandy shorelines, and ate picnics that he carefully packed for each day's excursion. And each evening, before it was dark, he returned her to her car at the beach in Empire and watched her drive away.

The day before she flew back to California, she met him in the late afternoon. This time she brought the picnic in a large wicker hamper—cucumber and watercress sandwiches and a bottle of French champagne. They found a protective alcove in the ridge of sand high above the beach. They ran down to the beach, swam out to the second sand bar, and played in the rolling surf until they were thoroughly chilled by the Lake Michigan water. They toweled off and, hand in hand, walked the beach for more than an hour.

Tired and hungry they returned to their bower high above the shore and ate, sipped champagne, and watched the sun slowly descend toward the horizon. There were bits of conversation and long periods of silence. In the final glow of the setting sun Allison crawled on top of him and kissed him passionately. He felt her pull her top loose, her warm breasts falling against his bare chest. She moved her moist lips along his neck and then kissed him again, her tongue meeting his. Even with the passing of so many years, Ray could remember the intensity of their lovemaking. They stayed for several more hours, wrapped in a blanket, looking at the stars, and talking quietly. At her urging they finally returned to their cars. As he held her door, she retrieved the copy of *Ulysses*. "A small gift," she said. Then they embraced for a last time. Ray remembered standing a long time, watching the taillights of her car disappear.

A few days after her departure a letter arrived—general delivery—at the village post office. There was no return address, just a California postmark. He remembered reading the two-sentence note several times, standing on the sidewalk in front of the post office. The letter was in his shirt pocket when he boarded the North Central Airlines flight in Traverse City on his way back to Germany. The copy of *Ulysses* was in his bag. He thought that after he was mustered out, he'd go to California and find her. But it never happened. A year later he was starting graduate school and trying to find ways to support himself. He picked up construction jobs during the summer and worked as a bouncer in a campus bar the first few terms. Eventually he picked up work as a teaching assistant and did legwork on some of his professors' funded research projects.

During the next several years, on the occasional weekends Ray came north, he looked for Allie. And a number of times during the ensuing decades he thought he caught sight of her in Leland, or Empire, or Glen Arbor, or Frankfort. But when he got close, it was always someone else—similar hair color, or facial structure, but not Allie.

Ray thought back to what Jack, the owner of the Last Chance, had said, that the local boys didn't hit on Ashleigh because they knew she was out of their class. That's probably what kept him from pursuing Allison; she was out of his class, beyond his milieu. His feelings of love and loss were mitigated by fears of humiliation and thoughts of inadequacy. He recognized long ago that he was into his thirties before he got beyond the psychological constraints of growing up poor in the woods of northern Michigan.

45

Nora Jennings met Sue in the driveway as she and her dogs were leaving Ray's house after she had returned and made him lunch. "I'm glad to see you," Nora said. "I'm concerned about Ray; he doesn't seem himself. I think you need to get him to the doctor."

"What's going on?" asked Sue.

"He's tense and tetchy. I've never seen Ray like this. He's behaving like my Hugh did before he had his stroke."

"How about his lunch—is he eating?"

"He made me go away for several hours, said he needed sleep. When I came back, he was up, asking me to mail this package," Nora showed Sue a package she had been carrying between the handles of her picnic basket. "I don't think he ever really napped. It was half past two when I finally served him lunch. I made him Welsh Rarebit, it's something he loves. And he just picked at it."

"I'll keep an eye on him," Sue responded. "He's lucky he has such a good friend, Nora. Thanks." She opened the tailgate of Nora's Explorer and helped her with the ponderous basket. She lifted the package off the top, scanned the addressee, *Orchid Genescreen,* and held it out to Nora. "Do you want this back here?"

"No, I'll take it up front. I promised Ray I'd get this in the mail this afternoon."

Sue stood by as Nora loaded the dogs in the back. She wondered about the contents of the mysterious package as she watched Nora's vehicle disappear down the steep drive. Then she looked toward Ray's house; she loved the small dwelling's clean, modern design and the way it blended with the wooded hillside.

Entering, she found Ray in the kitchen, sitting in his wheelchair, his leg elevated.

"I thought we were going to Leiston this morning," he snapped.

"There were other things that needed to be done."

"Well, why didn't you call and tell me?"

"I tried. Your landline was busy, and your cell was turned off." Sue sat down next to him and looked into his eyes. "Ray, are you taking the pain pills?"

"Yes."

"Today?"

"Maybe not today."

"Why not?"

"They make me feel depressed, cloud my thinking. So, where have you been?" he demanded.

"Let's see," Sue looked off at the ceiling, as if she was trying to remember; she then responded in a mocking tone. "What did I do this morning? I had my nails done. Then I went in for a massage. Those hot rocks, Ray, you've got to try them. And then the facial. I had my hair touched up. Let's see, after that I met some of the girls for lunch and . . ."

"Okay, okay, enough. Tell me what you were really doing."

"All your paperwork. Reviewing timesheets, signing off on the payroll, completing requisitions. I will be so glad when you are well, and I can hand this all back to you."

"I thought we were going to visit Warrington?"

"We are, but there are other things that need to be done. And there have been some new developments."

"What kind of developments?" Ray asked, his tone finally becoming less grumpy.

I don't know if this is in any way related to the case, but some incredible things have happened this morning," Sue said as she pulled a stack of 8-by-11 sheets from her soft leather case. She laid them out in front of Ray and, moving from left to right, started her briefing. "Early on I did criminal checks on the faculty and staff at Leiston."

"I remember," said Ray, nodding.

"I've now gone a step further."

"Meaning?"

"Curricula vitae. The curricula vitae for the faculty members and the administration are posted on the Leiston School website. I started checking them, Ian Warrington first." She took a paper clip off the first group of papers.

"Nothing much on Warrington. He got his degrees when he said he did. His job history has no discrepancies. Interesting enough, his publications seem to be padded a bit."

"What do you mean?"

"His record of publications is extensive and looks very impressive," she pointed to a long list of bibliographic citations, "but I couldn't find many of them. I think he even made up the names of a few journals."

"Unfortunately, that happens in the academic world," observed Ray.

"Your friend, Sarah James, seems to be who she says she is," Sue said in a light tone.

"Good," said Ray, allowing her statement to pass without comment.

"But Helen Warrington," she said, her tone becoming serious, "there are some major problems with her resume."

"How so?"

"According to the information on the Leiston website, Helen did her undergraduate and graduate work at Wisconsin, and she holds a Ph.D. in clinical psychology. But the woman I talked to at

UW could find no record that Helen had ever been enrolled in the graduate school."

"You had her maiden name?" Ray asked.

A long silence followed. Sue looked mildly irritated.

"Sorry," Ray said.

"Her maiden name is Gardner, Helen Gardner. The woman in the registrar's office then did a search using Helen's social security number. It turns out she did go to Wisconsin, but she dropped out in the middle of her junior year."

"Did you confront Warrington with this?"

"I was going to, but I got a call from Helen's sister, a Mary Hayden. She lives in San Diego. She had been trying to reach her sister, and Warrington told her that he hadn't seen Helen for several days and didn't know where she was."

"What?" asked Ray in an incredulous tone.

"That's right. Hayden called, wondering if she could file a missing person's report. She was upset that Warrington did not seem concerned about his wife's disappearance and felt something strange was going on. I took down the pertinent data and was indirectly able to learn a lot about Helen."

"Like?"

"She has a long history of mental illness, alcoholism, and drug abuse. She left college before graduation and spent years in and out of the Menninger Clinic." Sue stopped and looked at Ray, "You know about the Menninger Clinic?"

"Yes," he responded.

"I didn't," she continued. "I had to look it up on the Internet. Guess its got a big reputation in mental health circles. Anyway, eventually Helen returned to college part-time at the University of Kansas and got a degree in art history. I asked if she had done any graduate work."

"And?"

"Nada."

"Mary is the older sister and says that she and Helen haven't been in close contact for a number of years, but in the last few months Helen had seemed more interested in reestablishing a relationship; they had been phoning on a weekly basis. Mary said she sensed that things weren't right with Helen."

"But she hasn't been out to visit?"

"No. She's never been here. She's offered to come, but Helen discouraged her."

"Did you ask her about Warrington, their marriage, that type of . . ."

"Yes," she responded, placing a carefully printed page of notes in front of Ray. "Mary said that after Helen married Warrington, she didn't seem to want any contact with her or other members of the family. So, she couldn't tell me much about the marriage. I did learn that they've been married for about seven years, and they supposedly met on a flight from Chicago to L.A. or San Francisco. I also learned that Helen had inherited a fairly substantial sum of money when her mother died."

"I think we should pay Mr. Warrington a visit."

"We can do that. But first you have to shower and shave."

"That takes so long, Sue. I have to cover my cast with this plastic . . ."

"Ray, do you want me to play Nurse Kratchet?"

"I'll take a shower," he answered and moved off toward his bedroom.

46

It was late afternoon by the time Ray completed his ablutions and they drove over to Leiston School. Ian Warrington was standing outside his office talking to a student in an otherwise empty hall as Ray, Sue at his side, came slowly hobbling down the hall on crutches. Warrington quickly ended his conversation and moved to greet them.

"Sheriff, I'm surprised to see you up and around. I was enormously concerned when I heard about your injuries." He reached up and placed a hand on Ray's shoulder.

"We need to talk, Dr. Warrington," Ray responded.

"Yes, yes, of course," said Warrington, slowing his normally brisk pace as he led them to his office. "Why don't you sit here, I think it's probably the most comfortable chair?"

"I think I'll stand, it's easier. What we have to talk about won't take long."

"So, how can I help you?" responded Warrington, his tone cooler and becoming guarded.

"Would you ask your wife to step in here for a few minutes; we've found some discrepancies in the vitae she posted on the Leiston website. We'd like her help in clearing them up," said Ray.

"She's not here right now," Warrington responded, a mild look of panic spreading across his face. "She's away."

"Away where?"

"At a professional conference. Philadelphia, a conference of independent schools."

Ray waited for several moments, holding Warrington in his gaze. "Where is your wife?"

"I've just told you."

"You're a very poor liar, Dr. Warrington. Where is your wife?"

Warrington remained silent. He looked at the floor and then looked back up at Ray. "I don't know."

"What do you mean, you don't know?"

"Just that," he paused. "Sheriff, my wife is an alcoholic. Occasionally she disappears for a while. And it would kill her to know I'm telling you this. She's a very private person."

"This has happened before?"

"Yes, many times." Warrington stared at the floor, resigned to the sheriff's questioning.

"How long is she usually gone?" probed Ray.

"Some times a few days, sometimes a week or more."

"Where does she go, what does she do?"

"She drives off somewhere. Two, three, fours hours away, far enough that I can't easily find her. She buys enough liquor to stay smashed for days, checks into a motel, and drinks until she runs out of booze."

"And then?"

"She eventually starts sobering up. Is embarrassed by what she's done and calls AA for help. When she's back in control, she phones me to tell me she's on her way home. She goes away so no one can see she has this problem. It would annihilate her if people knew. She wants everyone to believe she's flawless."

"When did you last see your wife, Mr. Warrington?" Ray asked.

"Saturday, last Saturday, the day after the fire. I came over here to do some work. When I went back to the house she was gone."

"When was that?" Sue asked.

"After lunch, probably before two."

"And the car was gone, also?" she pursued.

"Yes, I was planning to run to town, but she had taken it. I ended up using one of the school's vans."

"Did she leave a note?" Ray asked.

"No. Actually, I wasn't worried until evening. I thought she'd gone off somewhere and forgotten to tell me beforehand."

"She's been gone almost a week and you didn't consider . . ."

"Sheriff, this has almost become the norm. I didn't think there was any special reason for concern."

"And even the events of the last two weeks . . ."

"No, in fact they made things even more understandable. This is all more than poor Helen can take."

"We've had a call from a Mary Hayden who identified herself as Mrs. Warrington's sister. She was concerned that she couldn't reach Helen, and she stated that you have been less than helpful. She's filed a missing person's report."

"Really, well . . ." Warrington paused. "Mary is quite meddlesome, and I don't think the situation is improved by having her mucking about. Helen's been clear with me that she wants no one to know about these episodes, and she means no one, not even her own sister. Helen's public image is vitally important to her—it's the one thing she can hang onto, it seems, and gossip or her sister's intrusions would only exacerbate her drinking problem. It could push Helen over the edge. I think most of Helen's problems go back to a very troubled childhood."

Sue and Ray left Warrington in his office and slowly retreated down the two long hallways to the mansion's entrance. With Sue's help Ray settled into the car seat and gingerly pulled his casted leg into the vehicle. Sue closed the passenger side door after he was finally situated and belted. She noted the perspiration on his face. He looked clammy.

"We should get you back in bed. This isn't what you're supposed to be doing," she said as she slid into the driver's seat and prepared to start the car.

"Interesting that Helen Warrington disappears after the Medford fire. We need to talk to her. Put out an APB."

Ray allowed his body to collapse against the seat and closed his eyes.

"I thought you'd ask Warrington about Helen's being a psychologist," said Sue.

"It can wait. There are other things I'm more interested in than her padded credentials," responded Ray without opening his eyes. "Warrington has spent so much time lying to cover for Helen that I doubt if he remembers what's truth and what's fabrication."

"How about the disappearance bit?" Sue asked.

"That's probably true. We need to find her."

Sue started the engine. "I'm taking you home so you can get that leg up. I'll go back to the office and get the APB out. Are you covered for dinner?"

"Marc and Lisa are coming over." Ray turned his head toward Sue. "Seems like I'm in custodial care. I've even noticed that there's a deputy lurking about all the time, too."

Sue smiled, but she didn't respond.

47

Ray was sleeping when Marc and Lisa arrived. He slowly became aware of noise from the kitchen, the sounds of food being warmed and carefully modulated conversation. Eventually his bedroom door was partially opened, a wedge of soft light illuminating the sparsely furnished room.

"Ray, are you awake?" asked Marc in a muted voice.

"Yes," Ray answered in a drowsy tone as he slowly pulled the world back into focus, the effects of exhaustion and prescription pain pills dulling his responses.

"It's after eight," came Marc's voice again. "Do you want dinner, or do you want to sleep through?"

"I better eat," responded Ray.

"Do you need help getting up?"

"No, I'm all right. Just give me a few minutes."

Ray carefully positioned himself, getting his good leg off the side of the bed and onto the floor, followed by the casted leg. After using the toilet, he combed his hair and looked at his worn face in the mirror.

The lines in his face seemed deeper than he remembered, and he was startled by the bags under his eyes. The loss of several pounds over the last week added to his gaunt appearance. Pulling on a fleece robe, he scuffled out on crutches.

Marc and Lisa, seated on the suede-covered couch, wine glasses in hand, rose to greet him. Marc helped Ray get settled in the wheelchair, elevated the left leg, and deftly positioned him at the dinner table.

After filling the wine glass in front of him, Lisa commented, "You can have a full glass tonight, I don't think you're going to get called out."

Without saying a word, Ray pulled a pill bottle from the pocket of his robe and pointed to a sticker on the side of the bottle. Lisa took the bottle from his hand, looked at the sticker, and handed it back.

"Anyone who continues to put himself in harm's way the way you do, can take a chance on mixing chemicals," she said in a tone that was devoid of her usually playful mocking. "But I promise that we will not allow you to operate machinery or drive."

Lisa watched Ray sample the wine, usually a precise ritual of swirling, looking at the color, sniffing the bouquet several times, and taking a small sip. Ray lifted the glass and took several large swallows; he paused a few seconds and drained the glass, setting it back on the table.

Without commenting, Lisa filled the glass a second time. She drifted back to the counter and uncorked a second bottle.

"I thought you probably needed comfort food, Ray. I made lamb stew, with new potatoes, and baby carrots," Marc explained as he worked at the stove.

"And a salad, a fresh baguette, and a very special dessert," continued Lisa.

Ray, halfway through his second glass of wine, paused. "I'm lucky to have such good friends."

Marc served the lamb in large steaming bowls, Lisa refilled the wine glasses, and they quietly settled into the meal. Conversation was unusually subdued.

After the bowls had been cleared away, Marc set a board

with a collection of English artisan cheeses on the table with a basket of assorted biscuits. Lisa removed the wine glasses and poured a tawny port into some clean glasses, setting the carafe on the table. Ray lifted the carafe and examined the richly colored liquid. Then he carefully looked at the cheeses. "A Colson Bassett Stilton, a farmhouse cheddar, and some Lancashire. Did someone make a special run to Ann Arbor?"

"Marc called Zingerman's yesterday, said it was a life or death emergency, and the package arrived FedEx this morning just before noon."

"And the port?" Ray asked.

"That's a bottle Marc has been saving for a special occasion."

"We're celebrating the survival of a dear friend," said Marc, without commenting on the somber mood in which they seemed to find themselves.

During the long silence that followed, they helped themselves to cheese and biscuits.

Finally Ray said, "This port is extraordinary. And the cheese, the stew, everything is wonderful. Thank you." He sipped the port and set it back on the table. "There's something I need to talk about."

Marc and Lisa waited in silence.

"And I don't know where to begin. I won't insult you by saying it needs to stay here, because I know you will never talk about what I'm going to tell you. But this is extremely painful to talk about."

"Do what you're comfortable with," said Marc.

"The dead woman, Ashleigh Allen." Ray stopped and reached for the copy of *Ulysses* at the end of the table. He opened the book and took the faded photo out and handed it across to Lisa. She studied it closely and passed it to Marc.

"That's Allison Ashton, Ashleigh's mother," explained Ray.

"With Empire Bluff in the background. Where did you get the photo?" asked Lisa.

"I took it," he said. "I had an old Leica that Marc's grandfather gave me when I went into the Army."

Ray carefully detailed his brief relationship with Ashleigh's mother, Allison. He also mentioned that during the early stages of the murder investigation he learned that Ashleigh's mother had died of cancer at a young age. After he finished, he passed copies of Ashleigh's birth certificate and a calendar so Marc and Lisa could do the math. With the calendar between them, they worked backward from the birth date.

A long silence followed. Marc drained his port and refilled his glass. "But you never heard from her again?" asked Lisa.

"Only this note," answered Ray, "that I got shortly after she left." He handed it Lisa. She inspected the envelope and postmark and scanned the short letter. Marc also examined them.

Neither was quick to respond.

"And you don't think there is any other way you can interpret this data?" asked Marc.

"Can you?" Ray responded.

"Probably not," said Lisa, looking empathetically at Ray. "What are you feeling," she asked, wiping a tear with her right hand.

Ray looked up to the ceiling and tried to find the words for the feelings he'd kept behind a wall of denial and disbelief. "Loss, confusion, enormous sadness," he responded. "I'm trying to understand what I'm feeling. I continue to ask questions for which there are no answers. Why didn't I pursue her? Why didn't she contact me? I have so many thoughts running through my brain; I have difficulty sorting them out."

"But you would have been back in Europe by the time she discovered she was pregnant," said Lisa.

"Probably, but she could have found me. I wasn't incommunicado. I was very taken with her, I would have adjusted my life to this situation."

He paused for a long moment. "She didn't want me as part of her life or part of her child's life."

"You don't know that Ray," said Lisa. "When you met her you weren't involved with anyone else?"

"No."

"But you don't know about her, do you?" she pursued.

"No."

"What if she was?"

"Are you suggesting that she might have been pregnant?"

"It's a possibility," Lisa responded. "Suppose she was involved with someone at the time she met you. And then she has a brief summer romance with you. She goes back to California and reconnects with her love interest. Soon after she finds out that she's pregnant. She might have become impregnated before she left California or soon after she returned. There weren't DNA tests back then."

"No," responded Ray. "On the birth certificate Ashleigh has her mother's family name, there is no father listed."

"Where did the Allen come from?" asked Marc.

"Ashleigh's stepfather. They were married shortly after Ashleigh's birth and divorced about a year later. We could find no record that he formally adopted her."

"What do you know about him?" asked Lisa.

"Little more than rumors. He was supposedly one of Allison's graduate professors."

"Well," said Lisa, "I don't want to go through all of our sexual histories, but wouldn't it have been possible when you or I or Marc were in our early twenties and our hormones were maxed to be involved with someone, and then go off on a trip and meet another person? And if the moon were right and the wine was good, after some time getting to know this new person . . ."

"Yes," Ray agreed, "but why wouldn't she contact me?"

"That's unanswerable. And if she had another lover, she might not have known who the father was. You're extremely responsible and caring. You would have done the right thing, whatever that might have been. If she is your daughter, it's a pity you didn't know her, and it's equally sad that she didn't know you."

Lisa paused and looked over at Ray. "How are you holding up?" she asked.

"Probably on the surface I look okay. I'm able to keep going."

"But below the surface?" pressed Lisa.

"I want to scream, cry. Sometimes I want to break something or get drunk. I want to find her killer. I want vengeance."

"Sounds reasonable," said Lisa.

"What do I do now?" Ray asked

"You might want to start with DNA," observed Marc.

"I've done that. I'll know in ten to fourteen business days."

48

~~~

Ray was awakened by the smell of coffee brewing. He could see light under the bedroom door, a door that had been standing open after Marc helped him to bed. He looked at his wristwatch; it was a few minutes before 10:00 a.m. As the world slowly came into focus, he became aware of a throbbing headache. *Hangover,* he thought. He could not remember the last time he had had a hangover, but the symptoms were clear.

A gentle knock was followed by the door opening a few inches. "Ray," came Sue's voice.

"I'm awake," he responded. "What's happening?"

"I found Helen," said Sue with great excitement, moving into the room.

"Found who?"

"Helen Warrington," answered Sue. "And guess who she's keeping company with?"

"Who?" Ray grumped.

"Denton Freeler."

"What? Help me get up," he commanded, followed by a slightly contrite, "please."

Sue helped get Ray onto his crutches.

She was pouring coffee when he emerged from the bathroom. He hobbled to the counter.

"You okay?" she said. "You look kinda rough."

"Hard night," he responded without elaborating. "Helen Warrington, Denton Freeler. What's going on?"

"Lots," said Sue, opening a folder with her neatly typed notes. "I went back to the office last night and entered the info on Helen Warrington into the National Crime Information Center. And as I was doing the paperwork for the APB, it suddenly hit me. I had one of those—your favorite term—cognitive leaps."

"What?" said Ray, still in a bit of a fog.

"Remember we had the names of two kids who were possible suspects in vandalizing Ashleigh's kayak?"

"Yes. One of the kids is in Europe studying and the other is dead," responded Ray.

"That's right. We didn't pursue that any further."

"So, you think the kid came back from Europe? What's his name?"

"Jay Hanson, and no, he didn't come back from Europe. Although the thought crossed my mind. It would be easy enough, eight hours to Detroit Metro, an hour to Traverse City, back to Italy the next day. But no, it's the other boy, Denton Freeler. We never went any further with him because we were told he was dead."

Sue paused and looked at Ray. "And where did the information about his death come from?" she asked.

"Leiston's alumni office—Helen Warrington," muttered Ray.

"Exactly. I called your friend Sarah James at home. I asked if I could stop by and talk to her. And when I got there I asked if she would allow me to look through Denton Freeler's records. We walked over to the office; fortunately Warrington wasn't about. She took me into a secure area where they store student records. We found his class year. And guess what?"

"What?" responded Ray.

"Freeler's name and social security number were on the folder, but it was completely empty. I asked Sarah if there was a policy of removing the records of deceased students. There isn't."

"Interesting. You're still not quite sure of Sarah, are you?"

"I was just being cautious; I think she's okay. When I got back to the office I did some quick checking. Someone named Denton Freeler has a Michigan driver's license, and there's a light-green Jeep Wrangler Sahara registered in his name. The social security number matches."

"Anything else?" Ray asked.

"Yes, he has a permit to carry."

"Wonderful, all the nuts want handguns. Address?"

"An apartment in Royal Oak," she responded. "So, going back to Jay Hanson . . ."

"I thought you dismissed him," observed Ray.

"I did. You know I talked to his mother on the phone, and she was very helpful and happy to tell me about Jay. She also told me that Ms. Allen had been a major influence in her son's life. Late yesterday afternoon, I called her back and told her I wanted to talk to Jay, that something had happened his senior year that might have some relevance to the investigation. She became a bit wary and was much less effusive, but after some gentle persuasion, she gave me his cell number. I called him immediately. I think I awakened him—time difference. He told me some amazing stuff."

"Like?" Ray asked, fully awake and focused on Sue.

"Like he and Denton were roommates. Hanson said Denton was a big, tough kid with a violent streak and that he was afraid of him. He also said Denton had a major drinking problem, and his family had somehow gotten him into Leiston after he got into big time trouble with the police in Birmingham. And here's the capper," she paused.

"Yes," said Ray.

"He was under a court order to go to AA meetings twice a week, and the school psychologist, Helen Warrington, accompanied him."

"Oh my God," responded Ray.

"And there's more. Freeler bragged to Jay that they only went to AA meetings for a couple of months. But by late fall they were going over to Denton's family cottage, smoking dope, drinking, and having sex. Hanson said Freeler was always bragging about how older women were hot for him. He also said that Freeler was obsessed with Ashleigh Allen, boasting while he was in school that he would 'bag' her before they graduated."

"Did you ask him about the kayak trip?" Ray asked.

"I was just getting to that," said Sue. "Remember the sleeping bag incident, the Billy Wylder hypothermia thing?"

"Yes."

"Hanson told me that evening, after they had set up camp and made dinner, he and Freeler went off and got stoned. As they were wandering back, they saw Ashleigh on the beach shampooing her hair. Freeler told him to go back to the camp, this might be his best chance to make it with Ashleigh. Hanson said he went back to the tent he was sharing with Freeler and fell asleep. Freeler awakened him some time later. Hanson said Freeler was furious and said that he was going to get even with the dirty bitch. Hanson remembers Freeler leaving again before he fell back to sleep. The next morning, when the students went back to the beach to start packing their kayaks, they discovered that Ashleigh's boat had been damaged. Hanson was sure that Freeler had punched the holes in Ashleigh's kayak with a commando knife he brought on the trip."

"Did he know why?" Ray probed.

"No. He said he asked what happened, but Freeler wouldn't tell him. Hanson speculated that Freeler tried to hit on Ashleigh and got turned down. He added that if Freeler tried to get physical with her, Ashleigh would have easily handled him. "

"Anything else?"

"No," said Sue. "That's about all. Hanson told me he loved Leiston School, and he couldn't imagine that Ms. Allen had been murdered. And he said that rooming with Denton Freeler had ruined his senior year; that Freeler was one sick kid."

"Did Hanson know the location of Freeler's cottage?"

"He had been there and gave me the general location. Turns out it belongs to Freeler's paternal grandfather. With the information he gave me, I was able to get the township assessor to come in very early this morning to pull an address off the tax records.

"We've staked out the property, and our friends from the Coast Guard did a slow pass this morning. They go over that area almost every day on routine training flights, so it shouldn't have aroused suspicion. There are two vehicles next to the house, a Jeep Wrangler and a Toyota that looks a lot like the one the Warringtons own."

"Where is this place?" Ray asked, now fully awake.

"Near the county line, in the southwest corner, nestled between federal land and a state forest. It's almost a full section. Access into the property is via a two-track that crosses state land. It's not much more than a sand trail."

"Only one way in?" asked Ray.

Sue unfolded a map and spread it on the counter in front of him. "One two-track," she said pointing to a tiny line, "and a couple of old fire lanes." She traced these with a finger. "But I don't know how far you can get a vehicle down them. We met this morning at 8:00 and worked out plans. The SWAT team will be in place by noon. The road is blocked in case they try to leave."

She sat two 8-by-10-inch pictures on top of the map. "Here are a couple of photos the Coast Guard shot this morning. There are three outbuildings that we will use for cover. As soon as the operation is complete, I'll call you."

"You got me up to tell me you'll give me a call?"

"If I hadn't run the plans by you, you'd never have forgiven me. But in your condition . . ."

"Condition, hell."

"Ray, don't you think it would be better if . . ."

"I'm going to ride along," he responded, doing a foot-and-crutches dance toward the closet. "Get me that jacket, please."

Sue was going to protest, but could tell it was futile. She

pulled a dark-blue winter uniform jacket off the hanger and reached back in for a bulletproof vest.

"I won't need that," said Ray, motioning toward the vest.

"Put it on," said Sue, "or I won't give you a jacket." She waited as he struggled with the vest, then pulled a shoulder holster and handgun and radio off the top shelf. With her help he got the holster on and then the jacket. He turned the radio on and did a battery check. Sue guided him to her Jeep, pushed the passenger seat back to the end of its track, and carefully helped Ray in.

They rode in silence most of the way. Finally Ray said, "Feels like it's blowing."

"That's the forecast, high winds and heavy rain, maybe even a thunderstorm. A cold front is blowing down from Canada. The gales of November."

"It's not November yet."

"We're on the cusp," Sue said. "The leaves are mostly gone; the days are getting shorter. Color season's over, almost." She slowed, looking for a road, stopped, reversed, and made a right turn.

They slowly jolted up a trail for several hundred yards.

"This is the access road?" he asked.

"No, this is one of the fire lanes. We wanted to make sure they were both blocked." She stopped behind another police vehicle and killed the engine. "I'll be back in a bit," she said. "I'll let you know what's happened."

"Be careful."

"You know I will." Sue opened the rear hatch, grabbed her gear. For a minute or two he could see her heading up the road. Then she was gone.

Ray moved around trying to get comfortable; his leg was becoming increasingly painful. He wished he had taken some pain medicine before they left. He squirmed about for several more minutes trying to find a less excruciating position. Finally, he shoved his door open. He slid his trunk toward the driver's side and pushed the heavy cast out, supporting his body between the door and the seat until he got his footing with his left leg. He reached back over the seat and slowly extracted his crutches, one at a time. Then he grabbed the shotgun from the holster mounted below the dash, and checked to see if it was loaded. It was. Realizing he couldn't hold a shotgun and his crutches, he left it on the seat.

Ray moved off from the road, carefully working his way up a small rise. A large ash tree lay in his path. He turned and rested against the trunk. The wind was howling through the treetops, the dry leaves of late fall rattled in the gale, a few torn loose with each gust. They swirled around him as they drifted toward the ground. A dead branch came crashing to the earth near him.

Ray could see that this was the rolling terrain common to the first few miles inland from Lake Michigan's shore. There was a rumble of thunder in the distance, and a second, and a third. He watched the trees bend and dance before the approaching storm. The air was dense and smelled of autumn decay.

The sky went dark as the storm closed overhead. Thunder joined with the wind in the roaring cacophony. And then came the rain, heavy sheets pulsating off the big lake through the dense forest, pulling more leaves from the frenzied branches.

Ray pulled his jacket zipper to the top and positioned the bill of his hat low over his glasses. As he scanned the road through the heavy rain, he saw a figure running in his direction. He recognized Helen Warrington. He positioned his crutches carefully and slowly pulled himself up from the log.

He heard a door slam, and Sue's Jeep came to life. He started down the slope as the driver reversed, pulling off the road into the soft swampy underbrush in an attempt to turn in the opposite direction. Ray could hear the motor scream as the driver frantically rocked the vehicle in the soft sand. Ray steadied himself, unzipped his jacket, and reached for his gun. Helen Warrington leaped from the Jeep, clutching the shotgun with her right hand. Ray, off balance, took an unsteady aim in her direction. He was falling forward when he heard the blast of the shotgun. Acute pain exploded in his chest; he toppled backward unable to breath.

49

Ray had been dozing; he opened his eyes—again—to the harsh lights of the trauma center. Saul Feldman came into view.

"Tripping on pain meds again?" Feldman asked. "Have you considered a career in talk radio?"

Ray gave Feldman a weak smile.

"So, what were my orders?" the doctor asked. "Let me see, that was just a few days ago." Starting with his pinky and ending with his index thumb, he made his points with his hand, finger by finger. "Bed rest. No excitement. Keep your leg elevated. Take your meds. No alcohol. Return in two weeks so the orthopedist, Dr. Stewart, can make sure the bone is mending properly."

Ray didn't respond.

"I think this time we'll just keep you hospitalized for awhile, in traction, with your arms and legs handcuffed to the sides of the bed. And we'll put you on a special diet."

"I can hardly wait."

"Your favorite, tuna casserole made the old-fashioned way, three times a day."

"When you're done with your audition tape for Comedy

Central, I'd like to ask a question," grumped Ray, noticing the pain every time he inhaled.

"Shoot," responded Feldman.

"Bad pun," muttered Ray. "What's the verdict?"

"You have four cracked ribs and your chest is going to be black and blue for months. But if you hadn't been wearing a vest, we wouldn't be having this conversation. As for your leg, Dr. Stewart hasn't reviewed the films yet, but the radiologist said things look pretty good. The cast kept everything in place, thank God. You're lucky as hell, Ray." He let the comment sink in and then continued. "I'm going to admit you. You've had a major trauma, and I'd like to keep you under observation for a day or two. Let's run a few tests and consult with Dr. Stewart. Then we'll discuss how long you'll be with us. I'll be checking on you this evening."

After he left, Ray held the button, bringing the back of his bed up far enough that he could see West Bay over the houses and now leafless trees. The storm was still raging, the streets were wet and black, and headlights glistened off the pavement. He watched the whitecaps on the bay—pushed by a furious northwest wind—crash into the seawall that extended across the front of the vacant marina.

He turned as Sue entered the room.

"You okay?" she asked.

"Think so. How about you?"

"Yes," she answered, grasping his right hand between both of hers and giving him a gentle squeeze before she withdrew them to the side rail of the bed. Ray noticed two shiny balloons were tethered to the foot of the bed.

"I'm pretty foggy on what happened. How about a chronology?"

"Chronology, yes. Everything went as planned, at least at the beginning. We had all our assets in place. Using the outbuildings and the terrain in front of the cottage, everybody was in a protected position with a clear field of fire if it came to that. I called Helen's cell phone. It was turned off or dead; I got her voice mail. Then

I used the bullhorn, again no response. We waited and then teams moved to the front and rear entrances. On command, both doors were kicked open. We found Freeler in a bedroom. He was dead."

"Cause?"

"Hard to tell, the body was starting to go. Probably blood loss or infection."

"And Helen?"

"She wasn't in the house. In fact, she really caught us off guard. We were doing a final sweep when I saw her sprinting down the trail."

"Where had she been hiding?"

"After everything was over, we found a sleeping bag in a little sauna building way behind the house. My guess is that she spent a night or two there after Freeler died."

"So, you followed her?"

"Yes, Reilly was with me. Helen was way out ahead of us, and it was pouring rain. We didn't close the gap until she jumped in my Jeep and got it stuck. If she'd engaged the 4-wheel drive, she would have been out of there."

"I remember her climbing out with the shotgun, then things get fuzzy."

"She was focused on you, I don't think she saw us coming. It looked like you were getting your gun out when she fired. I saw you tumble backwards. I thought you were dead. Reilly and I fired. She went down."

"Is she . . . ?"

"She has two wounds, right shoulder and left thigh. She'll recover."

"How are you?"

"Starting to get gray hair," Sue said. "You were out cold when I got to you. I couldn't find any blood, but I could tell you were having trouble breathing. It only took a few minutes for the EMTs to get there, by then you were starting to come to. I can't tell you what I was feeling when you opened your eyes." Sue wiped away a tear and took Ray's hand again.

"So, now I've got an important job for you," Ray said in the firmest voice he could muster.

"What's that?"

"Get me the hell out of here. Please."

50

During the few days that Ray remained in the hospital and the additional week he stayed at home in semi-bed rest, Sue had pulled all the evidence together and prepared a concisely written review of the case. After a consultation, Dr. Feldman determined that Ray could start back to work—half-days for the first week, and then a more normal schedule.

And the first item on Ray's agenda was to meet with the prosecutor and review the Allen/Dowd murders. In preparation for this meeting Sue had—with her usual attention to order and detail—laid out all the physical evidence, photos, sketches, and supporting documents on the large table in the prosecutor's conference room. At the extreme right side of the table were a military-style rifle, shell casings, and a large hunting knife.

Sue provided a commentary as John Tyrrell, Cedar County prosecutor, viewed the evidence. Ray stood on the other side of the table, rocking on his crutches.

"Wouldn't you be more comfortable in a chair?" asked Tyrell, looking over at Ray.

"He should be sitting with that leg elevated, but he's impossible," said Sue. "Maybe if we put him on Ritalin . . ."

Tyrell look over at Ray. "She's starting to sound like a wife."

"Just a dedicated professional," Ray responded. "Detective Lawrence has done a wonderful job organizing all of this evidence.

"Okay guys, what do you got?" asked Tyrrell, focusing on the table.

"Denton Freeler's grandparents are very elderly and live in an assisted-living facility in Bloomfield Hills. The cottage is a seasonal home. Their attorney told me that she had arranged for a cottage service to winterize the place in late August. She had no idea Freeler was camping out there."

"So, he had the run of the place?" observed Tyrrell.

"That appears to be the case," said Ray. "His parents have been living abroad for more than a decade; they seldom come back to the states."

Tyrrell loomed over the weapons. "You found this at the cottage?" he asked, pointing to a large, commando-style knife.

"Yes," answered Sue. "I think our search for the murder weapon is finally over. The blade—its size and shape and the serration on the back—seem to be consistent with the wounds found on Allen and Dowd."

"How about this gun?" asked Tyrrell.

"It's a Bushmaster .223-caliber rifle," said Ray.

"Looks military."

"It's modeled after the M-16. It's marketed to ex-military types who are nostalgic for the weapon they had in the service," Ray said.

"Great, that's just what we need people running around with. The dumb fucks who support this kind of lunacy should have to clean up the carnage," said Tyrrell derisively.

"These will be going to the state police lab to verify that the brass," Sue pointed to the shell casings, "we collected on the dunes were fired from this weapon."

"And the knife?" asked Tyrrell.

"Yes, that too. Traces of the victims' blood might be on the knife and scabbard," Sue said.

Tyrrell opened the folder. "How about these photos?" he asked.

"The interior of the Freeler cottage. The top one is a wide angle of the scene, then I move in."

"Great viewing, especially after breakfast. Our looks don't improve as we decompose, do they?" Tyrrell observed as he leafed through the photos. "Cause of death?"

"We just have a preliminary autopsy report, but it appears he bled to death," said Sue.

"So, you really nailed him," Tyrrell said looking at Ray.

"The knife wounds would not have been mortal," Sue explained, "if Freeler had gotten medical attention in a reasonable amount of time."

"Why don't you think . . . ?"

"They were probably afraid to go to the ER," responded Sue. "That's one scenario, but perhaps they didn't realize or want to believe how badly he was wounded. There was also a large quantity of oxycodone."

"Which is?"

"It's a synthetic narcotic, similar to morphine," answered Ray. "It's often abused with alcohol. And there were lots of empty Scotch bottles in the cabin. He might have comfortably bled to death."

"Where did they get the drugs?" Tyrrell asked.

"We're still working on that," answered Sue. "They obviously had a good source and the money to buy them."

"And the woman?"

"Helen Warrington," interjected Sue.

"Tell me about her," said Tyrrell.

"Right," agreed Ray. "We're just putting that part of the case together. Things are still quite sketchy."

"Give me what you got."

Ray nodded to Sue.

"Well," Sue began. "This is where things get interesting."

"How is she now, by the way?" Tyrrell asked.

"Physically, she's recovering. But mentally, she's way out somewhere," Sue answered.

"Tell me about interesting," Tyrrell prompted.

"The bio on the Leiston website said she had a Ph.D. in clinical psychology from Wisconsin. But when I contacted them, I found that she dropped out her junior year," Sue explained.

"So, she wasn't a college graduate?"

"Actually, she was. She had a nervous breakdown and withdrew from school. This was shortly after her father died from alcoholism. Helen's mother had her admitted to Menninger Clinic . . ."

"Where's that?"

"Topeka, Kansas, at that time. It's moved to Texas. I had a long talk with her sister, Mary Hayden. She was very cooperative."

"How did you find her?" Tyrrell asked.

"She contacted us to file a missing person's report. She was indignant that Dr. Warrington didn't seem to know where his wife was."

"So, give me a quick history," Tyrrell said, looking impatient.

"According to Mary Hayden, Helen was in and out of Menninger Clinic for years." Sue read from her notes. "She suffered from what's now called a dual disorder."

"Dual disorder, what's that?"

"She had both severe psychiatric and addiction problems."

"Addicted to what?" Tyrrell asked.

"Initially it was alcohol, but she also abused prescription and street drugs from time to time. Mary said that Helen's condition would improve for months and then she would have a relapse. When things were going well she returned to college part-time, eventually getting a degree in art history from the University of Kansas. As far as Mary knew, Helen had no graduate training."

"So?" asked Tyrrell, looking a bit bored.

"She advertised herself as having a Ph.D. in clinical psychology and worked as the school psychologist her first year at Leiston."

"How did she get away with it, was her husband part of the . . . ?" Tyrrell left the fragment of his question hang.

"I don't know. Mary said Helen had a rich fantasy life. She was an enormously convincing liar and a very skillful manipulator," said Sue.

"And did the sister . . . ?"

"Mary."

"Did Mary think that Dr. Warrington knew about his wife's . . . ?"

"Mary said that she has had little contact with Helen for more than a decade. She met Ian once, briefly, at her mother's funeral. Helen and Ian were newlyweds at the time."

"And you've talked to Dr. Warrington?"

"Yes, and he's sticking with the story that he thought Helen was a certified psychotherapist. He says he met Helen on a plane from Chicago to L.A.—at the time he lived in Chicago and Helen in Kansas City. He says that when he first met her she told him she was a clinical psychologist, that her specialty was multiple personality disorders.

"Dr. Warrington said they had a long-distance relationship for about a year, then she moved to Chicago, and they married. Shortly after that, her mother died. Warrington said Helen wanted to take some time off from working, and money wasn't a problem. By his account the first few years of their marriage were happy, and then Helen started falling off the wagon and having psychological problems. When he took the job at Leiston School, he encouraged her to take the school psychologist position. He thought working again might get her back on track, but before the first year was over he could see that it was just exacerbating her problems."

"Anything else?"

"He said the last six months have been especially difficult—Helen had become extremely difficult. He's been trying to figure out how to deal with the situation."

"What's her connection to this Freeler kid?

"When Helen Warrington was the psychologist at Leiston, she treated Denton Freeler. Denton Freeler's former Leiston roommate says that Denton bragged that his relationship with Helen Warrington involved drinking, drugs, and sex. We do know that his records disappeared from Leiston's files and assume that Helen removed them. Also, he was listed as deceased in the alumni file, and we assume that Helen made the change. And for the last few months he's been living in the area."

"How about Freeler?"

"I'm still trying to put that together, I've only got bits and pieces."

"His parents, didn't they know what was going on?" ask Tyrrell.

"His father works in Saudi Arabia. I talked to him on the phone—this is after their attorney informed them of his death. Very strange call," said Sue.

"How so?"

"There was no emotion. He didn't seem particularly upset by the death of his son. He said that Denton had been a very troubled child and a difficult teenager. After high school, he had flunked out of several colleges. His father said they did what they could to help him while he was growing up, but at some point Denton had to take responsibility for his own life."

"Did the father know he was living at his grandparents' cottage?"

"No, last he heard Denton had an apartment in Royal Oak and was going to the local community college. He said they had instructed their attorney to provide Denton with tuition money and a living allowance."

"So, let's cut to the chase. How did Helen Warrington and Freeler hook up? What provoked these crimes?"

"There's much we don't know; we are still collecting facts." Ray answered. "We believe that their relationship began when Freeler was a student at Leiston School. Based on the account of his former roommate, Jay Hanson, Freeler became involved with Helen Warrington when she was functioning as the school psychologist. Warrington, in addition to providing therapy, also accompanied Freeler to AA meetings. Freeler bragged to his roommate that rather than going to AA, he and Helen went to his family cottage for drinking and sex. That was more than three years ago. We don't know when they reconnected or when Freeler came back into the area. There seems to have been some powerful attraction—love, or hate, or addiction—that held them together."

"But why kill Allen and Dowd?"

"There's a complex history that we're still trying to sort out. But we think the event that triggered the Allen/Dowd slayings was that Ashleigh photographed Warrington and Freeler together."

"When was this?"

"A few days before the murders. Ashleigh had taken her biology class to Upper Bar Lake to collect water samples. Using a digital camera she took a lot of photos of the students. They were on a CD I took out of her camera. Several photos showed a couple on the east shore across from where the students were wading," explained Sue.

"Freeler and Warrington?" probed Tyrrell.

"Yes, they were in the distance at the edge of the photo. I didn't even notice them the first time I looked at the pictures on screen. And, given how far they were from Ashleigh, she might have not recognized them. But when I enlarged the photos, there they were, holding hands. No question about their identities."

"So," said Ray, picking up the narrative, "here's our theory. Freeler and Helen thought that they had been discovered. Freeler, on his own or with Helen's prodding, committed the murders to protect their secret."

"Great theory, but so what? They were consenting adults."

"We're not dealing with rational people," responded Ray.

"And the fire?"

"The arson investigator wouldn't commit to a specific cause, but I think there's a good chance that Freeler, or Helen, or both working together started the blaze. "

"Motive?"

"The photos, they wanted to destroy the evidence. Ashleigh's camera was in her apartment and lots of prints of her students doing field work."

"Why didn't they just take the camera?"

"Speculation again—perhaps he thought we would have noticed the camera was missing."

"Why did he try to kill you?" Tyrrell prodded.

"Again speculation," Sue answered. "But perhaps in their confused world they thought that Ray was getting too close. And if they killed him it would stop the investigation. It was just the two of them against the world. With Ashleigh dead, Ray was their most immediate threat."

"But you haven't been able to question Helen about this?"

"I've had several conversations with her psychiatrist. At this point she's catatonic," Sue said.

"Four deaths," said Tyrrell, "Ray shot. What an enormous amount of carnage."

"And Arnie Vedder," added Ray, "An unintended victim. We think he fled to his shack after he witnessed the murders or found the bodies."

"And Arnie Vedder," repeated Tyrrell. "What's happening with him?"

"He's been moved to a nursing home. He's made some progress," said Ray. "But the prognosis is uncertain."

"Poor bastard. That kid never had a chance," muttered Tyrrell. He dropped in a chair at the head of the table and looked at Sue and then Ray. "So, we can charge Helen with a lot of things, but she may never be competent to stand trial."

They both nodded their agreement.

"What an appalling way to save the county money."

A long pause followed, finally Tyrrell turned to Ray and said, "I hope you're going to take some time off. How long has it been since you've had a vacation?"

"It's been a while," Ray responded. "And as soon as I'm a bit more ambulatory I'm going to get away for a few weeks."

"Where to?"

"California. I've got some personal business I need to attend to."

AUTHOR'S NOTE

In the process of writing and revising this book I received help and encouragement from a number of people. Detective Sergeant Mark Henschell of the Michigan State Police provided counsel on police procedures and DNA evidence. Don Shapton lent his knowledge of the workings of rural fire departments and helped with cover concepts.

I am very grateful to the early readers of this manuscript, Anne Stanton, Anne-Marie Oomen, and Lori Hall Steele. Their insightful suggestions helped me grow the story during the many revisions.

My thanks again to Lori Hall Steele for her skillful editing and her help in bringing this project to completion.